CW00449274

TELEPORT 2

JOSHUA T. CALVERT

1

Doctor Adrian Smailov let the water of the river run between his fingers and enjoyed the coolness it sent through his entire body. It didn't entirely drive the heat from his skin or his bones, which seemed to glow from within, but it made him shiver and gave him goose bumps.

The path from the wall into the green forest landscape stretched to the horizon, with its strange buildings, had been arduous, especially since they had to carry Mette most of the time or support her in such a way that it amounted to carrying her. But now, at least, they had water, which raised their spirits. His lips were still chapped and cracked, but violent dizziness no longer plagued him, nor did his body feel like a wrung-out rag.

He gazed at his face in the rippled surface of the water, which distorted his reflection even though morning was approaching.

He recalled his last mission on the ISS, the International Space Station. Back then, Felicity Barnes was commander, a wiry NASA astronaut with a hawkish face that reminded him of his former elementary school teacher, whose name he couldn't remember though he did recall her stern look.

He had just zipped up his sleeping bag in the Swesda module, something he had not found easy to do even after two weeks on the station, when the alarm began to howl. From his rigorous training in Star City, just outside Moscow, he knew immediately it was the fire alarm and had freed himself. Since the Russian section of the joint international project was somewhat remote, he and his colleague Dima usually cooked their own meals on a day-to-day basis, so he took a moment to check whether the fire was in their modules or the western ones on the other side.

The most dramatic twelve minutes and thirteen seconds of his life played out in his mind's eye, as if he were there, living through them for the first time.

Adrian pushed off from the chamber with the sleeping bays, set into the wall side by side like upright coffins, and floated between the cream-colored wood-look compartments. He held onto the gray grab rails as he stared at the laptop screen in the Swesda. The European Columbus module was blinking red.

"Felicity, what's going on?" he called over the radio. "Is the passage to you clear?"

"Fire in PMA 3!" came the commander's breathless reply. "Everyone to Destiny!"

Adrian nodded and waved toward the Zarya liaison module when Dima emerged from the sleeping area. The other cosmonaut nodded and set off, nimbly using hand grips with legs outstretched, through the tin can they called their temporary home at an altitude of over four hundred kilometers.

A fire in space was, next to the impact of a micrometeorite with loss of pressure, the worst type of emergency they had rehearsed, and he could tell from the stench of burned cables this was neither a drill nor a trifle.

"*Blyat!*" Dima cursed in Russian as they slid through the modules as fast as they could without hurting themselves. "Why were we woken up by the alarm first?"

"It's extremely sensitive."

"Just what I needed."

Felicity and Roy from NASA and Max Erichsen from ESA were already waiting in the Destiny module. They were putting on their oxygen masks and holding out two to him and Dima. Between the locked drawers and computers attached to swivel arms on the wall—plus the thousands of cables—it was now so cramped that not even a Coke can would have found room.

Adrian knew it was probably bullshit, but he couldn't help but feel like a second-class cosmonaut now that he had joined the Westerners and the adrenaline was pounding in his ears like a jackhammer; they had arrived late and were the last to get their masks on. Although there was a distinct esprit de corps among astronauts, it was easy to feel like an outsider when you were Russian. Their modules were more obsolete, and they had little to do because their government could hardly fund research projects in space. Every cosmonaut on the ISS was here merely to show the nation that they could still keep up with the Americans and were extremely proud of their own abilities. However, the unvarnished truth was that the Westerners were working sixteen-hour shifts while they were taking pictures, doing maintenance work, or writing diaries and otherwise twiddling their thumbs. Everyone knew this, which meant that though they were respected as spacemen, they were still the smallest community in the world, they were still not considered equals. At least he was very sure of that.

"So, on with the failure analysis," Felicity said, the mask made her sound like she was speaking underwater.

"There are forty-eight electronic systems in PMA 3 with about the same number of cable connections. The first flames came up the blue groove, so we can at least rule out the locking mechanisms," Roy said.

The stocky American was the only wearing a headset and was connected to ground control.

The conversation went back and forth for a few minutes until they were startled by a loud bang. The acrid smell of burnt rubber got worse.

"We're evacuating!" Roy finally said, listening to Houston safety.

"No, we're not just abandoning the station..." Felicity said.

"But Ground Control has given the order—"

"She's the commander!" Max shouted with his German accent. He was upset. "She's up here; Ground Control isn't."

"So, what do we do?" Adrian asked.

"Roy, cut the power to Harmony! It's most likely a short circuit!" Felicity ordered. "Dima, get the memory cards out of Harmony. Max, shut down ventilation!"

Adrian's friend and colleague nodded and quickly pushed off with his feet, slid between him and Roy, and passed through the circular connector between the two modules to pull the massive memory cards out of the walls.

"Felicity, we're supposed to evacuate!" Roy insisted. He should have acted immediately, according to their training. Adrian had never liked him much with his gruff cowboy manner, but how someone like him had gotten through the tests was a mystery to him.

"I can shut it down!" Adrian suggested as Max prepared

the Soyuz for evacuation, which Felicity had just told him to do.

"You need the access code." She shook her head and glanced back and forth between her NASA colleague and Harmony, where Dima had pulled out the third memory card and given it a nudge in her direction. Now, like the other two, she flew through zero gravity to join them in Destiny.

"We should… immediately," Roy said, his face red.

"Protocol!" Adrian yelled at him. The brief shock seemed to help because the American suddenly nodded and quickly turned to a laptop on the wall and hacked furiously at the keyboard.

"Adrian, you—"

Felicity was interrupted by another bang and a vivid jet of flame shot through Harmony module, through the passageway where Dima was frantically trying to secure the memory cards. He cried out as several fire bubbles, moving like bullets in zero gravity, ate into his leg. Dozens of yellow red spheres flew past the technical equipment like little demons from hell, heading toward them and the Destiny module.

"Shit!" cursed Felicity, lifting the emergency interlock cover off the wall and slamming her fist down on the control. The safety hatch between the modules closed with a hiss, and Harmony was instantly vented. All the air was sucked into vacuum in one burst, and Adrian saw his friend twitch behind the thick porthole, the veins in his face now blue.

They later learned his death throes lasted two minutes, but Felicity didn't give them time to mourn. She shooed them to the Soyuz while she stayed behind. No one else dared object. Shock was written all over their faces. Minutes later they were seated in the cramped capsule and hurtling toward Earth under the guidance of Ground Control.

Weeks later, Roy was released from the program. It was Roy's fault because he hadn't followed orders and thus let the team down.

Felicity was revered as a hero for staying behind to keep the station in orbit and repair it as best she could until a multi-member relief team arrived.

Dima was only remembered as the one who hadn't made it, who had died tragically.

For Adrian, he never wanted to go into space again after that experience, which, contrary to the media reports, had nothing to do with heroic deeds or an adventure gone awry, but with an almost disappointing reality. There was nothing grand about it. In the log, he had noted he had disagreed with Felicity's decision to ignore Ground Control's evacuation order—although she had been right because an operator had misinterpreted a data set and believed the fire would continue within a few seconds by a cable running into Destiny. Still, they should have done it, at least then Dima wouldn't have died, and they wouldn't have had to prove with a precious life why there was a rule that the team worked as a unit even if one individual didn't like a decision.

"Hey, are you okay?"

Adrian looked up and saw Mette coming toward him from between two of the tall, slender trees. She waddled in her typical manner, which reminded him in a sympathetic way of one of those seals he had hunted with his father in Kamchatka as a youth, when the fiercest snows of winter retreated and made the wide plains off the coast passable.

Her cheeks seemed especially rosy now, where the heat made her skin glow. They had created a rough split for her injured foot with sticks and a frayed vine they had pulled from a tree. Still, she needed a massive stick to walk, against which she leaned visibly.

"Yeah, I'm okay," he said, taking one last look at his face before quickly washing his hands and splashing more water over his eyes, forehead, and cheeks. He filled one of the empty injector canisters with a swish from the river before handing it to her. She nodded gratefully and drank. Since the improvised vessel was so small, he repeated the process a few more times until she shook her head to show she'd had enough.

"You look so gloomy."

"*Gloomy?*" he asked, struggling to smile. "That's not even a word."

"If not, I'd make it up to describe the look on your face," she said, placing a hand on his shoulder, which he eyed, blinking. She noticed and quickly withdrew it as if she'd been burned. "Oh, sorry. I didn't mean to be too personal. I just—well, I-I'm here if you want to talk about anything and —" She broke off.

I'm not used to showing intimacy. My father was a soldier and woke me every morning when I was ten to run around the house in the freezing cold, and my mother was colder than the polar night. All I can remember is her face, which always seemed to say, "Concentrate. You won't be the best if you hang on my coattails. Be diligent in school. Stand up for yourself, and don't let others carry you!"

Aloud he said, "No, that's all right. Sorry. I—everything's fine. I'm just a little exhausted, that's all."

"This is my fault; I'm just holding you up and—"

"No," he said brusquely, and she recoiled, startled. She

looked like she might tumble over the uneven forest floor, but she caught herself and gulped. "You're not stopping us. You're part of the team."

"Um, thanks," she mumbled.

He tried to smile, though he still had a lot of worries.

They were drinking water from a river they knew nothing about. It could be contaminated or deadly because it contained an alien microbiome that their Earth-influenced immune systems couldn't handle because everything was alien. They had nothing to eat and the air was clearly radioactive or in some way toxic because the first signs of abscesses were forming again on them. Plus, they didn't know where they were, had hardly any real landmarks, and were groping in the dark regarding this world without being mentally and physically up to speed.

"Each of us is important," he declared. "Something can, and eventually *will*, happen to any of us, and we're not going to leave anyone behind, all right?"

"Sure." She nodded but stopped when he started walking.

He paused and faced her.

"What?"

"You didn't want any of this."

"What do you mean?"

"You didn't want us to trust Nasaku, to sneak out of the Air Force base, to use the teleporter at all without properly exploring it first. James's view that it was better to bite the apple rather than spend years surveying it was suspect by you from the beginning, and you spoke against it."

He waved it off. "It's not important. We decided, and now we're here."

"It does matter. You didn't like it, and yet you went along with it. You actively participated in Norton's strangely well-intentioned trap and helped Nasaku simply because we trusted her though we didn't have any concrete evidence," Mette said, eyeing him curiously. "Why? If there's a leader personality on the team, it's probably you. Instead, you followed."

Adrian carefully weighed his words to make sure he said exactly what he meant. "A leader is not always the one who makes the decisions. They can also be the one who shares them." He looked her in the eye. "Or the one who makes sure no one goes overboard. It's not the loudest voice in the room that leads, but each one in its own time, when it's the one that should be listened to. Norton was a good leader in his way. James is, too, in the appropriate situations. On the Nasaku thing, I didn't see it as right or wrong, and we had to take a chance. I'm a cosmonaut, not someone who likes to jump head-first in the deep end. I analyze problems and act as rationally as possible. That wasn't what was called for in the situation because there was no point where it could be engaged rationally. So, I joined in."

"You joined in?" she asked. Again, he saw more in her gaze than the shambling, round-faced woman with the slight smell of sweat and the tangled mane of hair let on. "Or did you purposely step back?"

Less alert minds would have thought that the two were the same, but she understood him better than she thought, so he merely smiled.

"Only those who know how to follow know how to lead," he said, deliberately vague. Mette smiled and gratefully accepted his arm and hobbled with him through the trees to the small clearing where the team was sleeping.

When they found this place, from which one could still see the huge shadow of the wall in the east through the canopy of leaves, they had all rushed to the river and, without thinking, drunk until they felt sick, and their stomachs rebelled. No one had even considered it might be dangerous. Of course, not, otherwise they would have died of thirst. Their instincts had taken over and made sure they survived the next few hours, or even minutes, and didn't consider a future they might never reach.

Now they slept, lying curled up on the dry moss bed between large roots surrounding the clearing like natural walls of wood, providing an archaic sense of safety and security. Meeks snored loudly, but James, Mila, and Justus, lay in fetal positions an arm's length away from each other, looking dead, so it apparently didn't bother them as much as it had himself and Mette.

"What do you think that is?" the Dane whispered as she leaned against a tree, pointing into the intertwining treetops above their heads that formed a complex pattern of branches and leaves. The leaves were as green as on Earth, but blue dots glowed on many, which could not be fireflies, or a xenoequivalent, because they did not move.

"I don't know," he answered truthfully. "A phosphorescent substance or a living thing that doesn't move, which I find hard to imagine. Unless it's fungal lichen. In that case, though, the infestation would be massive, and that in turn would suggest predators."

"But we haven't seen any insects or anything like that yet."

"Right." He looked up and enjoyed the sight of the blue lights. It reminded him of a romantic, starry sky. If it didn't look so alien, and if he didn't know it was an alien planet far from home, he would have found it beautiful. "It doesn't seem dangerous, anyway."

"At least not directly."

"Yes." He pointed to the others. "You should get some sleep. Your foot will thank you."

"My foot doesn't seem to thank me for anything anymore," she grumbled but nodded and slid down the rough trunk at her back until she leaned awkwardly against the tree. "What about you?"

"I'll stay awake. Someone has to keep their eyes and ears open."

She yawned audibly. "We didn't think of that."

Adrian nodded.

"We're pretty careless, aren't we?"

He waved it off. "We're traumatized and disoriented. That's to be expected."

"But you aren't," she said wearily.

"Sleep now, Mette. It'll be light soon, and you should at least catch an hour or two. I'll be fine, believe me."

Mette nodded after a moment and then closed her eyes.

"Fat Mette! Fat Mette! Fat Mette!"

She heard the chorus of her classmates' chant as she walked through the gate of Lyshøjskolen Elementary School with her head down and shoulders hunched.

She kept her gaze fixed on the ground, hoping the boys and girls would turn to other pursuits when they lost interest in her for not fighting back. She just wanted it to stop, just stop. If she could have screamed and blocked out the whole world at that moment, she would have. But if she screamed out her fear, *all* the children would look at her and that would make it worse. Every morning she went to the schoolyard with that heavy weight in her stomach, afraid it would happen again.

Don't get angry, Mettilde. Her mother's words echoed in her head. *The children are just jealous because you have such a clever little head.* Then she had kissed her on the forehead, as she always did, and frantically prepared breakfast, sugared cornflakes with milk, and gathered her rations for school, two packets of orange juice, two candy bars, and an apple, before looking at her wristwatch and suppressing a curse at being late for work again.

"Mommy, can I ask you something?" Mette asked.

"Later, Mettilde. I have to go to work real now or Said will fire me for being late for the third time this week. Today at noon, you go to Aunt Friga, don't forget."

Of course. Her mother had taken a second job as a cleaning lady at the local high school. Mette was already imagining how she would end up there later and be laughed at: *"Mette's mommy cleans the toilet!"*

"Okay."

She didn't like Aunt Friga. Whenever Mette went to her, all she talked about was how bad her dad was and how he had left her sister and niece alone. Then she would cry and cook lunch, and each time the tears would fall into the food, which Mette found repulsive.

"Mettilde, why are you crying?"

She looked up. Her mother was standing in the kitchen doorway which led to the cramped wood-paneled hallway where Mette's large satchel stood, with its many dark stains where her classmates had spit on her when they thought she wouldn't notice.

"I don't want to go to school, Mommy!"

"Oh, Mettilde!" With a sympathetic look, her mother embraced her. If only this moment, when she felt protected and safe, could last forever, away from all the naughty girls and boys who tormented her. "What's wrong with you?"

"The other kids hate me!"

"No, they don't hate you. Shh!"

Mette sobbed.

"They're just jealous because you skipped two classes. Just ignore their talk, you hear? One day you'll realize none of that matters and they'll be the ones cleaning your house and washing your car while you start a nice job as a professor at the university in Copenhagen, yep."

Mette didn't know what "one day" was supposed to mean and how it could be "unimportant" that she had to go to hell every morning, but she understood one thing, her mother cried at night, just like she did, and tried hard during the day to put on a friendly face and not let Mette notice.

"Hey, fat girl!" Her memories of the morning burst like a soap bubble. Helga, from the third grade, stood in front of her, surrounded by her friends, who stared at her spitefully and whispered mean jokes to each other.

"Hello," she mumbled meekly. *Don't attract attention. I have to ignore her.*

"Your satchel is huge!" Helga marveled, pointing to the boxy backpack she carried before looking to the other girls, and they all laughed. "What's in there? Definitely candy, right? You can't stop eating, can you?"

"Just stuff for class."

"Of course! 'Look what Mette can do already,'" the third grader mimicked her math teacher. "'Bravo, Mette, well done.'"

They're jealous, she thought, without really believing it. *Just as Mami had said.* If her mother said that, maybe it was true; after all, she was an adult and Mette wasn't.

She knew how that felt because she was often envious herself. Envious of the fourth graders who were already so big and strong and didn't have to put up with anything from third graders. Envious of the kids who were good at sports and didn't have misshapen legs like she did, who weren't immediately out of breath or teased for supposedly stinking. She envied the girls with short hair who didn't have their curls pulled constantly as they walked down the hall.

Envious of those with friends, who didn't have to sit alone on the bus. Envious of those who didn't feel like they were all alone, even though others constantly surrounded them.

"I can help you," she finally said, feeling sympathy for the girls in front of her. They were jealous that Mette was smarter than them and had skipped two grades. They were jealous of her good grades. Maybe they even got in trouble with their parents for not being good enough. That had to be terrible.

"Help?" Helga asked, looking surprised. Her eyes grew wide, and it was obvious she hadn't expected this. Her friends also gave each other irritated looks.

"Yes. I can help you with your homework so you can get better grades."

"That's really a great idea, Mette!" her counterpart said enthusiastically and turned to the others, who nodded and clapped their hands as well. Two ran around Mette and yanked so hard on her satchel so she tumbled backward and fell violently on her bottom. A dull pain spread through her legs. The top flap of the satchel unsnapped, and the contents scattered far and wide across the schoolyard, that was wet from the autumn rain. Helga pointed to the two candy bars.

"Ha! Sweets for the fat Mette!"

Before she realized what was happening, they took them away from her. They left the notebooks and pens.

"What's wrong?" Helga teased in a fake friendly tone. "Why are you sweating like that again? Are you afraid you can't eat enough candy?"

The other girls laughed and Mette started to cry.

"Is that what you do in first grade? Look, now she's crying like a baby. Like a first-grade baby because that's where she belongs!"

"I thought she was too smart to cry?" another girl asked as Mette scrambled around on the ground, gathering up her books and sheets of paper, which were already soaking up the dirty rainwater from the schoolyard, making the ink run. How on earth was she supposed to show her homework now? If she got bad grades, her mother would be even sadder than she already was. She was always so happy when Mette brought home good grades, and those moments were among the best. There hadn't been many since they moved Holstebro.

"When she crawls like that she looks like a pig!" Alma said, a blonde in Helga's class who was tall even for third a grader.

The others laughed, cackling.

"She's so fat. Do you think she'll get fatter in the rain, like a sponge?"

"Maybe all the chocolate is leaking out of her."

"She can't hear you; all she can do is grunt like a pig."

The school bell boomed across the schoolyard, calling for the start of first period.

"See you later, fat Mette!" Helge shouted, chuckling. Then she and the other third graders ran into the two-story building made of wooden slats and painted yellow. Mette stuffed everything back into her satchel, tears in her eyes. Half her school clothes were completely soaked, and the other half were so washed out that hardly anything was recognizable.

"Are you awake?"

Mette startled awake from her dream. Painful memories of several experiences at once, leaving her with a familiar feeling of sadness as she opened her eyes, blinking hard. Squatting before her was James, tall and sinewy with that handsome face of a modern New York intellectual who seemed to have fallen from their environment as much as she had.

"Uh, now, yes," she replied sleepily, rubbing her eyes. Her entire back was tender. The bark of the tree she was leaning against must have pressed its jagged pattern deep into her skin, the way she felt.

"Oh, I'm sorry. I thought you were—"

"It's okay." She waved it off. It was already bright, that is, if the dingy twilight falling through the leaves could be called bright. The glowing blue spots were barely visible. "Is everything all right?"

He nodded. "Yes. I climbed one of the trees and saw fires were burning to the west."

"Fires? You mean like forest fires?"

"No, more like campfires. Hard to say. We figured we'd go there. Maybe someone lives there."

"If someone really does live there," she said, "then is it wise just to go there? Even if there are other people living here, they might be cruel."

James nodded again and sighed dejectedly. "You're right, but we need food, and we don't know anything about this place. I don't think..."

"What?" she huffed when he made no move to finish his sentence.

He waved it off. "Ah. Never mind. I wanted to ask you what you thought."

They didn't want to present her with a fait accompli, which pleased her. She glanced over his shoulders and saw the others were awake. Meeks and Mila were gone, and

Adrian and Justus were crouched over some branches and creepers in the middle of the clearing.

"You don't think what, James?" she asked. "I don't think we're in a place where we can coddle each other and pre-filter the truth to cater to feelings."

"You're right," he said, his expression apologetic. "We won't survive long, I'm afraid. Wherever we go, it'll be far. And without food, we'll be in trouble."

He's really clever, she thought appreciatively. *Now he's steering the conversation as though I admitted to myself that clear words are necessary to survive here. I can no longer dismiss whatever he says from this moment on as too crass or dangerous because it was my own idea, although it had been his.*

"Where are the others?"

"Mila and Meeks went to wash at the river, and Justus and Adrian are building you a new crutch."

Mette smiled gratefully. "You are too good to me. I think I'll give you—"

"No," he interrupted her, "I don't want to hear about your foot slowing us down or about leaving you behind."

"I wasn't going to suggest that either," she lied.

"All right, then. Come on, let's see what happens when a former fighter pilot, a superconductor engineer, an astro-physicist, and a quantum researcher try to make a crutch without tools," James said, helping her to her feet. His breath smelled as unpleasant and sour as her own probably did. It wasn't just that they couldn't brush their teeth, the lack of food caused their bodies to excrete acetone through the mucous membranes of their mouths, much like fasting. In her case, it was probably worse because, absent food, the body drew on its own energy stores in the form of body fat and converted the fatty acids released into acetone, the simplest ketone of the carbonyl group. It smelled something like rotting fruit.

"Are you okay?" James asked after she leaned on his arm.

"Just the thoughts of a fat old chemist who feels about as out of place as a polar bear in the desert."

"Trust me, we're all polar bears here."

Mette eyed him out of the corner of her eye and had to smile. His one sentence was like a small revelation for her, a bright silver lining in her mind. For him it was just a mere remark he would forget in a few minutes. She wondered if she was in exactly the right place after all. Either way, she thought she had better keep that thought to herself; the others surely wouldn't understand or would rightly find it absurd.

As it turned out, the new crutch was considerably more comfortable than her improvised walking stick. It had a curved loop at the top made from a bent wet branch held to the stick with some twisted creeping plant fibers and rested reasonably comfortably in her armpit. She kept thanking them, and they seemed pleased.

Mila and Meeks returned, and they finally moved, following the course of the river, which led toward the remains of the city they had seen from the wall. It might still be something completely different, they might have misinterpreted it in the sparse moonlight of the previous night, but until they reached it, she wanted to hold onto the thought they would be sleeping with a roof over their heads for one night, or even meet people.

"What do we do when we finally meet others?" she asked after they had walked in silence for a while. She found it oppressive, although it was interrupted more and more often by birdsong the farther they got from the wall. "It's not like we can just say 'hello.'"

"Why not?" Justus asked, who was taking his turn supporting her. Even with the crutch, she could hardly walk on her own; otherwise, she would put too much pressure on her splinted ankle, which hurt violently with every step.

"Because we wouldn't speak their language."

"If they are human beings, then we can already communicate with hands and feet. After all, we share our facial expressions and gestures."

"A few years ago, didn't some primitive people in the Andaman Islands have their first contact with strangers from the 'civilized' world?" Meeks asked. "These guys with bows and arrows shot down the explorers because they were thought to be demons."

Mette nodded, trying to ignore the sweat that ran down her face and burned her eyes and the little fissures in her lips. "I heard about it. That's the kind of thing that worries me. A couple strangers wrapped in rags who don't speak their language could make for all sorts of reactions."

"When the first settlers landed in North America, the natives on Rhode Island received them very kindly and even got them through the first winter, which the Europeans would not have survived otherwise," James said. He was walking directly behind Adrian, who guided them past the largest roots and roughest moss beds. "The indigenous people of South America were also very welcoming to the Portuguese and Spanish with hospitality and gifts."

"And today, for the most part, there are only descendants of Europeans there," Justus grumbled.

"Yes, and we can make sure that doesn't happen here, too." James paused and snorted. "Maybe not a good example."

"If we run into anyone, we'll have your back," Mette said kindly, hoping he took it as the compliment she meant and not a cynical dig at his darker side as the con man Norton had told them about.

"If we do, let's hope they really are humans. Then we don't even need a common language for peaceful initial contact. Body language and tone make up eighty percent of the structure not only in negotiations but in pretty much every human interaction."

For the next few hours, they walked in silence beside the river, which was about 25 meters wide. The water brown and muddy like grainy coffee.

Exhaustion was noticeably affecting them. They moved in a trancelike state where they mechanically put one foot in front of the other. Soon the birds' singing and squabbling sounded like a mocking song accompanying them meter by meter, and in the monotonous grind of exhaustion, heat, and the uneasy sense of dreaming, one could almost forget where one was.

Mette soon believed herself to be on an energy-draining walk through the woods in her homeland that just wouldn't end. The trees and undergrowth, with its many ferns and creepers and damp bushes, looked more like a tropical, or at least subtropical, jungle, but everything, including the birds, was familiar enough to make one forget that they were possibly dozens or hundreds of light-years from Earth and everything they knew.

No, not everything we know, she admonished herself. *We are familiar with all this, too. There flows water, my feet walk on moss, it smells typical of a forest and the birds sound like those back home.*

Adrian didn't need to coax them when he suggested they take a break. They sat on a short grassy bank, where the river made a large bend, and collapsed, exhausted. The smell of acetone coalesced between them into an acrid cloud, but she couldn't muster enough strength to be disgusted by it.

Adrian scooped water from the river with the empty injector canisters and put one in each of their hands. Mette nodded and murmured a curt thanks. It tasted earthy, yet she greedily poured it into her mouth and gratefully accepted it when the cosmonaut refilled her glass.

"Did you hear that?" Mila asked as Mette lay on her back, eyes closed, trying to ignore the burning in her limbs so she could take a breath.

"Heard what?" Meeks mumbled, exhausted.

"I heard something crack!"

"Probably just a bird or small animal."

"What if it isn't?" she insisted.

"I'll go check," James sighed, groaning as he got up. Mette didn't open her eyes to look.

"I'm coming with you," Mila decided. She sounded worried.

3

Mila's eyes refused to open, as if they were smeared with viscous resin. It cost her an infinite amount of strength to move her eyelids, even a little. From somewhere, an unpleasant, uniform beep imposed itself on her. It seemed to increase in intensity, although she also knew that it did not change. Her throat felt as if it had been scratched with sandpaper and every swallow was a torment.

"She's awake!" someone shouted. The voice sounded excited. Why did it sound so excited?

"Pulse stabilizing," someone else said. A man this time.

Among the sea of overlapping spots of light and dark in her vision, something shifted. An unlocatable pain flooded her neural pathways like a pale memory under a thick layer of oblivion.

"Gospozha Shaparova, can you hear me?"

Shaparova, Mila, she thought lamely. The realization seeped slowly into her barely alert mind. *That's me.*

"Th-thirst," she croaked, and after what felt like an eternity, she felt a very strange object between her lips.

"Just a sip. Post-op, no more!" someone said, and she didn't like the voice. She was so thirsty.

"More!"

"I'm sorry, Gospozha Shaparova," said the woman. Her voice was soft as velvet, not at all matching the dark spot in her vision that could have belonged to a demon. "You'll have to wait a little longer to drink."

I don't know her voice. Who's that? Post-op? What does she mean by that? A prolonged groan escaped Mila, startling her. *The voice is wrong. Wrong! She should sound different. Where are they?*

"You need to rest first," the voice reassured her.

At least this speaker tried. At that moment, she wondered if she might have spoken aloud by mistake.

"No. Where am I, anyway?"

"Doctor?"

"I'll, uh, I'll take it from here," said the wicked voice that had denied her the water, the culprit that saw to it the straw was no longer being between her lips and the liquid soothing her battered throat. "You still have very little strength, Gospozha Shaparova."

Why do they keep stressing my name? I am not a stupid child!

"I have enough strength," she lied.

"I don't think so. Rest for a few hours and—"

Mila clenched her teeth and opened her eyes, tearing apart the resin in them with sheer willpower and kept them open.

She was lying in a hospital bed in a white-tiled room hooked up to several machines. Although she was covered with a blanket, she knew the many tubes peeking out from beneath them ended in her body and their number made her swallow, which her throat acknowledged with painful protest. Sitting diagonally on her bed was a doctor in a white coat with a stately belly and receding hair that made his forehead appear long and high. He looked very glum. A nurse with a clipboard under her arm was just leaving through a beige door. For a few seconds, the clamor of a busy hospital reached her ears: ringing telephones, nurses calling to each other, the beep of machines, the metallic clack of beds on rollers being pushed down the hall. Then it was shut out again, and a heavy silence hung in the air.

"Tell me what's wrong," Mila growled, fixing the doctor with a look that no one had ever withstood. As an engineering student, she had stood up to a whole lot of young men who had seen her merely as a pretty blonde, in addition to her professors. Ten years ago, when she had started her academic career after earning her doctorate in materials science and engineering, it had started all over again, and she had been seen as the blonde with brains, if not officially, then with looks and whispered comments. It wasn't until she received an award for outstanding research from the Ministry of Research that they fell silent. But by then, she had learned to appear as a hawk when she was seen as a mouse.

"You..." The doctor hesitated, then cleared his throat as her gaze darkened. "You are in the Novo Clinic in Novosibirsk and have just undergone surgery, Gospozha Shaparova. It was an emergency operation. You collapsed in the engineering institute during a lecture and the students contacted the emergency doctor. Due to a perforation in your small intestine wall, we immediately had to take you into surgery."

"What about my baby? Where is my mother?"

The doctor seemed surprised by her questions and blinked like he had something in his eye.

"Where are they?" she repeated.

"If you listed your mother as your emergency contact, then she has been contacted by hospital staff and is certainly on her way. Is there anyone else we can call?" The doctor was clearly uncomfortable. Judging by his body language, he wanted nothing more than to leave as quickly as he could.

"What else?"

"Excuse me?"

"What else?" she growled.

"Gospozha Shaparova, you—"

"I know what my name is! Tell me!"

"I'm not sure you understand. You had an undiagnosed intestinal tumor that had penetrated the intestinal wall. We had to remove it and were only able to save your life with great difficulty. Fifteen minutes later and you wouldn't be lying here talking to me."

"That wasn't my question." Mila held back the fear and terror as she had learned to do, packing it all into a tight ball of violent emotion and burying it under a layer of pragmatic self-control. She couldn't deal with it now. Every drama had its own time, and at this moment there were more important issues.

"This..." The doctor swallowed and avoided her gaze. Mila's heart stopped. "We couldn't save the child."

"But..." She fell silent. Her lips quivered violently and uncontrollably. She wouldn't have been able to speak even if she could. *"How can this be?"* she wanted to shout at the man. *In the eighth month! In the eighth month! Why did you save me and not her? She was all I had left of my husband!*

The pale doctor jumped up and straightened his coat, his wide eyes uncertain. He looked like he simply wanted to run away. Only then did she realize that she *had* yelled at him.

"Excuse me, Doctor." She forced the words out of her mouth, as if mechanically. Her vision was blurry, but she didn't miss the door opening and a nurse coming in with a flurry of sound.

"No!" The doctor replied to something she didn't hear because a sob escaped her.

"But—"

"No, if you inject her with anymore it can cause sinus bradycardia. We need to... call emergency psychiatric services and have them send someone over."

Suddenly, it was only the nurse, a pale figure with a white cap on her unrecognizable face.

"It's okay," she tried to reassure Mila, squeezing her hand. "I'm very sorry."

The woman's tone was unexpected and an eternity passed before she realized what it was. By then she had been alone in her room for a long while, accompanied only by the beeping of the machines beside her bed.

She had not only lost her child, but Anton's third. Anton had died in a car accident six months ago.

Saved her life, the doctor had said. *Saved her life. So, the operation was successful, but the tumor had already metastasized. A temporary rescue. Why wasn't the baby saved? Why?*

A week later it was finally time for her to be discharged. During that week her six-year-old son Yuri and her three-year-old Lyudmila had visited every day with their grandmother, who had looked after them and kept house for so long. She still felt like a bus had run her over, but she was hopeful, thanks to her children and a few conversations with the doctor. She had four more years in the best case, so she would make it twelve, somehow, so Yuri would be of age when the time came. Then he could take care of Lyudmila, as Anton would have wanted.

"It goes on and on, sweetie," her mother had said as the children played in the room next door with an old police car toy that the previous patient's son had left behind and never picked up. She had opened the curtains, so Mila had seen thick snowflakes dancing in front of them. "When you get home, you'd better take a bucket and rag in hand and clean the whole house. It will get your mind off things. In a hospital, only the sick languish, no wonder they tell such fairy tales here. You will live as long as you want."

Mila had cried.

"Yes, go ahead and cry, Milanchik." Her mother had brusquely waved her hand as always, not losing an ounce of love in her gaze. She had always been pragmatic, but it came from the bottom of her heart, which was why Mila loved her more than anything. The deep wrinkles in her parchment face looked hard, but a working-class mentality had steeled them. "What you cry, you don't have to piss."

"Very positive, as always," Mila laughed between her sobs, wiping away her tears.

"You can lament things or tackle them and make something better from them. When I see old branches in front of my dacha I see firewood, not a nuisance. When I see a hole in the roof, I'm glad that I won't be bored. Soon I'll have a new one, and nothing has fallen on my head. Everything is just up in here." Her mother tapped her temple. "So, you'd best clean up real quick and get to work. You've got two kids and they need you."

～

Two weeks later, she was dead, and with her Yuri and Lyudmila. Mila, at university and happy that the scars below her breastbone no longer itched so terribly, had just finished her first lecture when she got the call. Her mother had picked up the children from school and kindergarten, respectively, as discussed, and was supposed to drive them home until Mila got off work, but they never arrived.

A water main burst under a street not two blocks from Yuri's elementary school, it had turned into a sheet of ice as slick as glass. They had crashed into an old tree, the only one still standing after over two hundred had been removed from what had once been an avenue. This one was scheduled to be cut up and dug out the following week.

When the call reached her, she had simply stood shaking in her office, hyperventilating uncontrollably. Her field of vision shrank to a small tunnel whose black edges seemed made of viscous ooze, pulsing with the frantic beat of her heart. Her world had been reduced to pain so overwhelming that she became catatonic. Her entire body froze while her mind unconsciously turned into a wild hurricane and then became silent in one fell swoop.

She knew at that moment, deep inside herself, that she was alone and had no one. Whether there was a God or not —she had never believed in him and certainly wouldn't start now—she was alone now and secretly wished for only one thing, that the cancer in her body would spread fast enough that she wouldn't have to deal with the part of herself that considered a quick end to her suffering to be both brave and cowardly at the same time. In those moments her dark longing almost drove out her deep-rooted pragmatism.

Then came the call that kept her from making any final decisions, because something intolerable had come into her life that she would never get rid of. That call added something to the pain she had become and would be for the rest of her life—whether it was for weeks, months, or, in the worst case, even years. She couldn't calm her mind for several minutes following that call. What a redemption those minutes had represented. A temporary redemption.

"Was it this way?" James asked, exhausted, snapping Mila out of her heavy veil of memories. The creeping fatigue that held her tightly in its grip acted as an amplifier for musings.

"Yes, I think so," she said. They had just passed between two particularly large trees and had come across what looked like a deer trail.

"And you're quite sure it wasn't just a normal forest sound?"

She shook her head, which proved to be difficult. "No, I can't be sure, but it sounded unusual."

"Then we'd better look," he said, trying so hard to sound approving that she had to smile, because again he was trying to do the right thing. "This looks like a deer trail or unused path to me, don't you think?"

"It could be. If it really is a deer crossing, then that could mean—"

"—that we're close to a food source."

Hope resonated in his voice, and after a shared glance, they set about combing through the undergrowth along the narrow brown strip that ran through the forest. The path was barely visible. They had to stand right on it to see it, and use a little imagination to know it wasn't something natural.

The ferns, bushes, and grasses came up to their knees and they wandered among the trees, ponderous as zombies. Then, all at once, Mila saw color among the shades of green and brown: Red. Red dots, to be exact. The closer she got to them the more recognizable the fingertip-sized berries appeared amid the dense tangle of leaves at her ankles.

"James!" she cried hoarsely. She knelt in front of the gnarled bush.

Carefully, she held a hand under a fruiting bush weighed down with berries and lifted them. They looked like a mixture of strawberries and raspberries with little yellow dots on the skin and the finest of hairs.

"Oh," James said as he reached her and plopped down on the forest floor beside her like a puppet whose strings had been cut.

Mila picked one of the small fruits and twisted it between her grubby fingers. The urge to put it in her mouth, and then in quick succession all the others she could see, was superhuman, and she would have, had James not snatched them away from her and eaten them himself.

"Hey!" she protested weakly with some indignation.

"We don't know if they're poisonous," he said, chewing. "Red is usually a signal color of plants against possible pests. And this is a very different environment than our bodies are used to."

"Looks enough like strawberries to me to feel safe!" She started to reach for the next fruit when he grabbed her hand and held it back. The touch felt good and at the same time made her angry because she wanted to eat so badly.

Had to eat.

"Wait a moment," he told her.

When she saw that he wasn't taking any more himself

and probably fighting his own extreme hunger, she took a breath and barely nodded.

"Quite the gentleman," she said with no irony.

"I meant what I said." He looked her in the eye. "You are more important to the success of this mission than I am."

"Mission?"

"Yes. This is still a mission with a purpose, let's not forget that. We need to figure out where we are, how the teleporter works, and what's inside the marble."

"You mean we have to find this temple Nasaku was talking about?"

"Yes. Besides, we need something to keep us going."

Mila sighed inwardly. Quietly she said, "I know what you mean."

For a few moments, they just looked into each other's eyes, and she felt an exchange occurred between them that needed no words, providing an understanding beyond them. If only briefly, the all-consuming hunger within her disappeared and dissolved into a mere memory before returning even more strongly.

"Do you feel sick? Do you feel anything?" she asked.

"No." He shook his head, and then they both began frantically picking the berries and stuffing them into their mouths like mindless animals. Soon the fruit juice was running down both their cheeks and off their chins, dripping onto their sweat and dirt covered bodied, until they had picked the entire bush clean, and no red color was visible for miles around.

Exhausted, yet with a comfortable feeling, they lay on their backs on the moss, staring up into the treetops as if time had stopped.

Mila stroked her belly, just below her breastbone, lost in thought. "I can't remember the last time I didn't feel pain while eating," she mumbled, lost in thought, glad James didn't ruin the moment by saying something expected like "What's wrong with you?" or "Are you sick?" He stayed silent and gave her space. "You can think of it as an experimental result. The teleporter clones our bodies in healthy form, without the pre-existing conditions and diseases of the original body."

"That's a great insight," he agreed with her. "It means it doesn't make exact copies."

"Yes. Presumably, it creates an optimal clone based on the genetic starting material. I'm not sure I would have done it that way if I had been the designer, though."

"What do you mean?"

"We define ourselves by our sense of self and our sense of body, the two things that give a constant to our subjective experience," she explained. "One feels at home in one's body with all its peculiarities. It changes successively throughout life, at least through normal aging." She looked at the leaves rustling back and forth in the light wind high above them in the treetops. "But the 'I' feeling always stays the same. You have felt like you—mentally, I mean—as an observer of the world you perceive through your eyes, always, regardless of your age. You have learned, had experiences, but the feeling of 'being you' has always been the same. When you know you don't have long, that your belly is made of pain and is a ticking time bomb, it doesn't change that constant, but it does change the relationship of the sense of I to the body. Without that, I'm still me, but I've changed again. You know what I mean?"

"I'm not entirely sure."

Without looking, she could tell from the sounds he was making that he was sitting up and looking at her.

"But I'm glad you're feeling better."

"I'm not so sure," she whispered, thinking of her mother and Yuri and Lyudmila. "I'm not sure."

"Excuse me?"

"Oh nothing, I—" She heard rustling. Not what she had heard before, but as if a gust of wind was sweeping through the undergrowth, except that she also saw half a dozen shadows out of the corner of her eye before her sight went black.

4

The heat and hunger made it tempting to linger in his memories, as if in the straitjacket of a sedated psychiatric patient who had given up all resistance.

That was also true of Dr. Vincent Meeks, whose body roamed the woods, alternately yelling "Mila!" and "James!" over and over, as if his life depended on it. In a way, maybe it did.

Before the three dark SUVs pulled up in front of his Colorado home and Major Norton rang the doorbell to tell him about a top-secret project for which he had already passed the security check, he was busy strategizing his exit from Boeing. He loved his job—or rather *had* loved it—but it was also what had turned his life into a private roller coaster ride. As a senior engineer in research and development, he was always excited when confronted with new problems. How could a pump be made five percent more efficient? How to save two percent aircraft kerosene by subjecting the wingtips to a different molding process. What new research findings could be applied to new approaches to the aircraft development process? How could he push the boundaries further? He had enjoyed the twelve-hour shifts, working weekends, and throwing himself into the chaos of new approaches.

But he was also keen to have a haven of peace at home where he could leave all that behind. There, he didn't deal with all the offers from headhunters at other companies trying to lure him in with annual salaries that had others rubbing their eyes. He didn't enjoy his status as a luminary in his field; it bothered him.

"I'm just a simple Midwestern cowboy who wants to build the coolest Colt Wyatt Earp could have dreamed up," he once said to his wife, Jasmine, when she asked him on their second date at university what his big goals in life were. Today, he found this sentence to be richly horizonless and juvenile, but in moments when he was honest with himself, he had to admit it still accurately described his inner life later on.

After he and Jasmine married, everything had gone according to plan, as he had always wanted, as an engineer and out-and-out rationalist. His wife had liked to call him a "robot with hair." They had bought a house near Everett, north of Seattle, and he had made friends with the constant rainy weather in the Northwest. After two years, he started fishing, though he missed good old deer hunting. Then their first child was born.

Harry Lee Meeks had Down syndrome and had turned their entire lives upside down from day one. At first, he had been a normal infant, crying when he was hungry, crying when he was tired, even as the first signs of his condition had shown. In the next few years, Harry had become a test of strength for him and Jasmine.

He loved his son, yet he was completely overwhelmed by a child he couldn't reprimand without yelling because Harry couldn't hear well. Harry developed celiac disease at an early age and suffered from violent diarrhea that required planning every outing around the availability of sanitation. This was later compounded by pronounced forgetfulness, so Meeks had to constantly remind himself that his son had mild Alzheimer's disease symptoms, even though he hadn't even reached puberty. During every interaction with Harry he had to be wide awake, make sure he didn't react reflexively, say the wrong thing, or trigger him. There was no normalcy or relaxation, just a one hundred percent focus on Harry, which increasingly drained Jasmine.

That she later died of cancer had caused him to blame himself, even today. She had accepted the burden the birth of their shared son had placed on their lives and marriage and loved him as much as she loved Meeks. There was never anything like regret, only joy for their son, despite all the sleepless nights, the stares of others, the challenges Harry had brought. And yet, he had to admit to himself that he had thrown himself even more into his work at Boeing to escape the chaos at home.

He couldn't deny that he had wanted a son he could teach to hunt, whose baseball games he could attend, and who would wrestle with him on the couch without freaking out due to sensory-motor overstimulation and lack of impulse control. He had dreamed of building tree houses together and reading to him at night when he went to bed, and none of that had come true.

So, he'd done what he did best, worked and solved problems he *could* solve, that he *understood*, but in doing so, he had left Jasmine alone to manage everything. Year after year, he watched the wrinkles around her eyes deepen. Her mouth, once twisted into a permanent smile, the corners of which always pointed upward with a perky curve, gradually turned downward. Her cheeks became hollow, and she laughed less, and when she did it was no longer bell-bright and as fresh as it was when they first met. Later, he wondered what would have happened if he had taken responsibility and quit his job, or at least reduced his hours to take some pressure off her and not throw in the towel, or flee the ring, out of sheer insecurity and being overwhelmed.

Maybe I would have even done that if Patrick and Isabel hadn't been born, he thought.

Their son and daughter, who had come into the world six years after Harry, two years apart, unplanned, but not unwanted. He should have done everything differently. They were healthy and exceedingly low-maintenance children to boot, which was a distinct relief. They didn't change the attention and care Harry needed, but the three children living together became a whole new kind of challenge they hadn't even considered. Later, when Patrick hit puberty, Meeks could have made up for all the father-son time he had envisioned, but it had been too late. The many years of hard work had turned someone with a penchant for over-working into a real workaholic. He got up in the morning, drank his coffee, kissed his kids, and drove to work, only to come home late at night when everyone was already in bed. Today, those morning kisses seemed like an indulgence in the feelings of his children and wife. Like fleeting, meaning-less appearances that, in retrospect, he was ashamed of.

Jasmine's illness and death had only made things worse. Harry, Patrick, and Isabel were already of age when the diagnosis came, which, if they were honest, had surprised no one. She had looked so wan and ill.

She had always been the one constant in his life, who had known him even as a young man and not merely as a father who was always away. He mourned her, still did, and tried to help himself out with the only prescription he had ever known, more work. Instead, he should have been there for his children, whether they were of age or not, but it was too late. They liked him, he was their father after all, but there was also no denying that they could never form a close bond with each other.

Harry lived in a nursing facility in Boulder, Colorado, and Patrick and Isabel were both studying for their master's degrees in Germany and Sweden. He missed them, especially now that he had no way to see them, cut off from their lives. He knew he was too late with his feelings and would be met with incomprehension if he flew to Europe and introduced himself as a new, interested dad.

I did as well as I could, he wanted to tell them. *I was also once your age and overwhelmed with life and its challenges. I didn't have the maturity of character, maybe still don't, but I did what I thought was necessary to not break from the adversity God put in front of me. I loved your mother, have always loved her, as I love you, and I wish I had known better.*

I wish I had had some guidance on how to be a good father. My parents weren't very emotional and taught me things like "boys don't cry." That gets burned into your head. I always shook my father's hand. I can't remember him ever hugging me when we greeted each other. My mother, a staunch Methodist, didn't think much of "coddling" her child, which meant "putting emotions on the back burner so he'll be strong and self-reliant." That's how it was often done back then. Those were my role models. I wish you could understand that, but I'm not asking you to.

I just want you to know that I always think of you and love you and see your mother in you, and that fills me with pride that makes me endure more than I ever thought possible. If I survive this and can do something good for humanity—open the gateway to the stars—I would like to see you again, and not just tell you how I feel about you but to show you. If the Lord gives me the chance, I will do everything I can to make it come true.

"Mila!" Justus's call snapped him out of his thoughts, and the forest flooded back to him as if a muted movie was suddenly turned up to full volume.

"James!"

He joined in the shouts. "MILA! JAMES!"

"James! Mila!" The German sounded hoarse.

"Mila!" Meeks took his hands from his mouth, which he had shaped like a funnel to give his frighteningly thin voice more volume.

"Here!" Justus knelt beside a tree in the copse and beckoned him over. Beneath the low-hanging branches of a tree that looked like a particularly thick oak, all the undergrowth had been trampled-or flattened. "They must have been here."

"Hm." Meeks rubbed his chin and he hardly noticed the dirt and sweat coming off his tiny stubble. It was already becoming a habit, even though they hadn't even spent two days in this place.

"Did you find anything?" Mette asked excitedly, who, supported by Adrian, had caught up with them.

"I'm not sure," Justus said. "But someone's been lying here, or fallen from the tree and stayed there for a long time, but that would surprise me." As if to punctuate his words, he looked up into the apparently unbroken canopy of leaves.

Meeks bent down and picked up what looked like a bloodstained leaf, but the closer he looked, the stranger it seemed. It was too light for blood and the leaf had a jagged texture. He sniffed and didn't detect a metallic note, but a fruity one instead.

"Well," he muttered.

"What is it?" Justus stood and came to him. When he saw the leaf in his hands, the German gulped. "Is that—"

Meeks shook his head. "Blood? No. Unless blood smells like strawberries on this planet."

"Give me that," Adrian said, sniffing as it. "Hmm, more like blueberries."

Mette sighed. "What I wouldn't give for some blueberries. Or strawberries, I don't care."

"I'm already on the verge of just stuffing leaves in my mouth," Justus grumbled. Adrian nodded and looked worried. He went ahead, between the trees, looking for more tracks.

When he returned, Meeks realized he was sitting and had closed his eyes without noticing. Had he fallen asleep? A microsleep? It was so tempting to just give in to exhaustion and fatigue and shut out everything his senses were picking up; he just wanted to sleep. He felt like he was coming off a week of drinking, trapped in an endless hangover that wouldn't quit. Just opening his eyes because he was startled took almost unbearable strength from him. A hot rush of adrenaline shot through his veins and should have energized him, but instead he just wondered how his adrenal cortex could still function when he couldn't even think straight.

"Look," Adrian said. He stood in front of them, leaned down, and opened his hands. Inside were dozens of small red berries that shone enticingly.

A small voice in the back of Meeks's head screamed a warning, along with an uncomfortable tickle at the back of his neck, but before the worries could seep into his mind, they were already fizzling out in the heat of his biting hunger, and just like Mette and Justus, he was literally eating out of the cosmonaut's hand.

"Easy, easy, there's more!"

"More?" asked Meeks and Justus simultaneously, and Adrian nodded.

He was so grateful for that nod that he would have whooped if he weren't so exhausted. Every second, he regained some of his energy. It felt like an ancient power line that, after an eternity, was again supplied with basic voltage, albeit a low one.

The cosmonaut led them between the trees ,and they scrambled around like animals on the moss, ignoring scraggly bushes and falling onto a bush with more red berries as if their lives depended on it. They smacked their lips and sighed contentedly. They ate it all, pausing only when the last berry was gone, and their mouths were smeared red.

"Did we really just eat fruit unknown to us on an alien planet like it was popcorn?" Justus asked, suddenly pale.

"I'm afraid so." Meeks waved it off. "But we had to eat something. It's as simple as that."

"He's right," Mette said, agreeing with him. "If they were poisonous, we'll know."

"What if James and Mila ate some of them and it didn't

turn out well?" Justus asked. "They aren't answering our calls and we know they couldn't have gotten far in their condition."

Meeks remembered the leaf he had thought had been covered in blood and swallowed.

"We have to go find them."

"Where?" asked Mette.

"You stay put and we'll walk in a semicircle away from here. On the left is the river; they won't have gone in there, so only the other side remains. They can't have gone back, or they would have met us, so we'll aim northwest, but in such a way that we stay within sight of each other."

Meeks picked himself up and he felt sensation slowly return to his limbs, as if the calories he had ingested were rushing through his veins like a warm liquid, waking individual body parts from their hibernation. He stretched and rubbed his fingers together. He turned toward the river and waved to Adrian and Justus.

"I'm going this way."

They nodded and he set off, following the tiny path that looked like a drunk had built it with a plow. It had to be a game trail, which meant there was game. Which meant there might be more fauna besides birds. He became uneasy as he thought about wandering through the strange forest with nothing but empty hands.

He walked back to Mette, who eyed him silently, and then to their sleeping camp, where they had left the rifles without even thinking about taking them along. They had simply been too hungry, too exhausted to carry the bulky weapons, even though they were not even particularly heavy. Now, however, he had the strength, and he grabbed one. Before he left the clearing, Justus and Adrian also returned, one after the other, and they exchanged a few knowing glances before going back to their search.

Something had happened here. Mila and James would never have just disappeared, telling no one. It might have suited him, but the Russian would have told them. And James had become much more cooperative and team-oriented after going it alone with the teleporter. His willingness to sacrifice himself for the group and confront the monster proved more could be expected from him. This knowledge made Meeks more restless, which he did not like at all.

Again and again, he knelt where leaves or branches had snapped off, but he had to admit to himself that in a forest he was about as useful as a flamethrower in a fire department. To him, everything looked the same. Some leaves had a slightly different shape, and here and there the ground was churned up, but that might have been for any number of reasons.

He returned to Mette empty-handed, certain they were hopelessly useless in this environment. He realized with a sinking heart that the others had had no luck either.

"They're gone," Adrian said, voicing what they were all thinking. "Whatever happened, they're gone, and we have to help them."

"What if they…" Justus didn't finish the sentence, but he didn't need to.

"Until we know, we have to assume they're still alive," the cosmonaut said firmly, and Meeks envied his confidence. "Since we couldn't find any tracks, I suggest that one of us climb one of the trees and see if anything can be made out from above. A campfire, perhaps, or something."

"I'm sure Justus is a good climber," Mette suggested before anyone could object.

"Me?" the German asked, blinking.

"Yes. You're the fittest of us, even though Adrian is pretty strong for his age."

"Very charming," the Russian said laconically at her comment.

"I'm just saying that—"

"It's okay." Adrian waved it off and turned to Justus. "Can you do that?"

"I think so." The astrophysicist didn't look enthusiastic as he eyed the massive tree trunks around them suspiciously. But he finally nodded. "All right, then."

5

When the car pulled up, Justus had just sunk his hands into the kitchen sink and was using a rough sponge to scrub the leftovers off the plates from the dinner he had just finished with his wife, Sarah, and their two sons, Friedrich and Michel. The mixture of warm water and dish-washing detergent made the skin on his fingers wrinkly, and every time he moved them back and forth in circles, smaller pieces still left over from the entrecote and broccoli florets struck against the back of his hand. Others probably thought it disgusting, or at least annoying. Even Sarah shrugged her shoulders today when she saw he wasn't draining away the dishwater but was putting more into the sink. He, however, loved this ritual.

Twice a week, he cooked because he loved cooking, with its meditative simplicity and the feeling of creating something with his hands that gave others pleasure afterward. This included washing the dishes, where he enjoyed the warmth on his hands. Although simple and relatively mind-less, he was often able to solve simple problems by moving his hands back and forth, rather than at work, where he pored over complex astrophysics theories and spent hours dwelling on tiny partial aspects of an idea that he might have to discard after a few months of thinking about it. He would pick up a tool, in this case the sponge, and get going, and it would only take a few minutes to discover the solution. Then the plates and cutlery would stand wet and shiny in the rack to dry.

That's it. No more thoughts, no more back and forth.

Sarah was putting their twins to bed, who had to go to school the next morning, when his cell phone rang. He awkwardly placed the last plate in the designated rack and dried his hands on the towel hanging over his shoulder before answering.

"Falkenhagen."

"Should we ring the bell?" the man from the federal police asked.

"No, I'm coming. Give me fifteen minutes, please."

"We've planned for it, doctor. The plane takes off in two hours, so we have a half-hour buffer."

"Thanks." Justus hung up, sighed, and placed his cell phone on the countertop next to the sink. The last remnants of dirty water gurgled into the drain, leaving stained foam as he stared, lost in thought. A slight rustle announced the gradually bursting of the myriad small bubbles.

Finally, he turned away, deliberately placing the towel neatly over the wide handle of the oven so it could dry, knowing full well it would be the last time he did so for some time. It was a mundane task, and yet it felt charged with special meaning. He walked from the kitchen into the hallway and up the stairs; the fourth plank creaked slightly, so he skipped it. At the top, he leaned the doorway of the room Friedrich and Michel shared. Now that they were in school, he and Sarah had tried to put them in separate rooms at the end of the summer, the house that once belonged to his parents was big enough, but the two had cried instead of rejoicing because they thought Mom and Dad wanted to separate them. Even after six years, they were still learning new things about life with twins.

He smiled wistfully as he watched Sarah sit diagonally on Michel's bed and stroked his blond hair off his forehead. His little eyes were already closed, and his chest rose and fell in a steady rhythm. Friedrich was already asleep in his bed under the window, wrapped in his dinosaur bedding. The dinosaur phase would probably never pass with him, whereas Michel inexplicably seemed to prefer cars. Not everything was the same with twins.

Sarah noticed him and threw him an amorous smile, which slowly faded as she noticed the sadness in his eyes.

"Is it time?" she whispered, her face serious as she came to him, and he nodded mutely. She put a finger to her lips and slowly closed the bedroom door before they went downstairs to the large living room with its wingback chairs. Two wheeled suitcases stood next to the fireplace, packed and ready for his three days away.

"My cab is here."

"Do you really have to go?" Sarah asked, the plea in her voice almost breaking his heart.

"I'm a laboratory astrophysicist, honey."

"The best in Europe!"

"It's just a prize."

"The most important one."

"How important can it be if I don't even have a five-figure salary, huh?" he said, grabbing her upper arms. They looked deeply into each other's eyes then embraced intimately.

"But we have enough. I don't want you to go to the U.S.,"

she murmured against his chest, her voice muffled by the thick fabric of his wool sweater.

"My contract was only for one more year, and then I would have to transfer to the university."

"They'll take you. You're a luminary."

"University careers work differently," he said, inhaling the scent of her hair. He would miss it. "This job in the US is just to a few months and the salary is enough so I won't have to work for at least ten years. I could finally start my own institute."

"Six months sounds like an eternity to me."

"You can visit me anytime."

"At least once a month!" she demanded, detaching herself from his embrace and looking him in the eyes. "Understood?"

"Yes, honey," he said, smiling.

"You always said astrophysicists weren't needed in the private sector. Now a telescope builder wants—"

"Manufacturer of radio telescopes," he clarified, and she waved her hand in front of his face as if his words were smoke.

"Whatever. Big mirrors. Now someone like that wants to shower you with money. If that's the case, it can work here too, can't it?"

"If I do it, then at least I have a foot in the door, and I can use it as a reference. It's the right thing to do for our family, honey. Believe me, I wouldn't be doing it otherwise. We've talked about this for a long time, haven't we?"

"If you call a week-long—"

"That's not fair. I involved you in everything from the beginning. I could have said no."

"I know," she sighed and leaned against him. "It's just...

now that it's come to this... I'm just being emotional. It's not like you're leaving the planet."

"Right." He kissed the top of her head. *Besides, the lab fired me two weeks ago,* he thought, feeling a deep shame rising inside him.

Sooner or later, she would find out he no longer had a job and was just leaving in the morning to sit in his car for hours, wondering what to do next. He had decided, against his late parents' advice, to become an astrophysicist rather than a teacher. That he had turned down various modeling jobs was something they could understand, but in exchange for a secure degree followed by civil service status at a high school was something else entirely. In the end, though, they had been right, and all because he had been too impatient.

Had he allowed the experiment to continue, he might have been able to detect his xenomolecule, but instead, in all his hope, he had started data analysis too early. He went against the advice of many collaborators to collect more first. The initial results had been sobering, even though he was so sure he had won. A bumbling mistake, born of hubris after his award from the European Research Commission and the desire to show it to the committee at CERN, who had preferred a colleague from France for purely political reasons. He had been so ashamed that he had not even told Sarah. Stupidly, because this had only made things worse for him. For the first few days, he had struggled with himself, always on the verge of telling her. They had always been open with each other and proud of their relationship, which thrived from this openness.

But that morning, after he had turned around and said goodbye, and since, he had felt even more ashamed, because the next day he would have had to admit he had already lost his job the day before and had merely pretended to go to the lab as he did every morning. Each morning the same reasoning, the same shame, only a little stronger, and so a mistake had become a habit.

Who does that? he asked himself, not for the first time, while he stroked her head and looked at his wristwatch. Twenty minutes had passed. *Michael Douglas, maybe, who doesn't want to admit he lost his job at the Department of Defense, but not you. You are forty years old!*

But then came the phone call and the meeting with the head of the chancellor's office, which had thrown everything he thought he believed over the edge. An alien artifact was found in South America, a secret research project to explore its mysteries, and, of all things, they wanted *him.*

Him!

Someone who lied to his wife and, out of sheer hubris, sabotaged one of his scientific dreams through impatience and carelessness. Of course, the chancellor didn't know this and her informants considered him, perhaps after a few phone calls, the number one choice for what was being researched. Only he didn't know why. Presumably, it was for political reasons, as it always was with politicians.

"I really have to go now, honey," he said with some reluctance, feeling a slight pressure behind his eyes and a not-so-slight tugging in his stomach as she pulled away from him. It was like taking away his coat in the middle of a snowstorm. "I'll call you as soon as I land, I promise."

"Yes, please arrive safely."

I did it, Sarah, he wanted to shout to her. *I got fired, but I pulled myself out of the mess again. I'm getting almost as much money a month as I was getting a year before, and I'm researching an alien artifact. An alien* artifact! *Can you imagine that? Your husband is going to collaborate on something that could effortlessly push the boundaries of what we know up to now. You can be proud of me again.*

But as he walked across the small path of the front yard to the waiting luxury sedan with Berlin license plates and tinted windows, accompanied by the hollow scrape of the wheels of his suitcases, he felt regret along with the cold drizzle on his face. He would prove himself on this project and show that his mistake was only a one-time thing. That he wasn't just some exuberant young man with the beaming smile whom everyone thought was a poster boy, not a serious scientist. His reputation testified to what he could do, and his appointment to this project was not merely proof that the chancellor apparently did not care about the animosities of his colleagues, but about facts, and factually he had a lot going for him, no matter what personal mistakes he had made.

In the armored limousine, two beefy federal police officers in suits sat in the front seats. One of them got out and put his luggage in the trunk, while Justus got into the rear. He didn't turn to look at Sarah because he was afraid that he would cry, and he would have felt childish. He missed her already, just like his two sons.

It's only for a few months, maybe a year, he thought. *When the project becomes public, or at least bigger, it will probably become a long-term thing. You don't do something like this on the side. And the first scientists involved become the veterans of the first hour, whom you can't do without. We might move to the US, who knows?*

Justus's hands ached from the rough bark of the "prime oak," as he had christened the tree species with its serrated oval leaves and mighty branches. The first few meters of his ascent were the most difficult, and he had needed help from Adrian and Meeks to reach the lowest branch and pull himself up. Finally, he was surprised he had mustered enough strength to pull himself up. At home in the gym, he probably would have laughed about it since he always stayed fit, but here he felt like a wrung-out can of energy drink, with only a tiny residue of the once-energizing beverage reminding him of its contents.

Now he was climbing between increasingly intertwined branches, pushing smaller branches and leaves away from his face, trying to determine the best way up to the top of the tree without seeing very much.

If I'd known it was the last time I'd see them, he thought, resting both feet against a mushroom bulb growing out of the trunk like a rock-hard tumor to push up and grab the next branch with both hands, *I would have turned around. Should have turned around! What does she think now when I don't return her calls? Don't get back to her? Did the Air Force contact her and give her a death notice? He didn't even know what had happened to his body after they got into the teleporter. I wonder if it's in a coma. Did Sarah arrive with the children? Was she now sitting and crying next to the lifeless shell of her husband, the father of her children, while the machines beeped and droned, keeping him alive like a mere vessel without contents? What were the doctors telling her? Were the paramedics able to get him on life support fast enough? The entire complex was being cleared, and there had been quite a few of them.*

His head seemed to explode amid the many circling thoughts.

I did what I thought was right, Sarah. If there is no way back, I hope you and the kids will someday know the truth and be proud of me. I didn't want to run away one more time and live with the shame of having done something wrong. This is bigger than me, bigger than us, and the team needs me. Maybe humanity, though that sounds very grandiose.

With grim determination, he pulled himself to the next branch and squatted on it, startled by how thin the branches had become. His palms were cut, not deeply, but enough that they itched and burned, and tiny droplets of blood stood out in some places.

"Can't be far now," he muttered to himself and listened to the chatter of the birds around him for a few moments.

A moment ago, it had been loud above him, as if a whole flock of sparrows was nesting among the dense leaves. But as he climbed higher, they had fallen silent, probably waiting for the troublemaker to disappear. Now heard the varied calls of other birds in the other trees and enjoyed this constant proof of life. Never would he have thought that something so banal could warm his heart so much. It was comforting to know there was something else breathing this air with him, that he was not surrounded only by death, monsters, and the stinking morass of organic decay.

His muscles were burning and trembling. So, after his short break he continued, groaning and struggling through dense foliage until his head finally reached free air. He stood on two branches and clung to two twigs thinner than his fingers. He swayed slightly without secure footing, but he was able to keep his balance. Enough, at least, to survey the land.

The view was sublime and took his breath away. It even made the hammering of his heart fade. A pleasant, undulating sea of lush green spread out before him, gently swaying back and forth in the breeze. The leaves, bulging with chlorophyll, seemed to rustle and applaud the gentle breeze, and every now and then the horizon glistened blue. Though the sky was overcast and the clouds looked just as dirty as always, a brown yellow like the chemical-swollen exhaust of an industrial plant, something was giving off light. Perhaps the glow of the many tiny dots on the leaves created a brighter glow. He felt like a surfer whose head had broken the surface of the water and was breathing deeply for the first time after a fall. Amid the canopy of the forest, there was only him and the clouds above. No fear, no tense muscles that ached all over, no worn-out limbs and no nightmares of roaring creatures in the night.

He took one last deep breath and absorbed the sight of the endless greenery, then admonished himself to his task and searched the leafy landscape, which was incredibly dense. He could imagine himself walking on it as if it were soft grass.

Far to the west, were the gray brown towers of solid material that looked like concrete, a city of unfinished skyscrapers, dotted with regular dark patches, possibly windows. He estimated the distance at twenty or thirty kilometers, at least. At this distance, the buildings looked like they were growing out of the uniform vegetation like morbid growths.

He blinked and let his gaze wander and noticed a golden glow along the terminator line between the forest and the sky, for which he could think of no explanation. He wondered if the forest ended there.

Further south, there was something else. Where the wall stretched undamaged as far as he could see, it looked like there was an open area amid the trees. There was a large dark patch that could only have come from shadows. The hillside of leafy canopies was undoubtedly broken at this point, and he thought he saw thin wisps of smoke.

Under different circumstances and in a different place, he might have thought what he was looking at was the crash site of an airplane that had burned out, due to its somewhat wedge shape but without any blazing flames.

Back on the ground, the others were calmly waiting. They sat in a loose circle between the towering roots, which they used as backrests and seemed to doze. Only Adrian was somewhat alert and keeping an eye on the surroundings. The sight of the team, or what was left of it, reminded him that eating the alien berries—which had tasted incredibly good—had given them energy but not really made them fit. They still had far too few calories and were starving, just not so much that he feared collapsing. Justus had fasted once before when Sarah had been on a healing fast before her pregnancy, but that had been without the constant anxiety and physical exertion in an oppressively tropical climate.

"There seems to be a large clearing to the south, near the wall," he reported when the others noticed his return. "I saw smoke coming from there. I don't know what it is, but other than the structures to the west, I couldn't see anything but leaves as far as the eye could see."

"Smoke, huh?" Meeks asked, rubbing his chin thoughtfully.

"If there are no other suggestions, I think we should look into it," Adrian said, looking at everyone. No one disagreed, and Justus was glad that they didn't think twice about looking for James and Mila, no matter what shape they were in.

So, the Russian and the American resolutely picked up their rifles, while Justus retrieved and shouldered his before helping Mette to her feet and wrapping her arm around his neck.

"Let's go!"

6

J ames's world was black, but only before his eyes. Someone had put a sack over his head, and the air inside was becoming increasingly stuffy. He was being carried but felt no restraints, so his imagination kept hitting walls.

What had happened? Who had kidnapped him? And where was Mila? Images of aliens ran through his head, dragging him through the forest, either with tentacles or telekinetically, abducting him. Nobody said anything.

He could not utter a word, not even to call for Mila. A fear had crept over him that with the slightest sound he might provoke a reaction that would end badly for him. Or worse, for her.

So, he had no choice but to listen to the snapping of twigs surrounding him that possibly came from footsteps. With time, his hearing became more and more refined, and he imagined he could hear the grass being crushed, the moss smacked, and the ferns gently brushed. There was also the rustle of the wind in the treetops, which was unmistakable, mixed with the birdsong, which was not equal to the choirs in earthly rainforests, but at least had a calming effect on him.

The worries, of course, still remained. Besides the immediate fear from the uncertainty of what was happening to them and who had taken them, there was the fear that the rest of the team might think they had run away or were dead. Would they ever find each other again?

"Tak tu!" someone shouted, and James froze.

"Mak ta tu!" replied another voice. Both were loud and harsh in the silence that had reigned before, like axes striking a tender twig.

"Mila?" he whispered cautiously.

"James?" came the answer, close by, and a great weight fell from his heart.

"Are you okay? Are you hurt?"

"No, I don't think so. And you?"

"I'm all right."

"Do you hear that?"

James listened and nodded, unseeing. He heard voices, many voices, farther away and so numerous that they were a jumble.

"Do you think these are the locals? The ones Nasaku was talking about?"

"I don't know. But I hope so," she said softly.

"Malak tan! Uluk hanan?" They were interrupted. The man was nearby, and James froze. But when someone else answered in the foreign tongue, he relaxed again.

"I'm not so sure that's cause for hope right now."

"Nasaku was obviously not hostile," she objected.

"But she lied to me and used me," he said.

"You mean the story about her children and that she came here from another planet?"

"Yes. She told me that her way back was cut off, and her children had died here. That obviously wasn't the case."

"At least she was able to tell you that. Your Sumerian wasn't very good," Mila said.

"That's true, but she also lied to me about her language skills. After all, she clearly knew English later," he replied, surprised by his cynicism.

"Up until now you've always been protective of her and tried to convince us to trust her. What happened to that?"

"We were kidnapped and—oh, I don't know. I just feel like a pawn in a game whose rules I don't understand. He sighed and tried to remember Nasaku's face, to fathom what was going on behind it. But she remained a riddle. Something about her had been so smooth and aloof, as if he was dealing with a robot that simply could not be read. After all that had happened, he didn't think that was impossible, even though he had seen her bleed.

"I know what you mean."

"Nak lok tuun!" someone barked, and he swallowed his next retort, irritated by the harsh tone of the stranger near him.

The sounds of a large gathering of people steadily increased and were now loud enough to make him think they were close. The birds continued their chorus of sound underneath it all, but the wind in the trees was barely audible. He tried to pick out something, recognize it, look for patterns, but he found only what sounded like human speech that he could not understand. He imagined he'd been carried off by Amazonian natives in loincloths, cannibals carrying him on a pole through the jungle like hunted game that would soon roast over the fire.

He shuddered.

After a while, during which he tried to absorb every

sound to create a virtual picture of his surroundings, it abruptly quiet and noticeably cooler. He was set down and he felt damp ground under his buttocks. Footsteps moved away, creating a strange echo, then silence. Only now he noticed his hands and feet were free, and he moved the joints gingerly. They did not hurt but felt a little rusty.

"Mila?"

"Yes?"

He grabbed his head and pulled the fabric off. Mila was sitting next to him on a damp stone floor in the middle of a cave in semi-darkness. It was about the size of a small room with a vaulted ceiling, roughly carved into the rock and a small exit he could have ducked through if it hadn't been for the crude, cobbled-together lattice of thick branches blocking the way.

James turned to Mila, grabbed her by the shoulders, and examined her for injuries with narrowed eyes.

"I'm fine," she assured him, looking at him with an expression he couldn't read. There was something in her gaze beyond the gloom that always surrounded her. A new life, perhaps, that hadn't been there before. Even if it was a misinterpretation on his part, after all, he couldn't think of anything that could have provided any comfort in their situation.

"Are you sure?" he asked, checking her wrists. They were a little red but not bleeding.

"I'm all right, James!" she said, almost laughing as she looked around. "Although I'd feel more comfortable if I wasn't locked in a cave."

"Did you see who brought us here?"

She shook her head. "No, when I took the bag off my head there was no one here but you. But if they wanted to kill us, I think it would have happened in the forest."

"I hope so. I didn't even see them coming."

"No wonder, we were lying on our backs, exhausted. Like Adam and Eve in paradise. We were preoccupied with the sight of the leaves above us. I don't know about you, but I feel pretty naive, especially for a scientist."

"You're too hard on yourself. Instead of naive, you could say hungry and scared."

"I wasn't scared," she objected, and the serious look in her eyes confused him.

"I'm sorry, I didn't mean to—"

"It's okay, I didn't mean it that way." She was lost in thought as she rubbed her belly. "It's just..."

Mila seemed to wrestle with herself and looked around again, this time more cautiously. It reminded him of a cornered animal.

"Hey." He grabbed her again by her shoulders. "Whatever it is, you don't have to say it."

"Yes, I've had to for a long time."

"I hope I didn't—"

She shook her head. "No, not to you, to myself. You poured your heart out to me in your quarters. The whole thing with Joana, and I just listened."

"Yes, and I'm still grateful to you for that. It was really liberating to get that off my chest. I'd had all that buried inside me for so long I didn't know how to get rid of it. It was like trying to squeeze a mountain through a bottleneck." James sighed. "If you had to sum up what's bothering you in one sentence, what would that sentence be? When you have it in front of you and it scares you, it's the one you want to admit to yourself."

Mila considered and nodded.

"I didn't want to live anymore."

James blinked in surprise. "Excuse me?"

"I didn't want to live anymore," she repeated, swallowing visibly. Her nostrils quivered, as did her full lips. When she continued, her voice was firm, determined, underlaid with a tapestry of pain to which he could instinctively sympathize from his own experience. "They're all dead. All the people I loved. If there's a God, he's taken everything from me. If there isn't, I'm the definition of bad luck."

James felt the urge to take her in his arms, but his own experience stopped him. She was about to realize that her own mountain could fit through the neck of the bottle and at this stage he was wise to not interrupt her before it was through. He remained silent and was just there for her, in the middle of this cave, where he was supposed to be afraid, and yet he only had eyes for Mila, and nothing in the world was more important than the pain she had to get rid of.

"I lost an unborn child a few months before I was selected for the project. My husband, Dima, died six months before that," Mila said, her gaze fixed on her memories, which he could not see but could feel. "Two blows, and in the midst of my grief, my mother crashed with my other two children in the car. I had no one left, James, and though I have always considered myself an extremely strong and pragmatic woman, I did not know what to do. I just felt so lonely and wanted it to be over ."

"You were thinking about killing yourself," he said.

"Yes," she breathed.

"There's no shame in that. I've thought about it over and over myself and even Googled the quickest and most effective ways." James pressed his lips together. "I was probably too much of a coward to do it, and instead found reasons to live."

"Sneaking money from kidnappers that you gave to your ex-fiancée's charity?"

"Yes. And that was good."

"That's how it was with this project. I saw a silver lining on the horizon for the first time, but that horizon was cloudy." Again, she rubbed her belly, lost in thought. "The tumor that led to my baby's death... I only had weeks left, James. And here it's gone, I know it. I've told you, but the pain of what happened weighs worse than the tumor."

"And you'll never get rid of that, but it gets a little easier every day. Sometimes that's all we can hope for." He considered and impulsively took her hand. "But if there's one thing I've learned, it's this: We're never given more than we can handle. You're the best example of that, aren't you? When I hear what happened to you, I just can't imagine how anyone can get through it. Just thinking about it makes my heart go cold, and I almost feel ashamed for falling into such darkness just because the love of my life left me and I had to keep a secret. What's that dilemma against losing everyone you love? But when you thought your life was crushing you, this project came out of nowhere."

Mila nodded thoughtfully. "My mother once told me, if you need a light, go turn it on. I never understood what she was trying to tell me, but she was the most pragmatic person I've ever known. Today, I think I understand what she was trying to tell me."

"She was wise in her own way."

"Yes, she was." Mila nodded again and squeezed his hand. "Thank you."

"So, did the mountain fit through the bottle?" he asked gently.

"No, but the bottle is no longer there."

James smiled.

"This is a fresh start for all of us, maybe more so for you and me than it is for them, but it is a start."

"I just wish it didn't start out in a wet, cold prison."

"At least this place is better than what was waiting for us inside the walls."

"You're right about that." She turned his hand over in hers, so the back of his hand was facing up. On it was a penny-sized red spot, the beginning of an abscess. "Have you noticed it hasn't gotten any worse since we left the death zone around the teleporter?"

"No, but you're right. There's no abscess yet." He pursed his lips and exposed his knee to look at the spot on the kneecap, careful not to let go of her hand. There, too, he saw only a large red spot that looked exactly as it had yesterday. Within the walls, it had taken no more than an hour or two. By now, a suppurating abscess should have long since formed.

"I wonder how that's possible," Mila said. "After all, a big wall isn't something that keeps pathogens or toxins in the air from spreading. Maybe it's something to do with this forest. On Earth, after all, there are terpenes secreted by trees that stabilize the immune system."

"Terpenes?"

"Something like essential oils. However, their effect is much more subtle and long-term and requires long exposure."

"I would imagine it had something to do with those blue fireflies," he said. "They didn't look natural to me."

"What is certain is that this place raises many questions." Mila's expression suddenly hardened, and James turned his head toward the entrance.

"Someone's coming!"

"Yes."

The figure was definitely humanoid, with two legs, a head, and arms, but seemed made only of shadows because the daylight shone from behind. Only when it reached the grate and opened a clasp on the side could he make out details: It was a man with powerful muscles that stretched under almost chalk-white skin. He was shorter than James and had a large head covered with long blond hair with large bright eyes that fixed him and Mila. He wore simple shorts woven from flax or something similar and gaiters of the same fabric, but was otherwise unclothed except for a dark sash. When it became clear he was coming into the cave, they both stood, and James stood protectively in front of the Russian.

The stranger pulled the grate closed behind him and James noticed that he did not fasten the latch.

"Did you see that?" he asked Mila quietly, carefully raising both hands in a gesture of appeasement but would also allow him to use them quickly if it came to a fight.

"Yes," she said. "And he's unarmed."

"I saw that, too."

"Should we try something?"

"No," he said without taking his eyes off the pale figure who stopped two steps away and examined them.

"What if he attacks us?"

No weapons, no obvious threat, tension in the features, a slight twitch in the corner of the mouth, but eyes are relaxed. James analyzed the man as he had done dozens of times before with warlords, pirates, kidnappers, and other criminals he had dealt with. *I'm not just analyzing him, he's analyzing us.*

"He won't," he said, keeping his voice soft and calm. Then he addressed their visitor, "Hello." He placed a hand on his chest and said, "My name is James." He pointed to Mila. "This is Mila."

"Tuk mak," said the man in a full-throated voice, and

even as James wondered if that was his name, he turned and strolled out. Only now did James see two knife handles in the back of his trousers, protruding from frighteningly long leather sheaths.

"And what was that?" Mila asked when the grate was closed again, and the stranger was gone. She exhaled loudly.

"I'm not sure," he said. "But he didn't attack us, even though he was armed and could have overpowered us. We have no weapons and are physically weak. He was tense, but I couldn't see any fear. I think he was testing us."

"Testing?"

"Yes. The door was obviously left open, he was here alone and armed. Many prisoners would have flanked him and tried to overpower him to escape. Hell, I might have done that if I wasn't so exhausted and been tested by men I was much more afraid of."

"They want to know if we're a threat. That's a good sign, I suppose."

"I think so. But these people not only look different, they speak differently and they're from an alien planet. I could be wrong; body language could have evolved differently here. After all, symbolic interactions are very different between cultures on Earth. It won't be any better between other planets."

"And then there are other problems, such as diseases. Contrary to how history is read today, the conquistadors did not wipe out all of Central America with their few hundred fighters, but rather the pathogens they introduced. The simplest flu viruses, measles, and rubella, possibly even simple cold viruses were responsible for over ninety percent of the deaths and for the demise of the Maya and Inca," Mila explained, "because there was an ocean between them. There's a vacuum between us and them."

"No, just a teleporter," he reminded her, tapping his chest. "This body here is mine, but it also belongs to this planet. It was created here, so let's hope the teleporter builders thought of obvious vulnerabilities like this."

"Good point," she admitted. "I just wish…"

"They would bring us food?" he asked, gesturing toward the entrance. On the other side of the door, a woman was holding a woven basket with the outline of fruits and vegetables in front of her belly.

7

The woman did not speak to them, only placed the basket of raffia-like material in front of them and left. She seemed shy, but perhaps it was just the extreme paleness of her skin and the dark circles around her eyes that gave him that impression.

As soon as she was gone, he and Mila tucked into the fruits and vegetables offered: juicy fruit with a sweet aroma and starchy, leafy vegetables that looked like kale. He was particularly fond of an apple, which was the same shape as its earthly equivalent and reddish in color, but tasted more like a cross between a pear and a cocoa bean.

Under all the food, what he had first thought was cloth or fur laid at the bottom to protect the food, was a leather water skin. The water smelled of old feet but tasted good, and they emptied it, down to the last drop.

Afterward, they both had stomachaches from the sudden amount of food they had eaten far too quickly, as if there would never be anything to eat again. His stomach rebelled with wave after wave of cramps after two days of hunger, and more than once he thought he would throw up.

"If these people aren't just feeding us so they have more to bite on after they cook us over their fire, they really are friendlier than I thought," Mila said after a while. With gentle force, James urged her to use the empty skin as a mat so she wouldn't get cold in the humidity. He sat right next to her, shoulder to shoulder, keeping the entrance with the irregular grating always in view.

"I think so, too. After all, even the monster didn't kill us, although it had the power to do so."

"Because Nasaku told you how to overcome it."

"She implied it, and her actions and statements suggested it."

"For all I care, it can go on like this." Mila sighed and held her stomach. "No bellyaches, a roof over our heads, we're fed, and we're safe."

"So are animals in the zoo," he replied, earning a sour look. They were silent a while and he realized how tired he was. His full stomach meant exhaustion was joined by an almost blissful stupor that made his eyelids heavy, even though he didn't want to sleep. He had to stay awake and alert in case something happened, and he needed to react. What if another person subjected them to more tests?

But was no use, soon he fell asleep.

He dreamed of snow-white figures visiting him in his New York apartment in Manhattan to bake bread with him, but when he found there was no salt in the house, they became displeased. Joana had left him a letter saying she could no longer live near pink salt and was going to Africa where it was never pink.

He took a handful of pepper and his late father appeared to him as a ghost, warning that pepper came from Mars and must be used in good doses. But the pepper turned his white guests into monsters with razor blades for teeth, giving him five minutes to bake the bread. But the oven was actually a cave where Mila lived, a very small version of Mila, whom he desperately wanted to kiss, but she was just too small. Afraid he might accidentally swallow her in the attempt, he stumbled back and tumbled out the open window into the depths.

While he fell he realized that he was dreaming and he woke up with his heart pounding. Sleep fell away and with it the illusion of the extremely strange fantasy world his brain had knitted together.

"Are you all right?" Mila asked.

"Yeah," he mumbled, bashfully wiping saliva from the corner of his mouth. "How long was I asleep?"

"I don't know." She held out her freed wrists. "It's light outside, anyway."

"Still or again?"

"I'm afraid I don't know that either. I've been asleep myself until a while ago, and while I feel tight in places I didn't even know I had, I don't feel the least bit tired anymore."

"Someone's coming," he said, pointing ahead.

Two bulky silhouettes approached through the tube-like entrance, their heads bowed, their gait a bit crabbed. The one in front fiddled with the latch and pulled open the grate. He, unlike his companion, was portly, with mighty mountains of flesh on his powerful torso and a jiggling double chin. His skin was also white as lime and his hair a silver gray.

"Nak taku," he said, tilting his head slightly. The other man, muscular and with the look of an eagle, stood diagonally behind him with his arms folded.

James stood slowly, hands outstretched so as not to appear threatening, though he didn't know how he could have looked threatening in the first place, and Mila followed his lead. Their visitor seemed to expect an answer and looked at her patiently, waiting.

Body language, anyone can do that, James reminded himself, and bent to pick up the empty plate Mila had been sitting on. He held it with one hand and tapped the empty water skin, then his chest at heart level, and bowed.

"Thank you!"

Mila nodded and rubbed her belly before lowering her head as well.

To her surprise, the man laughed and clapped his greasy hands. His chin wobbled back and forth and his eyes grew moist with amusement.

James exchanged a glance with Mila, who seemed as irritated as he was and merely shrugged. He also decided to smile but was careful not to show his teeth, which was considered rude or even a sign of aggression by some primitive peoples on Earth.

However it was received, the stranger seemed satisfied and held a hand over his solar plexus.

"Monka'Ka!" he shouted cheerfully.

"Is that his name?" Mila asked.

Monka'Ka pointed at her. "Issas no nursi?"

"Uh, no, no. My name is Mila." She mimicked his gesture and said slowly, "Mila."

James hurried to do likewise, repeating his own name.

"Milla ke James." Monka wiggled his head. "Mak to, mak to!"

He turned toward the opening and waved at them with a very earthly gesture.

"Shall we...?"

"I think so," James said as Monka waddled off and his

companion, who appeared to be something of a bodyguard, stood back, waiting, but kept the passageway clear.

They walked out into a large clearing about the size of two soccer fields side by side. Round wooden huts with palm-frond roofs formed a tight circle in the middle, leaving a clear twenty-meter boundary to the trees. One or two hundred chalk-white men, women, and children were gathered in the dusty village square as if at a reception. They wore little clothing except loincloths and the simplest of pants. It was notable that the women showed their breasts openly but hid their hair under tightly woven scarves that stretched along their backs and appeared rigid.

Old and young, man and woman, child and infant, they all stared wide-eyed at James and Mila. Not frightened, not aggressive, *fascinated.* It would have been easy to feel uncomfortable at so much attention, but, strangely, James did not. On the contrary, he felt secure, without being able to say exactly why. Was it because he had secretly expected to have fallen into the clutches of cannibals and so only now could relax? Or was it because his trained gaze unconsciously absorbed all their body language and, in an automated part of his brain, deciphered them all at once and concluded that no harm lay ahead of them here?

Monka led them to a rug, spread out on the ground amid all the staring villagers, with an irritating pattern of jagged lines and concentric circles that made him dizzy if he looked at it too long. He sat down rather awkwardly, and James and Mila followed his lead after he spread his hands invitingly.

"Monka mak to!" the chief exulted, at least James thought he was someone in that or an equivalent position.

"Monka mak to," he repeated, and peals of laughter went through the ranks of the villagers, spreading out in waves and passing back and forth. Even the chief's mighty belly bounced up and down under his enthusiastic laughter. James decided to be polite and laugh as well. At least he tried, and Mila joined in after some hesitation.

Once the general amusement subsided, an hour-long back and forth of foreign terms began, a cultural approach of the third kind. They were shown various tools, axes, hammers, and knives, and given emphatically pronounced words. Then fruits and vegetables, rugs, jewelry, and clothing followed in the same manner. The tribe's interest in their strange visitors, with much darker skin and dark hair, foreign bodies among the natives, did not break, and only the smallest ones eventually got bored at and moved away in cackling and shrieking playgroups toward the huts or trees, so the ranks thinned a little at least.

Soon they were all sitting cross-legged on the ground, improvised seating furniture, or their own blankets and rugs. Besides Monka, other residents brought things to show and explain to him and Mila, and they didn't hesitate to use English or Russian to name something in return. They were greatly interested in learning as much as they could from their guests.

James was no expert on such situations but knew that in similar ones on Earth, after a promising initial phase, many things had often gone wrong.

Again and again, Monka and the whole village fell into merry laughter. Eventually, he and Mila felt so comfortable they became more and more free and optimistic in their body language. Soon they were trying to explain in elaborate pantomime why their skin was darker—possibly the sun hardly ever shined here in the extreme cloudiness—that they were not a couple and what the difference was between him as an American and Mila as a Russian. She put it quite pragmatically by creating four circles from small branches and placing five apples in the center. Two of the circles were to represent America, James, and Russia, Mila. She first took the Russian circle and put it around an apple before saying "Russia," then she said "America," shot at the other circles, broke them apart, and put all the fruit in the American circle.

"Very funny," he commented on her curt look while her audience appeared irritated. But he was not bothered by the teasing and waved it off with a smile before becoming more serious. He took six of the unbraided branches and placed them in front of him, then he looked Monka in the eye and pointed to two of them. "James and Mila." He tapped them gently and then touched the remaining four before pointing into the woods. "Friends. Our friends."

Mila also became serious and a little pale. It had been easy, in the general excitement of this first contact with real people on an alien planet, to forget for a few hours that they were part of a team. But he couldn't forget it, and so the concern about Justus, Mette, Meeks, and Adrian suddenly grew stronger like a storm gathering on the horizon faster than they could get to safety.

"They are our friends," he repeated, vigorously tapping the four branches he had separated from his and Mila's. "We thank you for your hospitality, but we need to find them. They're out there all alone, probably looking for us. Please."

Monka eyed him, his brow furrowed, and seemed to think. One of the burly men from the front row went up to the chief and whispered something to him.

"Ahu," he said, then looked concerned before placing a hand on his chest and pointing to the four lone sticks. A whole torrent of words left his mouth and he turned to the group. Several men joined him and finally disappeared between the huts, heading toward the forest.

Shortly after that, the gathering broke up, and many villagers were obviously disappointed He and Mila were taken back to the cave, which was not a cave in the conventional sense at all, but something like a walk-in burial mound covered with sod and overgrown with moss. From the outside it looked like an oversized stone oven with a stone tube in front of it, the entrance. Before they could fear being locked up again, Monka sent an entire column of women and children after them, who dragged in blankets, raffia-like mats, more food, and two water skins.

The only thing that was irritating was that a man closed the gate.

"I guess they'd rather play it safe after all," Mila said, voicing what he was thinking.

"Maybe there are predators and they're just trying to protect us."

"You're right." She didn't sound convinced but also didn't seem to want to pursue her theory any more than he did.

"That was amazing," he said. "These people seem so open and happy to me."

"Then why do you sound like you're about to give a eulogy?" Mila asked as they unrolled their raffia mats and laid the roughly woven blankets over them.

"Because I don't understand it."

"I know what you mean." She paused and looked at the exit. "The clouds look toxic, if you ask me. Toxic, just like the teleporter's surroundings inside the wall. These people, however, are healthy, just like the flora, and apparently the fauna. Acid rain would make everything wilt or at least get sick. They probably don't get enough exposure to the sun to produce enough vitamin D. The trees seem sturdy and should protect against wind and the roughest weather, but everything else makes little sense."

"They hardly seem afraid. They were cautious with us but surprisingly good-hearted. We could have played them and then attacked."

"Hardly, with so many of them."

"Just imagine if we had met complete strangers. It doesn't matter if we represent an entire state, we would have wet our pants. We're always afraid of the unknown. Just look at how Pavar reacted when Nasaku escaped. She was *a* stranger among billions of people on our planet and almost everyone freaked out. These people here are different. Very different," he said, rolling his extra blanket into a pillow since it wasn't likely to get very cold at night, even in their shelter.

"They look a little creepy, like ghosts..."

"Happy spirits, perhaps."

"Yes. But you're right, I got the same impression. Let's just hope things keep going this well and that they find the rest of the team."

"They have Adrian with them." He tried to sound encouraging while also addressing his own concerns. "He seems pretty competent at handling unforeseen situations. He was an officer before he became a cosmonaut, wasn't he?"

"Yes. Fighter pilot. But jungle combat might not be one of his areas of expertise."

"That's not needed here. After all, the worst thing they could do would be to attack the village and try to gain access by force."

But as darkness fell and they sprawled out on their now comfortably cushioned mats, that's exactly what happened. At first, James only heard a suspicious *crack* followed by a dull *thud*, like someone had hit a watermelon with a base-ball bat but failed to burst it. A silhouette fell like a wet sack in front of the entrance, and a figure emerged with some-thing in his hands, which James immediately identified as one of their rifles.

It was Adrian, whom James recognized by his sinewy build. It didn't take him long to unfasten the latch of the grate and yank it open.

"Are you hurt?" he hissed into the darkness. "James? Mila?"

"No, we're okay! You shouldn't—" James started to protest, but the Russian didn't give him time.

"Shh, we'll get you out! Can you run?"

"Yes, but—"

"Shh!" Adrian said again and ran to the entrance, where he could hear restless, suppressed voices.

"Adrian!" someone whispered excitedly. "We're out of time!"

"Damn it!" Mila cursed and gestured for James to follow her. "Adrian!"

It's likely he didn't hear them because of their footsteps echoing in the cave. Outside the entrance, a visibly agitated Justus was waiting, holding his rifle against his shoulder, almost like a soldier but awkward.

"Where are Meeks and Mette?" Mila asked.

"In a small clearing nearby," replied the cosmonaut, barely audible. He was about to walk toward the forest, where the cave was located near the edge, but suddenly two men in short cloth pants appeared right in front of him. Their upper bodies were strong and seemed to shimmer like moonlight. They had to be some of the fighters from the village who had gathered around Monka.

James closed his eyes and suppressed a curse. Two more

appeared on their right and others behind them, slowly forming a semicircle, their expressions serious and shadowed in the half-light of the night.

"Blyat!" Adrian cursed and aimed his rifle at the locals near him. Justus did the same on the other side, standing protectively in front of James and Mila.

"Don't!"

"Stay back, they're unarmed. We can still make it if we hurry. When I say *go*, you rush after me, understand?" Adrian hissed.

"No!" James said. "You must drop your guns."

"But they'll tear us to pieces!" the cosmonaut protested. "We're not leaving you behind! And we have to take care of Mette and Meeks; we can't leave them alone."

"Wait!" Mila jumped in to help James. "Look at their faces. They know what those guns are, I'm sure of it, and that means they know they could all die."

"And that's why you have to drop your weapons."

"Are you crazy?" Justus asked, his voice quavering. He aimed nervously at the heads of various locals who had stoically surrounded them.

"These people are not what you think, and I think the tranquility here is part of a greater system," James said. "Please, trust me."

"System? What kind of system?" the cosmonaut wanted to know.

"The monster, Nasaku, these people—I think they are peaceful for a reason."

"That's a big ask, man! If you're wrong—"

"Would you rather kill these unarmed people instead?"

There was a long silence, and James noticed Monka was standing a dozen meters away, watching the scene with a serious look on his face.

"Please. No one has to die here."

Adrian slowly lowered the rifle. "I hope you're right this time, too."

"Thank you. If you trust me, trust me completely."

With a mumbled Russian curse, Adrian threw the gun on the ground, and Justus did the same after a brief hesitation.

James held his breath.

8

SIX MONTHS LATER

J ames sat by the river, which the Tokamaku called
Thunder Stream because a long rapid near the village
roared and it could be heard from far away. He liked to
spend his days here, alone with the loud noise that swallowed everything else. Here he found peace and quiet,
which he needed again and again, so he was no longer be
the center of attention. The Tokamaku were kind and curious, and they wanted to know everything about him and the
team, especially now that he and the others knew their
language. It hadn't been difficult. The vocabulary was
largely based on social interaction symbols and references
to their lifeworld, which was not comparable to a fully technological civilization.

They didn't seem to have any religion, not even basic
animism as found among primitive terrestrial peoples. This
simplified the terminology to communicate with each other.
The tenses were also simple, and as with Indonesian and
Malay. There were no proper tenses; a verb was simply
supplemented by a tense. Thus, "I went hunting yesterday"
became simply "I hunt yesterday" or "I hunt today," "I hunt

tomorrow," instead of "I go hunting today" and "I will go hunting tomorrow."

James was extremely happy to sit here today on a washed-up tree trunk, his feet in the wonderfully cool spray, well-fed, and clearly more muscular than when he arrived. After that night's attempted rescue by Adrian and Justus, he had initially feared that his theory about the nature of the tribe might turn out to be naive, but he had been proven right, again. Despite their apparent superiority, laying down their weapons and submitting had been exactly the right reaction. The team later found out that they abhorred any form of technology, were downright afraid of it. The guns had been burned far away from the village that same day and the remains had been buried. Afterward, they were treated as if nothing had ever happened. Violence was rare and there was a high level of social cooperation. In six months, James had not witnessed even one real argument, only minor discussions that always ended quickly with an amicable settlement.

Nearly three hundred Tokamaku were the descendants of six villages in the Blue Paradise, what they called their forest. During extensive hikes, James had seen the remains of the old villages, which had not been abandoned out of absolute necessity, as Monka assured him, but through the desire to live closer together and better support each other in case of food shortages or natural disasters, of which there were probably a large number.

After about two months, once he'd mastered the language fairly well, James was sure he misunderstood when they were told of fierce snowstorms and floods, of monstrous sandstorms and heat waves that one could only survive by hiding in underground holes.

Justus had explained to him this was not unlikely because of the shattered moon in the night sky.

"The moon is larger than average for a planet of Earth's mass," the German astrophysicist explained, looking up at the string of debris in the night sky as they sat on the sod above the cave. "And it's very close. A least it seems so when I look at the remains up there. Such proximity of large bodies to each other causes strong gravitational forces, which we notice as the tidal ebb and flow, for example. Due to the fast rotation of the Earth, tidal accumulations are pulled away from the moon. The moon's gravity directly counteracts this and pulls the mountains back again, thus restoring the balance of forces and, as a side effect, gradually slowing the rotation of the Earth. This is a stabilizing process, you might say. If it had happened on Earth"—Justus pointed to the shining debris of the local satellite between the wispy clouds —"we would have had real problems. Fewer tides resulting in less nutrient and mineral exchange in the oceans followed by mass underwater deaths. The Sun's gravitational pull is not even a third as strong as the Moon's and would not compensate. Most of the mass that makes up the oceans would end up closer to our planet's axis of rotation, reducing its inertia. The angular momentum as a whole would be preserved and thus increase the speed.

"Without the moon, the days would be shorter, not twenty-four hours. It might only be eight hours long—it is similar here. It's light for only a few hours and then dark again. You've felt the effects yourself. We're constantly tired and stressed because our biorhythms are disturbed. I don't have the means to take measurements, but if things run even remotely as they would back home, it's a disaster in the making up there.

"The Earth without an intact moon would be like a spinning top shortly before falling over; it would spin and its axis would sway back and forth. The climate changes would be devastating in the long run. Some regions might regularly become the poles or the equator, turning tropics into icy landscapes and vice versa.

"The Tokamaku seem to have lived with such effects for a long time. I'm sure they don't live very long. A day is only a few hours long, offering little time for gathering food, and the night allows little time for sleep and regeneration. They are quite small and compactly built, real energy-saving models, if you can say that. Since we've been here, we've had eight storms, one a week, and they've been as terrifying as anything I've experienced on Earth. That's on top of everything else. But this forest seems to have adapted to it. The trees don't become uprooted and don't even lose many leaves. That tells me that whatever destroyed the moon must have happened a very long time ago. Otherwise, the flora wouldn't have had time to adapt."

"Or someone has artificially helped it along," James said, looking at the glowing blue dots on the leaves. They still hadn't figured out what those were all about. Of course, they had examined them, but without instruments, the individual dots were just tiny blue beads a millimeter in diameter that were surprisingly hard.

"Yes, I wouldn't rule that out, either. Anyway, we should be prepared to be surprised by more things as we learn more."

And they had.

Mila had warned them, rightly in his opinion, that they should proceed carefully and deliberately so as not to stumble over cultural ambiguities. They had no reason to hurry. A resumption of teleportation was not to be expected anytime soon when the president, apparently with the approval of Russia and the EU, had ordered the entire main silo of Francis E. Warren Air Force Base filled. Here they had plenty of food, shelter, no apparent danger from predators or major natural disasters because the forest protected them from the worst, and they didn't get sick, at least not after the first three months.

Their health had been bad and had scared him at first. Sometimes alternately, sometimes simultaneously, they were repeatedly plagued by violent bouts of fever, rashes, and headaches. But as the symptoms gradually subsided, Mette, as a chemist with skills closest to human biology and medical knowledge, believed that their bodies were acclimating to the local microbiome. Which meant the clones had to be robust genetic copies of themselves and that their immune systems learned quickly.

Since then, they had never become seriously ill, besides latent fatigue due to the short days and nights. But they even got used to that.

Week after week, they dared to ask more questions of the Tokamaku, who answered them quite innocently. They knew the name Al'Antis, not in reference to themselves but their ancestors, and not directly, because their name for them was "Ukmak," which probably meant something like avatar or protector. It was irritating that Ukmak was the singular of Ukmaka and Ukmak belonged to the Al'Antis. But why they said Ukmak and not Al'Antis were their ancestors, or even Al'Anta, could not be discovered.

They did not seem particularly interested in their prehistory and passed on large parts of their history orally, but not in writing. The older members of the tribe told mainly of great heroic deeds, not of individuals but of groups that had worked well together after a catastrophe or a long dry season when there was little food, of the clever minds of a certain time that had dug the first holes in the earth to cool food, and of another peculiarity: the Tokamaku felt it their duty and perfectly normal to kill old and infirm members of the tribe. Old people who began to suffer from pains that their healers could not control, or who could no longer walk, were one day hit from behind with a large club by so-called "experienced" people, so they did not see their end coming. It seemed cruel to James and the team, but the Tokamaku did not feel that way at all. They revered those who mustered the "courage" to put them out of their misery, and even the old ones did not seem concerned that they might suffer the same fate. It took some time for them to overcome their social conditioning to not protest, to remember they were guests here and had no right to feel morally superior based on their experiences on Earth. Mila explained to Monka that old men and women who were no longer productive were shunted off to nursing homes so they would not become a burden on their families, which he had found shocking, apparently without understanding what a nursing home might even be.

"Everything dies in the end," the village spokesman said. "If a leaf is wilted, you cut it off so that the rest of the plant will continue to thrive."

They could barely respond in a way that did not sound like moral hubris. Their team reached a consensus on this relatively quickly. Meeks was the last to have reservations, calling the killings "barbaric" until Mila told him about a book she had read as a child. This was probably a science fiction story about the first human spaceship to encounter aliens, the T'llnnt, large, two-headed figures with pink skin and horns on their heads. According to the guidelines of the future government, the protagonist of the story decided not to show his cloaked spaceship and limited himself to observing this new civilization he had discovered. They had colonized the far corners of their world and lived in competing nations, waging wars, making peace, building industrial plants, and even sending satellites into orbit. Their planet was similarly biodiverse, harboring millions of species, some of which the protagonist found so cute that he took photos of them to bring home. Many did not live free, however, but were confined and fattened in large facilities, the young were taken from their mothers after birth and some were slaughtered as a delicacy at the youngest age, while the mothers were kept in standing cages for the extraction of a nutritious secretion. The offal was then shredded and fed to their own kind in an efficient cycle. In these industrial breeding and killing camps, meat was produced for the population who, after work, watched acted recordings at home of others of their species murdering each other, torturing each other, or fleeing in agony from ghosts and nightmare creatures. They called this entertainment.

"I get what you're trying to tell me," Adrian said. "I hope aliens never find and observe us."

Finally, they agreed they were in no position to criticize the ways of the Tokamaku and had accepted it.

Other things were less frightening but still interesting: They couldn't swim, for example, because the only bodies of water they knew of were two rivers. One was the Thunder River and the other was the Sand River, further east, which owed its name to the sediment it carried. Both had strong currents and were considered dangerous, so they didn't fish either, until Adrian and Meeks taught them to make simple fishing rods and bait. Eating fish, wide-mouthed specimens with flat tails and an alien blue coloring, appealed to the

Tokamaku, especially Monka, and was accepted with much enthusiasm.

Another thing was the villagers' lack of desire to expand. They knew nothing but their forest and, when questioned by James and the team, merely said that the forest was "the land" and that there was nothing beyond it. However, the farthest point they had ever explored was a pyramid-shaped rock two days' journey, or eight hours walking, to the west and the wall to the east, which they called "the end of the world."

"If my day had only four hours, I wouldn't feel any particular urge to travel," Justus said. "As it is, you'd spend half the time just collecting food and eating."

And he had been right. Monka had found the idea of simply setting off in one direction and exploring the country absurd. There didn't even seem to be a word for explore in their language, the concept was so foreign to them.

He had merely asked, "What do you hope to find? Is the tree in front of the hut no longer the tree in front of the hut?"

Joana certainly would have been more fascinated by the Tokamaku than he already was. Their thinking was completely different from his and the team's and yet under-standable in a heartwarming way, except, perhaps, for the end that the aged and infirm experienced, although he real-ized he was also preloaded with societal conditioning. Was it better to die pumped full of drugs in an intensive care unit or lonely in a hospice? He didn't have a definitive answer to this question but could not answer it with an unreserved "yes" either.

As the months passed, they felt more and more at home, befriending the Tokamaku and enjoying their ease as they went through what could have been a short life. They seemed to have no fear of death, and no belief in an afterlife or redemption.

"When you're dead, you don't look anymore," Monka had explained with a shrug, not showing any particular interest in the subject.

They learned to hunt *bruutak*, a small animal that looked like a cross between a rat and a squirrel with a bushy tail and pointed head and erect ears and tasted metallic, like beef liver. The villagers showed them how to make knives from obsidian they mined from a cave under the wall, how to tan hides, and make fire with a fire bow. They learned three kinds of plants for healing wounds, insect bites—large bugs with long spines launched veritable bloodsucking festivals at dusk—and digestive ailments. About two dozen edible berries and herbs existed and about half of those were poisonous. Mushrooms were also available, but they were advised to keep their hands off them.

"Hey." A voice mingled with the sound of the river, and he shook his head to free-his thoughts from it. He smiled when he saw who was taking a seat next to him, dangling her bare feet into the water.

"Hello, Mila."

In the last two months, they had spent less time together than before, when they had met almost daily for long explorations of the surrounding forest and philosophized about God and the world. He sorely missed that time, but something had changed. One of the Tokamak, who was quite tall and strong for the natives, had taken a special interest in the Russian and had offered himself as a kind of private instructor. From him, she learned to make bows and spears, sharpen knives, build traps for the bruutak, and cook *kuumpa*, a stew of bruutak meat wrapped in large *fuurak* leaves and then buried in a hole in the ground with burning coals for an entire night. She seemed to take great pleasure in it, and he didn't want to act like a jealous boy, so he hadn't pressed her and instead spent a lot of time with Justus, Mette, Adrian, and Meeks.

But that was beneficial, too, because getting to know them better had been touching. Each had their story about what had brought them to this point, just like him, and each was very open and free, though Adrian a little less so, which may have had something to do with being far from home, and so their shame and all their baggage was now only in their heads.

"Brooding again?" she asked, and he looked to see if she was joking, but she didn't appear to be. He saw only the frothy reflections in her green eyes, which shimmered like emeralds.

"Yes," he admitted candidly, turning back to the rushing whitecaps before him.

"Because of *her*?"

James was surprised. Not by her question, he heard a slightly tense undertone in her voice, but by the fact that he hadn't thought about Joana for several weeks. Well, he had some thoughts about her, but not with a heavy heart. Thinking about it that way, he had spent more time wondering if he had somehow upset Mila because she hardly sought his company anymore.

"No." He shook his head and turned away as his cheeks grew warm, and he was afraid he was blushing. "I was just thinking about how the Tokamaku can't swim and are afraid of the rivers."

"Why?"

"Well, they're not explorers, that's for sure, but I wouldn't be either if I were just on foot. The forest is pretty rough, and you don't cover a lot of distance in a day even if you're in good shape." He pointed to the rushing floodwaters. "But you'd get pretty far on the river, I guess."

"I guess you're right." She nodded thoughtfully, then gave him an expectant sideways glance. "Well?"

"What?"

"When are you going to ask me?"

He frowned, confused. He looked at her and tried to interpret the gleam in her eyes, and then he wanted to slap himself for his stupidity.

A great judge of character you are. Ransom negotiator, huh? he scolded himself, almost horrified by his lack of comprehension. *Don't be a coward!*

James gave himself a nudge and did what he had been thinking about for weeks. He had to do it. If that made her want to see him even less, so be it.

He leaned over and kissed her on the mouth. To his horror, she flinched back.

"Sorry!" he said quickly and wanted to slide into the water and disappear in it as quickly as possible, or drown, at that moment, either would have been all right with him. "I-I didn't mean—"

"I thought you were going to ask me to build a boat with you!" she countered and grinned mischievously.

"Oh, uh, well..." He clenched his hands into fists and licked his lips thinking a thunderstorm would be handy about now. With lightning to strike him. *Oh, Lord...*

"Ha!" she laughed happily, grabbed his cheeks with both hands, pulled his face toward her, and kissed him long and hard.

James's world was abruptly reduced to two sensations: The touch on his lips and tongue and the warmth in his heart that spread like hot lava. It was a reduction to the essentials, to the only thing that mattered at that moment.

Mila and him, and the fulfillment of a deeply cherished desire he only now dared to admit. A dam of feelings burst in their physical fusion here and now to the applause of the rustling leaves above them and the roar of the river rapid's spray, and it was all he needed.

9

"And I was beginning to think you'd forgotten about this 'Temple of the Winds,'" Meeks said. The "cowboy," as Adrian often teasingly called him, chewed on a long blade of grass and pointed toward the river. The entire team was sitting on the mossy bank, not ten minutes from where he had sat with Mila yesterday.

"Temple of *Heaven*," James corrected him.

"See, I even forgot the exact name Nasaku used. How come you're thinking about it again now?"

"I never forgot it. But we needed to learn more about this place before we stumbled through it like a couple of blind men in a hall of mirrors." He glanced around. Mette had lost her extra weight and was hardly recognizable. She looked older, with sunken cheeks and her straw-like hair, but she was as hearty as ever. Meeks's handsome potbelly was gone. Justus had lost some of his tan but still looked like a surfer, even if a sad shadow had settled over his eyes. James could relate only too well. Only Mila and Adrian looked the same as before, even if Mila's melancholy look now had a happy glow that warmed his heart.

"He's right, you know," Mette interjected. "We now know the main plants of the forest, how to get food, what the dangers are, how to talk to the Tokamaku, and how to deal with certain diseases and injuries. As we discussed at the beginning: haste is not a good advisor. Even if we had set out immediately, the teleporter is still off-limits until further notice because there is no place to go. Haste wouldn't have helped us."

Everyone nodded.

Adrian pointed vaguely toward the village, which was about an hour to the east. "It was also right to first gain the trust of the locals and find out if they could help us. But then, that wasn't very fruitful. They don't know anything about a temple and don't even seem to be familiar with the concept of a temple."

"Although they are with Ukmak, the protector," Justus objected.

"Or the protector. That could mean Nasaku," James replied.

"I wouldn't be so sure, but let's assume it's so. Then Monka and the Tokamaku consider her their ancestor."

"Except the concept of ancestors has a different, less evolutionary meaning here."

"I know we have a responsibility, and we made a promise to Nasaku—" Mette said, but James quickly interrupted her.

"*I* made it with her. It would be unfair to impose that promise on you, you never made it."

"Good, so I promise you now—redundantly, I should note—that I, for one, will see your promise through to the end."

"We decided this together and went through the teleporter as a team knowing full well that there might not be a way back," Justus said in a strained voice. "You shouldn't take that cohesion away from us, it's the only thing that doesn't make me perish with worry and longing for my family. That and the knowledge that we're doing something important for humanity here. That sounds kind of stupid while I'm sitting in the dirt, bare-chested and wearing scratchy cotton shorts, talking about things that seem like fantasy."

"He's right," Meeks agreed, uncomfortable that they were all looking at Justus with pity.

Each had had a reason to run away, some more, some less, but the German had had all the reasons to stay on Earth. This meant that of all of them, the one whom James had previously thought of as an overprotective doubter, had made the greatest sacrifice of them all. James had learned to appreciate him as an extremely thoughtful, circumspect man who approached every problem from multiple angles. Even in the few arguments among the group, Justus had always held back, but not because he was wary of conflict, but because he weighed things carefully and always tried to consider both sides rather than following an emotional impulse.

"Man, if only we had a bottle of whiskey and some hot dogs right now," Meeks said, rubbing the sturdy beard that covered half of his neck.

"Oh yes, a Kogt hot dog," Mette said enthusiastically with a dreamy look.

"Kogt *what*?"

"*Kogt hot dog,*" she repeated. "A *real* hot dog with røde pølse and remoulade!"

"I don't know what that is, but that doesn't sound like a real hot dog to me."

"You guys don't even put fried onions on yours. Something like that shouldn't be allowed to be called a hot dog!"

"The hot dog was invented in Germany," Justus interjected, apparently happy to jump on the deliberate change of subject, much to James's relief. "By a butcher from Coburg. As far as I know, the American version also came from a German, a migrant."

"If we were in Denmark, I'd make you a Kogt hot dog and you'd never touch one of those things from the States again, I can guarantee you that," Mette appeared unusually combative but winked at Meeks.

"Then I still have my whisky," he grumbled.

"Only an American could say something like that." Justus rolled his eyes. "First of all, it's called *whiskey*. And it was invented by Christian monks in Ireland or Scotland. If it was, they get to argue about it. Just make friends with the fact that anything with cultural significance was invented outside the United States, okay?"

"Yes, yes, the culturally conscious Europeans and their ego. No wonder you've gone downhill. Always resting on the old. The main thing today is that you all watch Netflix, order from Amazon, and go to Disneyland or eat at McDonald's."

"Touché."

"Cultural dick comparison, wow," Mila said drily.

"Now the Klingons are coming to tell us that Shakespeare can only be enjoyed in the original Klingon." Meeks sighed, and they all laughed, releasing the tension they were carrying. This new world had been surprisingly good to them, after what they had come to expect considering the Death Zone and the monster and all, but there was never any mistaking that this was not where they belonged.

The Tokamaku were undoubtedly human, though significantly smaller and had such white skin and bright eyes that a mere glance in their direction was enough to know you didn't belong. The forest was different enough to feel as if they were in a dream. They probably would have felt lonely if they were in the jungles of Borneo with aboriginals, but here there was the added knowledge they couldn't leave. They were far from Earth and everything they knew and considered normal. It could not be wiped away and certainly not ignored, no matter how hard they tried.

"I think we should check that town for clues about the temple first," James suggested after a while, feeling guilty that he had to break the relaxed mood.

"You mean the ruins that we think are there, at least?" Adrian asked.

"Yes," Mila said. "They're the only thing Justus saw that wasn't trees or wall. If there's a clue where we can start the journey, it'll be at the ruins."

The cosmonaut looked from Mila to James and then nodded. Something resonated in him that James didn't know how to interpret because Adrian showed no emotion on his face.

"The river goes about that way, doesn't it?"

"Yes. And we have more than enough raw materials to build a raft or even a boat."

"A boat, for sure," Meeks decided firmly. "We've got three engineers here with Adrian, Mila, and me. We'll to do it right and build ourselves a sleek boat so we don't capsize and drown at the next rapids."

"Are you sure?"

Mila shrugged. "We have time. And if the six of us work together and don't rush things, we should be able to build something good. A boat has a lot of advantages. We can carry it ashore and turn it over to give us a roof, as just one example, and we wouldn't be as susceptible to turbulence and rapids, as Meeks pointed out."

"I have to confess that I'm reluctant to leave here, and I

don't have a good feeling about this," Adrian said, folding his beefy arms in front of his chest in his typical manner. "But we have work to do, and our grace period is over. We've learned enough, and it's time to take the next step."

Which is what they did for the next four weeks. James had expected it to take a few days, maybe a week, which, in retrospect, was probably naïve because the three engineers spent the first seven days discussing what type of boat to build. A dugout, which would be labor-intensive but relatively simple, was discarded because of its susceptibility to water movement and the danger of capsizing on a river with rapids.

Next, they decided to go with a fairly large boat they could lay in the sand. Then they had to make saws and files using obsidian, which presented them with a whole new set of challenges and took another week, and the results were unimpressive. By the third week, they managed to saw boards that were reasonably equal in size and could be laid together with a simple plug system, after countless blisters and reamed areas. For the filing work they were fortunate to get the help of over thirty of the Tokamaku, who thought it was great fun. They didn't really understand what the team was up to.

Once that was complete, the boards were heated over a fire and bent to shape in a frame made from tree trunks, and after some time the shape of the boat could be guessed. After the boards were assembled and cooled, resin was smeared into the remaining grooves, which Mette had gathered, to seal everything. Cross braces, which they fastened into the boat with improvised obsidian nails, stabilized the walls, and a thick layer of dried ferns provided a flat, reasonably comfortable, if scratchy, floor for them to sit on.

While all this was drying, the engineers built rudders, a simple but sweaty job.

They watched the engineers and lent a hand wherever one was needed, which was as frustrating as it was amusing: They constantly argued about details, drew complicated formulas and models in the sand, only to try again and again because they were hardly ever sure, and often failed. Then they'd try something new, and someone would claim they'd been right.

Mila and James got their own hut, offered to them by Monka, who apparently understood that something was going on between them. That they no longer slept with the others in their "burial mound," as they called the cave, irritated the chief, however.

"Because you want to make love?"

"Uh," James hesitated, and the many locals, who were as usual listening in as if it were a big event, had joined in the uproarious laughter. Only when they made it clear to Monka they were not joking, that where they came from privacy was prized, had he calmed down a bit and, chuckling, decreed that someone should let them have a hut.

As a result, James and Mila were plagued by a guilty conscience, which they effectively knew how to distract themselves from at night. One of those nights was the last they would spend in the village. Monka had been informed they were leaving and, unexpectedly, had shown no disappointment or surprise, but had merely stated that what happens in the day happens in the night in his typically wise-poetic way.

His light-hearted attitude seemed inherent in the other villagers, as well. From the scrawny Miktak, who had helped them weave the ropes they used to set the bent boards, to little Ilktak, who did not even reach his chest and had provided them with meals every day, or Taka-Taka, a youth with big eyes and a genial look, who had watched every step of their work in amazement for the entire four weeks and had asked again and again if they really wanted to drown in the river. Finally, they had given up and said yes, since it seemed impossible to explain the concept of a boat to him. None expressed sadness they were leaving, they merely wished them health and happiness, and that was the end of the subject.

"I wonder what effect we've had on them," Mila asked against his chest as they lay on their mats, looking up at the round ceiling where the interwove fern fronds formed a complex pattern.

"What do you mean?"

"We're taller than them, hairier, darker, and we talk differently, but they never asked us where we came from."

"But they have asked if we are a threat to them and if more are coming," he said.

"Yes, that's true, but when we tried to explain that we came over the wall, they just laughed at us." Mila snorted. "They don't even seem to realize the danger that lurks there."

"By *danger*, do you mean the monster or the teleporter?"

"Both. They know so little about their surroundings that I wonder if there's something wrong with them."

"They are different from us in many ways. For example, they're more positive and much more careless. They don't have ulterior motives and no hidden communication like we do. When they say something, they mean it, and when they don't say anything, it's because they have nothing to say," he said, summarizing what he thought he had learned about the Tokamak. "They're amazingly adaptable and are extremely culturally and intellectually related to the present."

"That would also explain why they haven't developed any technologies, hardly any mythology or religion. They don't tell themselves fictions and, as a result, they don't believe in future things to which they would devote their lives."

"You mean they'll never build pyramids."

"Yes. When I look at their way of living and thinking, it's possible their people are ancient and lived exactly like this ten thousand years ago and will live the same way ten thousand years from now." Mila rested her chin on his chest so she could look him in the eye. "But that doesn't match the structures we saw. They looked like skyscrapers. Even if they're not, they're not natural."

"Perhaps they're the successor civilization of a past advanced civilization," James said. "The pyramids of the Egyptians can still be admired today, some five thousand years after they were built, and there is no trace of the Egyptians of that time. Not culturally, not linguistically, not mythologically."

"I think certain anthropologists would disagree with that."

"That is their job, after all."

"Do you think it's a good idea?"

"Where we're going tomorrow?" he asked, trying to buy himself some time.

"Yes. We're not adventurers. Though Adrian is close. I hope we don't just drown as the Tokamaku seem to think we will."

"That's not what scares you, am I right?"

Mila returned his probing look and nodded.

"That city kind of scares me. Don't worry, it's not stopping me from taking the next step, which I think is the right one, but something about it feels off."

"I know what you mean. Your reaction is logical. A hidden city that we don't even know is a city. Our brain has merely made one out of a rough pattern on the horizon. Why do primitive people live unsuspectingly within sight of such a remnant of a sophisticated civilization? I think I once read that it would only take a few hundred years for our concrete to disappear and only the steel beams would be left. After a few thousand years, even those would disintegrate. Stonehenge is four thousand years old and still very visible, but it's also a lot sturdier than what we build today, even if you don't think so." James paused. "So, either humans or aliens lived in that mysterious city until a few hundred years ago, or less, and they were significantly more advanced and never made contact with the Tokamaku, or they were better builders than we are."

"Or it's not a city at all," Mila added.

"What then?"

"I don't know, but we're going to find out, and I think we should prepare to be surprised by the answer."

"You sound like you think it's going to *scare* us."

"Perhaps it's just a bad feeling, but maybe it's the fear of a woman who, for the first time in a while, has something to lose and is leaving the safety of the nest behind," she replied, smiling as he pressed a heartfelt kiss to her mouth.

"We're never really safe, are we?" he mused when they pulled away from each other. "A tree may fall on our heads before we get in the boat, take your pick. There's no point worrying about it. Believe me, as you know, I've done this for many years."

"You're right. Don't listen to me."

"Can I make that a rule for our future together?" he asked teasingly.

"I'm Russian, you can be macho outside if you have to, but at home you're my doormat, let's get that straight right now."

"Good thing you have such small feet."

"Hey!"

"Little lumps at the end of your legs—"

"Did you just say I have *club feet*?"

"Not exactly, I—"

She snarled at him, and he laughed wildly, a premonition of his own stirring in the back of his mind; that it would be the last time for a long time he would be able to show this kind of joy.

10

E ven though the Tokamaku were very fixated on the present, it didn't stop them from giving them a big send-off when they left. The whole village had come a very long way, for them, to the riverbank, which cost them half a day round trip. Men, women, and children stood wide-eyed among the trees, watching as the Earthlings launched their strange thing of wood and resin and moored it with vines. They still did not understand that their guests wanted to float away on the river.

"You want to meet your end in the water?" Monka asked, squatting on the embankment and tapping the wooden planks. The fat on his arms wobbled as he did so, as if taking on a life of its own. "Water is for drinking, isn't it?"

"You're about to see how well it works. Besides, we can swim," James explained as the others stowed water skins and supplies in the stern and bow. The Tokamaku had virtually showered them with smoked bruutak meat and forest fruits. They had had to turn down most of it because there simply wasn't enough room.

"We can still teach you," Mila called out mischievously

holding a liana net full of makchi, a kind of reddish colored pear, under her arm.

"But no, I enjoy my life," the chief replied. "I would also rather meet my end in the forest."

James sighed and gave up. When Monka stood, he unceremoniously embraced the much smaller man, which seemed to irritate him at first, but then he felt his chubby hands on his back and his body was shaking with boisterous laughter. The other villagers shared his amusement and rushed toward them to imitate the gesture. So, one by one, they had to hug all the natives and share a few kind words. It was like a big farewell ceremony with no tears, although James was kind of sad. He appreciated these people, who were as open and warm as one could wish for. They were naïve, but in a disarming way with the charm of children.

When they finally sat in the boat and untied the vines wrapped around some young trees on the shore, the Tokamaku waved laughingly in awkward imitations of the team, and James found the whole scene increasingly unnerving. He was sad to leave their hosts, and they seemed pleased. At the same time, he envied them their ability to live with so little mental baggage. He had always thought it was part of the human condition to constantly dwell on the past or the future, grieve over what had happened, or worry about what might happen. There was always something that wouldn't leave one's mind. A careless word from your partner, an emotional or physical injury from someone, something your parents had done, or neglected to do. If you were in love, you were afraid your affections might not be returned; if you were together, you feared a future where you were not.

Once he saw a woman whom he had thought was Monka's wife having fun with another man in another hut. He had a stomachache for two days because he felt obliged to report it to the chief. When he finally did so, he was once again surprised because all he had received in reply was laughter.

"Doesn't it bother you that she's sharing camp with someone else?" James had asked.

"But she doesn't."

"But I saw it."

"When?"

"Two days ago."

"Aaah," Monka had said and chuckled. "Show me this one 'two days ago.'"

"Excuse me?"

"Show me this one 'two days ago' that makes you so unhappy. I cannot see it."

James had remained silent, carrying his confusion with him to their hilltop shelter, where he pondered the chief's words and the deep wisdom that lay within them. How he wished he could think as pragmatically as the chief. Jealousy had seemed so normal to him that he had never questioned it.

Jealousy is a passion that seeks with zeal what creates suffering, Franz Grillparzer had once written. Even though he had appreciated this quotation for its linguistically pointed finesse, he had not understood it. Not in his heart. He had been jealous for half his life. If he was honest with himself, he couldn't even separate his thoughts of Joana, with all the affection he felt for her, from his jealousy, which seemed firmly interwoven with his image of her. But after Monka's almost casual rejoinders, he kept getting stuck a rut. Until now, he had always believed there was a basic human condition from which they all suffered to a greater or lesser degree. Perhaps he had simply become too cynical.

James sat in the back of the boat with Adrian, paddling.

Justus and Meeks paddled in the front, while Mila and Mette sat in the middle and held on. The Tokamaku seemed to find the scene amusing, laughing and waving, as they headed downstream in the current.

He felt wistful, and he sensed the others felt the same way. It was like a self-imposed expulsion from paradise, a place where they had been safe, not only from danger and hunger, but from human weaknesses such as jealousy, resentment, and hatred. All this was foreign to the Tokamaku. Would it have been so bad to stay there to the end of his life? He had Mila were warm and safe around each other. They had food, companionship, and always enough to do to bring meaning in their lives. More sense and meaning, at least, than on Earth, if one disregarded the project.

Here, people knew every day why they lived because there was direct evidence of their activities in relation to the world they lived in. They went to the forest to gather food because it gave them enough to eat. They made pilgrimages to the river to fill water skins because they needed to drink. They repaired huts so they were protected from the rain and wind. They knotted bast mats to sleep on, and they mixed ointments in mortars to heal minor injuries and prevent infections. Everything that was done here had a purpose.

At home, it wasn't so easy to tell since most people had abstract jobs. They pushed paper from A to B and answered emails that referred to fictional items like stocks, purchase orders, official certifications, or other documents that followed a whole chain of abstract meanings and symbols. But how was the brain to derive evolutionary meaning from this? The longer he lived here, the more he understood how easy it was to be happy as a human being. You just had to know why you got up in the morning. You needed a functioning social environment where you felt secure and activity that was meaningful for you and others.

It was actually quite simple, and the Tokamaku demonstrated it.

"The expulsion from paradise, huh?" Adrian asked, nodding in understanding as James looked at him, blinking. "I was thinking the same thing. Life here was almost too good to be true. I kept wondering why I became an astronaut and didn't join the Ewenken."

"Ewenken?"

"A primitive people in Siberia. They hardly use any technology and live like nomads. Supposedly, they are the happiest Russians, but I always dismissed that as anthropological romanticism," the cosmonaut explained. "I won't do that anymore."

"They are very wise in their way," James said, and his heart grew heavy as they rounded a bend in the river and the Tokamaku vanished out of sight. They probably felt nothing of the sort, just returned to their village and lived as happily as before.

"We always ask ourselves what we have lost and what we can gain. We never ask ourselves what we have now. At the same time, it is usually enough. We always had enough to eat and drink, enjoyed a high level of security, and could learn anything we wanted. On earth, I mean."

"And what did we make of it?"

"A civilization with growing rates of depression and anxiety disorders." Adrian nodded and, with paddle applied, steered them around a log jutting into the water in front of them. "It's crazy that we would dismiss the Tokamaku as *uncivilized* if they were a natural people on Earth. I found myself thinking of them that way. What hubris."

"I would have preferred not to leave at all," James muttered.

"We were able to enjoy life there, but we can't forget that we're not like them, James. We are still us, even though we certainly learned a lot from them. In the end, we would have merely carried our problems into their midst like black mold slowly spreading on a pure flower. It's better this way for them."

"That's pretty grim, and I'd like to think better of us, but I'm afraid you're right."

"We wouldn't have wanted it that way, of course, but it would have happened."

"You have a strange way of glossing over our parting." James smirked and Adrian flashed a rare smile.

"That's the Russian way. If you can't fix something, just leave it and admire its morbid charm, which, conveniently, can only increase with time."

They silently followed the river, which remained about twenty, sometimes thirty, meters wide for the next few hours, and meandered through the seemingly endless forest. The banks were mostly overgrown with dense bushes that blocked any view into the undergrowth, but they could hear the high-pitched calls of the bruutak females and the occasional the rustle of *gecklings*, as Mette had christened the small, six-footed lizard-like creatures.

The trees barely changed. Their merging crowns formed jagged silhouettes against the gloomy sky and the dirty clouds that passed overhead, casting their ochre hue as they did every day. James would have liked to see the sun just once, but the only cloud-free time seemed to be at night, and there wasn't a real moon to gaze at, only its remains, the sight of which always sent cold shivers down his spine. Even after seven months, he could not get used to it. What kind of force was able to act on a celestial body of that size to destroy it so fundamentally? An asteroid impact? Justus had assured him that was hardly possible. Not because an asteroid would have been incapable of destroying a moon that size, but because much of the debris would have fallen on the planet, not moving like a string of pearls orbiting across the night sky. When questioned about what could be responsible for such destruction, the astrophysicist had merely replied that he was not a military expert but a physicist, which had not exactly calmed James's uneasiness.

Perhaps it was the stark contrast between the happy-go-lucky life of the Tokamaku and the mysterious and threatening world in which they lived that unconsciously made him so uncomfortable. The natives dwelt on an island of carelessness, surrounded by signs of the greatest destruction, desolation, and poison. To James, they gave the impression of a blind man threatened by a horde of criminals with their weapons drawn, merely for enjoying the fresh air he breathed. He could only hope the weapons were not loaded.

There were only two hours left of the first day's travel, so after a very uneventful push, at the first signs of dusk—when the clouds took on the color of milky coffee—they searched for an accessible embankment. It grew darker and darker, and they had no success, so they tied up to a tree overhanging the water that looked like a giant hand with the lower third bent to create a perch. They tied a vine to the improvised benches that doubled as braces, they were able to stabilize the boat in the current.

Adrian suggested having two keep watch at all times while the other four slept, which drew protests. Mette objected, citing there was nothing dangerous in this forest, while Meeks pointed out that the night was already far too short, and Justus added that not even a bull could break through the thorny bushes along the shore. But it was all to no avail. Adrian prevailed and insisted that they did not know how far they were from the village and whether they might encounter something new.

"From now on, we have to be more careful and not act recklessly," he said, and that settled the issue. Unfortunately, Adrian volunteered for the unpopular guard shift in the middle and asked James to join, which he could hardly refuse.

"I didn't want you to take a watch with Mila," the cosmonaut finally admitted in a whisper as they sat in the bow watching the rippling reflections on the ever-moving surface. There was something hypnotic about the play of light with the shimmering lines created by the remnants of the moon that James could hardly escape.

"Why not?" He tried to keep his tone calm, but he was annoyed and even felt a touch of injustice. Perhaps living with the Tokamaku had made him gentler.

"We all know what's going on between you," Adrian replied blandly. "Don't worry, it's your business, and no one is upset about it. I just didn't want to risk you two lovebirds getting so busy with each other that you overlooked the big bad monster poking its head through the surface of the water and trying to eat us."

"Thanks for the foresight, Dad!" James snorted.

"You're welcome. At some point, though, it is going to become a problem."

"What?"

"Your relationship."

"Now you want to—"

"Shh." Adrian put a finger in front of his thin lips and pointed at their sleeping friends. "Not so loud."

"I'm really too old for a father-son conversation."

"I didn't mean it that way."

"No? How then?"

"Just look at your reaction. I've rarely seen you so thin-skinned. What's the reason for that? Do you think that what you have is still too fragile to be true? Do you think my words will be like a needle against your balloon of feelings? Do you not believe in it yourself? Or are you worried about what this place might do to you?"

James, annoyed, wanted to retort but instead took a deep breath and thought about what Adrian was saying. Listening to himself, he detected a certain restlessness he thought he had covered fairly well. For the first time in a long time, he was happy, or at least he thought he was. He didn't even know the last time he had been happy. Mila was the first woman who had made him take a breath, who didn't make him think about Joana all the time. He didn't want to run away from her as he had from all the other women he had tried to get to know over the years. Each time he'd had to admit that he just wanted to distract himself with them and realized how unfair that was. Besides, his fear of feeling and suffering again, like he had with his ex-fiancée, was far too great.

"What is it?" asked Adrian.

"What do you mean?"

"Why her?"

"She is heartbreakingly pragmatic; she doesn't make small talk. When she talks, it's because her words mean something. I know where I stand with her. I can see in her eyes what she's feeling." James searched the cosmonaut's face for signs he might be teasing him but found only interest, so he continued. "It's probably normal for you Russians, but I come from the country that practically invented small talk. We like to talk about everything without talking about anything. Empty words that are supposed to lead to having a good time without revealing anything, and certainly without talking about feelings. With us, you always have a good time and would never admit that you're not feeling well or sad."

"We are different," Adrian confirmed, nodding. "Call it the Russian soul, or a reflection of the cold that has our country in its sights most of the year. Some even say it's our melancholy woven into our genes."

"Whatever it is, I like it," James explained and paused. "Why are you asking me all this?"

"I don't know what else awaits us here, but I believe it will be more dangerous than we imagine. I have recovered from the hours spent in the death zone inside the walls, although I admit I still dream about them sometimes, but I have not forgotten them. All the chirping birds and the green colors, as if someone turned up the saturation, can make it seem like we are in a Garden of Eden, but I don't believe it. Something's not right here."

"I know what you mean. This may sound strange, but I have the impression that this place has lost its soul."

"You are the only one of us who is not a scientist. If anyone can say something like that, it's you," Adrian joked without smiling.

"You didn't answer my question, though."

"Actually, you know what I'm going to say," Adrian said seriously.

"If I'm scared for her I'm not going to act rationally, and I am going to be scared for her," James whispered, and it was equal parts answer and admission.

"I know you can't change feelings by repressing them. You have to go through them, but at least prepare yourself for it."

"Didn't the Tokamaku teach us just the opposite without knowing it?"

"Did they?" the cosmonaut asked seriously, and James had to admit to himself that he couldn't find an answer to that within himself. He *hoped* they had, but he didn't *know*. He feared they would find out soon, and the next day at about the same time, they reached what they thought was a city.

11

They reached the first foothills of the "city" in the evening hours of the next day. The light of the local central star, dimmed by the thick layers of clouds, seeped unseen toward the horizon like a pastel painting, and the first stars appeared through the initial cracks in the clouds.

"There!" Justus shouted, pointing to what looked like a chimney of smooth obsidian.

But the closer the boat got, the river gurgling about the bow, the more details became visible. The base was about ten meters high and five meters wide from which a conical tube stretched upward, held by four metallic clamps connected by ball joints to the tube, which rose another thirty or forty meters into the air.

As soon as they rounded a bend in the river, which was much wider here than anything they had seen before, they found an identical structure on the other side. Both structures were overgrown with moss and creepers that covered the thick base, but thinning toward the top.

"They look like howitzers aimed upward," Meeks said.

No one responded, and that was depressed approval enough.

James also thought they looked like guns. Guns of a strange shape but still recognizable as cannon barrels.

"The weed growth extends exactly to the height of the treetops," Mila said. "Above that, it's clear for the last few feet. Do you see that?"

"Yes, why would that be?" Adrian wondered.

"Probably due to an interaction between the different parts of the flora here. An exchange of microorganisms, gases, nutrients—take your pick."

"Or it's related to the blue dust."

"Or that," she agreed. And indeed, the blue glow that made the entire forest to either side of the river shimmer softly ended at the same altitude, and the two structures showed no signs of blue spots.

Unhurried, they floated along, keeping to the middle of the Thunder River as it slipped out of the forest, which they had considered a temporary home. The "blue dust," as they had christened the phenomenon, also ended, forming a sharp boundary. It was a strange feeling, and, again, James couldn't help but think of it as a kind of expulsion from paradise. A self-imposed expulsion, true, though that didn't make things any better. It increased the danger and he chided himself for trading something safe and pleasant for the unknown. Of course, it was the right thing to do, and he did not doubt that sooner or later he would have felt guilty if he had ignored his promise to Nasaku just because it was convenient.

Beyond the blue dust, the vegetation changed abruptly. Trees and plants looked gnarled and dry. The smell of muck spread, like in a swamp, giving off the sweet, acrid note of decay. Foliage and branches were more sparse, and the former was no longer rich green, but yellow or brown and looked pale. Trees became bushes and bushes became shrubs, no longer inviting and vibrant, but looking as if they struggled to survive against disease.

They remained silent, but the sensation that they had lost something valuable became a depressing heaviness. The two futuristic, though apparently ancient, guns did not help to alleviate this feeling.

They gradually saw more outlandish things. On the right-hand bank a pyramid dozens of feet tall with a broken top was surrounded by large statues on an overgrown square. From all sides, trees and shrubs pushed toward the structure in a siege that had lasted thousands of years. The statues were only recognizable as such in the moonlight because their jagged outlines looked remotely humanoid, and they stood on massive pedestals. Close to the embankment in front of the river, one had been stripped of its creepers and much of its moss and what it revealed made James hold his breath. The statue, nearly ten meters high, showed a man with his arms crossed in front of his chest, ending in fists, each containing a long ankh and a sickle. His head was not a man's but a bird's, with a powerful beak and large eyes, and the back of his head was adorned with jewelry weathered by erosion.

"It's Osiris!" he gasped.

"Ra," Justus corrected him. "The Egyptian sun god."

"What's an Egyptian statue doing on this planet?" Mette whispered, as if afraid to awaken sleeping spirits.

"The question should be, what were representatives from this planet doing in ancient Egypt?"

"That's utterly impossible! The teleporter has been underground for hundreds of thousands of years, kilometers deep," Meeks objected. "The Egyptian culture is how old? Five thousand years? Six thousand? There's no way they had contact with Nasaku's ancestors or the Tokamaku. Even if the teleporter miraculously sank that deep into the ground under Lake Maracaibo within a few centuries, there was no contact between Africa and South America at that time."

"We've talked about something like that, haven't we," Mila said. "There must have been an exchange earlier. How else could Nasaku have spoken Sumerian? And the Sumerians lived in Mesopotamia, which is even farther from South America—not that it would have made any difference. Even though the sight is disconcerting, I'm not surprised."

"But how is that possible? You're not going to tell me those pre-astronautics people were right, are you?"

The Russian shook her head. "I don't think so. At least not completely. I still think it's unlikely that aliens visited Earth in spaceships. The teleporters are the best proof of that, after all."

"Proof?" Meeks quietly lowered his paddle into the calm waters of the river to keep them midstream. He looked back to the right, where the plaza was slowly being left behind, along with the massive overgrown pyramid.

"Yes," said Mila. "We found a teleporter made of a material that has managed to remain undamaged for hundreds of thousands of years, despite all the forces that must have acted on it. This is so far beyond anything we can manage today that we can conclude from this alone that it was built by an extremely sophisticated civilization. Not to mention, the teleporters can send consciousness back and forth between planets without significant lag."

"She's right," Justus agreed. "Otherwise, we probably would have found the remains of a spaceship. But teleporters are a much more logical solution to the problem of interstellar travel than spaceships. Many of my colleagues—and I'm one of them—consider spaceship travel between solar systems to be all but impossible."

"Impossible?" Meeks snorted. "With the right propulsion technology and the right material, it's doable."

"Feasible, but the timescales would be too great. Even at the speed of light, we would need more than four years to reach the nearest star. But we will never fly anywhere near the speed of light. Even at half *c*, a single dust molecule hit by a spacecraft in the interstellar medium would have the explosive power of several atomic bombs, leaving nothing behind. The mass needed for an equivalent yield..." The German waved it off. "Add to that the amount of reaction and propellant mass. And even if you could solve all that, we're talking about many centuries of travel to the nearest star, but the nearest star systems are all practically empty and uninhabitable. By the time you find a habitable one, it could take millennia because of the distances involved. Mila is right, the teleporters are evidence that spaceships have not visited Earth."

"And what is that flying toward Earth?" Meeks asked.

"I don't know, but it could be anything. It could even be an asteroid swarm that happened to cross the telescope's line of sight at an awkward angle. These data evaluations take forever, and it may well be that Norton and Pavar have given the all-clear by now because, after months, it's became clear that it was a coincidence. Wouldn't be the first time."

"What worries me more," Adrian said, "is the environment here. It's gotten hotter, it smells again, and I'm sure we'll start seeing red spots on our skin soon enough. We've reached the end of the forest and the end of the blue dust. That tells us something."

"Then our theory is correct: the forest is an artificial structure of some kind. Perhaps a technologically protected preserve, or a testing ground, a kind of open-air ark," Mila said. "The dust seems to keep the toxins out of the air, like a filter."

"Not only that. The trees are also more resilient than average to storms and flooding." Mette pointed toward the shore, where the few visible trees were barely ten meters tall.

As far as the eye could see, great cubes of gray shadows rose from the ground and grew larger and larger as they moved further inland. Amazed and intimidated, they sat silently in their boat, accompanied by an eerie silence they had not experienced in a long time. No birds chirped, not even the few that usually let out their shrill calls in the night. There were no high-pitched whistles of the bruutak females, no rustles or squeaks. This place was dead and had been for a long time. The built-up area on the right bank was at least as large as a small town, the tallest shadows against the dark blue horizon, with its button-like stars, as mighty as skyscrapers. However, on the left-hand bank stood only more guns like they had seen at the beginning and the land faded into pale tundra as far as the eye could see. Small hills became gentle rises to the west, but even those eventually faded into a flat plain that took on a pale-yellow hue along the horizon.

After a long silence, they arrived at a lock—or what looked like a lock. The river had been dammed to form a wide lake that ended in a dark, massive wall made up of round segments with gray honeycomb patterns along the front. To the right of center, a large piece had broken away the structure and the notch created a rapid flow in the water visible from afar, its current increasing the closer it got to the breach.

Adrian gave swift commands to paddle as hard as they could toward the right bank, where the water flowed into a corner between the embankment and the base of the structure where the current subsided.

Startled by the cosmonaut's sudden orders, James frantically sank his paddle into the cold, slushy brown water and pulled long strokes from front to back, stretching as Meeks had shown them. Their boat swayed precariously, and Adrian barked at them several times to make corrections as he leaned alarmingly over the stern on the opposite side to evenly distribute their weight.

A small maelstrom formed in front of them, threatening to pull them into the depths should they go overboard. The size of the swirls was enough to make his blood run cold. As they passed the first, their boat pulled to the left, even though they were paddling at full strength, and the bow turned frighteningly, inexorably toward the breach in the lock wall, which barely fifty yards away. The ominous roar grew more and more intense, heralding the impending disaster. Beneath this background noise, he heard an ugly *crunch* and felt a sharp vibration that went through the entire hull of their boat.

Once they were out of the whirlpool, Adrian ordered Mila and Mette to lean over the right edge of the boat and they realigned themselves. After more wild paddling, during which they all got wet and were breathing so hard that it was louder than the roar of the break, they finally made it. They slid into the space where the currents canceled each other out, and it became quieter.

James leaned forward and propped his elbows on his knees to catch his breath and calm his pounding heartbeat.

"That... was... close..." Meeks panted from the front, dropping his oar inside the boat.

"I was starting to think the current was just going to sweep us away," Mette said.

"It didn't," Adrian responded. "But we have another problem: we're sinking."

James wrenched his eyes open and stared between his legs at the water spreading between the dried reeds lining the deck. Little by little, his bare feet were submerged and got cold.

"Damn!"

"Keep calm," the cosmonaut told them. "The shore is not far away. The most important thing now is food and water. Mette and Mila, I'll hand you the water skins and you pass them forward to Meeks and Justus. You take the paddles from them and start rowing slowly and carefully with me and James. Meeks, Justus, see to it the food and water get ashore first. If we get wet, we won't die from it. Move carefully, so the boat doesn't tip too much, understand?"

Everyone nodded silently, their faces extremely pale, and not because of the dim, fragmented moonlight. They quietly set to work. It was strange for James to proceed almost methodically under such cool guidance and not give in to the adrenaline burning in his veins after the brief rest.

He and Adrian were the last to leave the boat, the muddy water up to their waists, and they were pulled up the embankment by the others.

The short bank was covered with diseased grass and moss that were saturated with moisture and made smacking sounds with every movement.

"It should be easy to look around at night, here in the open," Adrian suggested. James instinctively wanted to object because the night cast shadows, and he had to admit he was afraid of this place. But the Russian continued as they caught their breath. "It was darker in the forest because of all the trees blocking the moonlight, but during the day with the smothering clouds, I don't hold out much hope of seeing any better than we do now."

No one objected, so they shouldered their bags with the rations and medical injectors they had picked up, and made their way deeper into the dilapidated complex. James took Mila's hand in his. They walked behind the others as they left the shore.

They were on the southern edge of the complex, across the river from the gun artifacts, where the foothills formed. The area was mostly populated with cube-shaped buildings and later tall square-cut stones so overgrown they could have passed for bizarre trees if there had been less light. However, on most they passed, a shiny black material could be seen underneath when they removed the layer of dust, creepers, and mold. It was hard and made no sound when struck, could not be nicked, and there was a faint when they put an ear to it.

The open areas between each building were covered by dense undergrowth, which mostly consisted of intertwined creepers that were dry and scraggly and often bore thick thorns that cut their lower legs.

After what felt like an eternity of stumbling back and forth between the shadowy monoliths, Mette asked for a break and pointed to a small open area to their right at the foot of a skyscraper—the mighty structures could hardly be called anything else, even if they had no windows.

This space was a shaded semicircle of stinking grass adjacent to a wall of hard, wild growth that curved slightly inward. James settled in front of it with Mila and inspected the minor and major wounds he had sustained during their trek through the vast canyons. He took out some of the bundles of medicinal plants they had brought along, chewed them, and rubbed the resulting paste on the bleeding cuts and scrapes.

"I expected a little more," he said to Mila, wiping the sweat from his forehead so it wouldn't drip onto his treated legs.

"More than brush that wants to rip the flesh from your bones? More than vegetation so dense we might have made two kilometers in two hours? More than geometric shapes of black something that nature has reclaimed? More than a place as dead as a place can be?" Mila smiled away her frustration.

"All of it," he said.

"Well, I don't know what I expected, but the more I think about it, the more I realize there could be worse alternatives."

"Like what?"

"How about a monster?"

"All right. You win." He shuddered as he looked into the deep shadows surrounding them. The skyscraper at their backs was in the center of the complex, along with the other overgrown giants, creating shadows the stars and moon couldn't banish. "It's strange that there's grass here and everywhere else those nasty creepers are taking over. What do you think all this was built for?"

"We don't have much, but we do have some clues. You heard the buzzing in the walls?"

James nodded.

"Something's vibrating—that is, energy," she said. "Even in concrete buildings, you can hear it, or rather feel it, if the power or water lines are close to where you press your ear. But what we heard was a deep, steady sound."

"And what does that mean?"

Mila shrugged. "I don't know. Either these buildings still have power, or they go so deep we can hear the lava below. Take a guess and you'll be as close to an answer as I am."

"Whatever we were hoping to find must have been gone for millennia," he thought aloud.

He gratefully accepted a water skin from Adrian who was handing out rations. No one spoke, but James understood what was going through everyone's minds as they recovered from the exertions of the last few hours: Had it been the right decision to leave the Tokamaku? Should they go back? Even if they decided to—which no one dared say —there was the problem of *how* to get back. How would they get through the undergrowth? It was untamed outside the immediate area and would make progress as difficult and energy-sapping as it was dangerous to their health. They would have to stay near the river to avoid losing their bearings since they couldn't find their way by using the sun. But the bushes were so dense they hadn't been able to see a step beyond the growth from the boat.

There was only one way forward, and none of them liked the answer, especially since it had not been productive.

"We need to climb one," James muttered absent-mindedly.

"Excuse me?"

"We need to climb up," he repeated. He blinked and looked Mila in the eye. "So we can get a better all-around view. How are we going to know where to go next?"

"That's way too dangerous!" she protested, glancing up at the overgrown green facade. "That's a good two or three hundred yards!"

"The alternative is to keep wandering endlessly back and forth between these things, using up our supplies." He pointed to a red spot on his right hand. "I don't think that's an option."

"Hey, guys!" Justus shouted. He sounded so upset that James and Mila jumped to their feet.

The German was standing two steps away from them, groaning as he tugged at the wall of creepers behind them. It moved as a whole, as if it was a connected carpet, but without resistance. James grabbed the thicker pieces of wood and pushed them inward. There was no resistance.

"There's no wall!"

12

Helped by their obsidian knives, they cut through the dense, interwoven undergrowth blocking the hollow space in the side of the huge green cuboid in no time. James slipped through a slit just wide enough for one and entered a featureless darkness. The sparse moonlight that penetrated the few spaces between the creepers faded away after only a few inches. He stopped Mila, who had started to follow him, so she wouldn't injure herself on the cut branches and thorns protruding inward and returned to the others.

"We need light. Do you have the fire bow?" he asked. Adrian nodded silently, grabbed his pouch, squatted in front of the opening, and pulled out the archaic device.

With practiced hand movements, he threaded the string from one end to the other, so the tool actually looked like a bow. The others found another stick and sharpened it. It took longer to find a larger piece of wood into which they could carve a notch. They had no shortage of tinder since most of the diseased leaves nearby were withered and dry along with some smaller twigs that had not made it to the damp ground through the dense undergrowth.

"We shouldn't do this out here," Meeks said. "If we're unlucky, the whole area will burn down, as dry as it is."

One by one, they climbed through the opening and crowded inside, close enough to the light to see. It was a strange feeling to be standing in such impenetrable, almost solid, darkness. James felt he would hit a wall if he took half a step forward, yet judging from the echo of their voices, it was likely they were in a large room.

They took turns with the fire bow so no one got calluses or blisters, and after a frustratingly long time, the first glowing sparks appeared and ignited their tinder, which they quickly covered with the smaller twigs. Mette carefully blew oxygen into the beginning fire so it wouldn't die out before it had really begun.

Soon they had lit several thick branches Meeks and Justus had gathered and the darkness was easily dispelled.

They were in a huge room that must have encompassed the entire base of the building. Although the light was sparse and unsteady, he made out a semicircle of debris that looked to have come from the collapsed wall through which they had entered. Here, too, the creepers were everywhere and had taken over every nook and cranny. Here and there, between individual columns that supported the high ceilings, they found outlines of things that might have once been furniture or fixtures, but was now impossible to tell with the naked eye. The green carpet had smothered and hidden everything.

Sparks fell from his improvised torch and dripped like molten lava onto the ground. At first, he shuddered violently, worried a fire could quickly get out of control, but he noticed the high humidity and realized there was no great danger. The embers quickly died.

"Looks like the entryway to an office complex," Mila said.

"Only without windows," Justus said, who had walked a dozen feet along the wall, holding his measly torch up to some black material that was as smooth as soapstone and free of weed growth over a large area. "Nothing seems to grow here. It stretches along this length at waist level, to the corner back there."

"A skyscraper with no windows?" Mila asked, incredulous.

"Different planet, different customs." The astrophysicist shrugged and traced the wide strip with one hand. It didn't appear covered with mold, either.

James walked over to him and touched the wall. It felt cool to the touch. The others joined them, and James took a few careful steps back, careful not to trip over a creeper or a stray root that might have grown through the solid floor.

"Move aside a bit," he urged the others, while eyeing the vague shape he thought he saw beneath the growing weeds.

"What is it?" Meeks asked, tense, squinting into the darkness around them.

"I think I can show you." James pointed and directed the others to stand along the edges of the rectangle. "Try to cut or burn that stuff away."

After a while, they had uncovered the entire rectangle and, sure enough, a finger-thick joint appeared, running vertically along the sides, connected by a horizontal line. In the middle, where the strip was suspended, as if by magic, there was a depression.

"Is that a... *gate*?" Mette asked.

"Looks like it."

"So, we have a skyscraper with no windows and a gate on the first floor," Meeks summarized.

"Or several," Adrian added.

"A business park or something like that?"

"Who knows."

They took a long time to explore most of the first floor. They had to keep finding thicker half-dead branches of creepers that were dry enough to light quickly and burn for a long time. But to do this, they had to go outside because everything inside was too damp. Finally, they were gathered in front of a bulge on the north wall with a two-meter-deep semicircle in front of it. To the right and left were several waist-high mounds of green growth, under which, after some work with knives and fire, they found empty cages made of thin wire. The blocks between the wire were empty, but sealed with a transparent material. The first two were empty, but under the third they had found, to their horror, a head with two eyes. After further examination it turned out to be part of a robot, folded up like a person crouching and hugging his own legs. It was impossible to exactly tell its shape since the individual parts blended perfectly into one another with hardly any contours.

"Seems to be offline," Justus said. The sight of the robot that had silenced them all.

"The cage is vibrating slightly. I'd bet my ass it's still being powered somehow," Meeks said.

"Maybe just the cage and not the robot?"

"Let's hope so."

"It's a good thing there's no switch," James said.

"Don't tell me you would push it." Mila looked at him reproachfully, and he made a dismissive gesture.

"I'm the only one of us who's not a scientist, okay? And I want to know where we are and what this is."

"It's not a temple, anyway. We've already seen one of those."

"You mean the pyramid?" he asked her.

"Yes."

They had visited the pyramid, and Mila had voted to spend more time there in case it was the Temple of Heaven Nasaku had mentioned. After all, the statues of Egyptian deities, which were very similar to their earthly counterparts yet differed from them in details, at least invited them to investigate further. But she was the only one who thought they might be in front of a temple. Justus, who had logged a semester in archaeology because he had to wait for his admission to astrophysics, turned out to be surprisingly well-read in these matters and had objected, believing the pyramids had been tombs, not temples, unlike their counterparts in South and Central America. The presence of the statues of the gods outside and the lack of an entrance also tended to indicate this. Besides, they had been impatient to learn what the large, square structures in the center of the presumed city might be.

Mila had gone along with the majority, but James had felt bad. Maybe she was right after all. Just because they hadn't found an entrance didn't mean it wasn't the temple they were looking for. But how was he supposed to know? He could hardly hope to come across a sign that said: "This way to the Temple of Heaven and a connection for the marble."

"It can't be a coincidence that the six cages are close to this one," Justus said, tapping the tangle of growth making it rustle in protest against the wall curving toward them.

"An access point for robots?" Adrian asked.

The small group stood in front of the plants with smoldering, crooked branches in hand, as if at a seance, their faces red in the purgatorial light that diminished with each breath.

The cosmonaut pointed to the left, outside the small, illuminated area, to the west wall with the gate they had discovered. "And there's a doorway. Maybe those are maintenance machines."

"Maintenance of what?" Mette wanted to know.

"I don't know, but there has to be a way up if not stairs."

"An elevator shaft?" James asked, approaching the web of creepers.

"I don't think robots ride elevators, but something like that."

He sighed. "Then we'd best get back to cutting and burning."

The work was again sweaty and it spoke to the strength of the team and the friendship that had formed that no one objected or even grumbled to vent the frustration written all over their faces.

The heat was almost unbearable, and they were all showing the first signs of eczema and abscesses again. The air reeked of rotting biomass and was so thick they felt like they were drowning in it. James was constantly thirsty because his body was expending vast amounts of energy to regulate its core temperature and help it with a basic level of evaporative cooling through sweat.

"It's not an elevator, anyway," he noted as they uncovered two holes with the remnants of weathered metal hinges still visible around the edges.

They led to two chimney-like tubes, first to the front and then to the top, and here, too, everything was overgrown—at least on the walls. The vertical tubes were at most a half meter in diameter, perhaps twice that without the creepers. James felt like a chimney sweep in a nightmare as he lay on his back, staring up into the darkness that opened like a black hole above him.

"I'm climbing up."

There were murmured questions from outside, indistinct since the plants seemed to steal the consonants from all speech. So, he slid out like a clumsy crab and eyed the others, who looked at him like a crowd of concerned relatives at the deathbed of a close relative.

"Are you crazy?" Mila asked. "You want to climb up there?"

He nodded. "Yes. I took a climbing class once in college."

"For how long?" Meeks wanted to know, and James gave him a sour look.

"Two months."

"Far too dangerous," Mila said, shaking her head firmly.

"Actually, it will be very easy to climb. The branches of these nasty shrubs, wind and intertwine like snakes on the walls and provide perfect footholds. And if we want to know if these robots did use the shafts for maintenance, then there's no other way."

"I can go," Adrian suggested with a meaningful look in his direction, but James immediately shook his head.

"No, I'll do it. I'm slimmer than you and have experience with this kind of thing."

"With xenofauna in claustrophobic shafts? Why didn't you tell us about this before?" Mila glared at him, and he blinked in surprise at her cynical tone.

"Gonna be a piece of cake." He looked into her eyes and smiled at her in a way he hoped she would understand that this conversation would not and could not happen here and now.

"You can't see anything up there," Mette objected. "And you need both hands to climb."

See, Mila seemed to tell him wordlessly by tilting her head and pursing her mouth.

"I'll feel my way through. You can hold one of the torches, so I have a fixed point and don't get cold."

No one laughed at his joke. There wasn't even a hint of a smile on any of their faces.

"Look," he said taking a deep breath and resting his arms over his bent knees. The uneven roots and twigs under his buttocks pressed painfully in places he would have preferred to avoid, but he had to look relaxed lest they talk him out of it. "You're five smart eggheads. I'm a professional babbler, as I was once certified to be, and I can climb quite passably. Let me do what I can do, and you check out these robots. Maybe you can activate one of them?"

"How are we supposed to—" Mila started to protest, but he interrupted her.

"I don't know. As I said, I'm not a scientist. You'll figure it out." Then he crawled back into the shaft and twisted and turned around until he was standing, or rather stuck, upright in the tube. His shoulders touched the walls, or the brush, and only when he reached up with his hands did he have enough room to move. Because of the curvature of the walls combined with the limited space to move, he had to keep his hands and feet equally in front of him and could barely reach right or left or behind him.

"All right," he said to himself, before blowing hot breath into his hands, rubbing them together, and groping to find a suitable grip.

"Take care of yourself," someone whispered below him. It was Mila. Her face appeared between his feet. She looked worried.

"I promise," he replied earnestly, absorbing the sight of

her sweaty face glowing red in the torchlight like a drug. She was as beautiful as ever.

Then he climbed, accompanied by the muffled rustle of creepers, and here and there an ominous crack or creak as he shifted his weight more to his feet or his hands. Every now and then, he took short breaks by leaning backward and resting his shoulder blades against the leaves and branches with pressure on his knees. It would have been almost pleasant if there hadn't been so many thorns tearing small holes in his skin again and again. Soon his fingers felt wet, and he knew it wasn't just sweat, even if the heat was almost unbearable.

The faint torchlight, the dark red glow that covered the ground far below him like the vent of an active volcano that had run out of power, offered him little help. He was practically blind, barely able to distinguish between lighter and darker areas and, if he was lucky, to recognize particularly thick branches and not reach haphazardly into the worst thorns.

Although his hands soon shook and his arms vibrated with exertion, he did not give up and continued into the darkness, undeterred.

I must find it, he thought, blowing drops of sweat from his upper lip that appeared as glittering, shooting stars in front of his dilated pupils and faded so quickly he thought they were mere imaginings. *I must find the temple. Where is it, Nasaku? Where is it?*

It was as if a voice was calling to him, like the sirens to Odysseus, only it was no voice his ears could hear. The thing that drove him was a vague feeling he was on the right track. A feeling that had been there ever since they had come ashore at the lock and had grown stronger as they got closer to the center of the complex. Here in the shaft, it became a steady pull. The voice beckoned to him, urgent and emphatic.

James *knew* he was in the right place, and he had to keep climbing. The answers he sought were close. Before, that instinct had guided him when he'd negotiated deals with militiamen and kidnappers in the shade of baobabs, gauging how much he would have to offer to avoid getting shot and how little he could offer to keep his job. He had rarely thought about the tickle in his nose and the prickle on the back of his neck, simply dismissing it as his ability to read situations and the people in them. If he was honest with himself, though, there had always been that sense of the right way, at least when he had allowed it.

This, though, was something different and had a different quality and intensity.

"No problem," he growled, and the pain in his hands pulsed from the tips of his fingers to the back of his head at increasingly shorter intervals.

He refused to give up, even though the glow beneath him was only the size of a pinhead, and he wanted to scream that it had finally ended. The sweat on his forehead grew cold and left him feeling feverish.

Suddenly, he bumped his head against something hard and almost fell from fright. His hands jerked and tore some of the creepers from the wall, which clung to them with tiny, hairlike roots, and he wobbled back and forth for a moment. Carefully, he disengaged a hand from the brush and felt around with wet fingers for what he had collided with. It was cold, perhaps metal, and barely vegetated. With short prods and scraping motions, he dislodged it, coughing and spitting when bits of dust, dirt, and wood fell into his mouth and nose. Eventually, his fingers found a notch with a round handle and a moving piece. He pushed it.

It made a hollow squeak, and the resistance eased slightly. He groaned and pushed his hand up with as much force as his trembling arm could muster, and the resistance was suddenly gone. There was a hiss, followed by a gust of cool, extremely dry air blowing around him.

He pulled himself through the hole and the tug subsided. He knew he had arrived where his instincts had drawn him.

In total darkness, he rolled onto his back on a cold, slick floor. There was a faint smell of ozone and disinfectant. His chest heaved as he gasped violently for breath. Suddenly, the light came on.

13

J ames rolled onto his side and came to his elbows and knees, exhausted. He breathed deeply, in and out, trying to ignore the trembling in his extremities that were on the verge of failing him.

Slowly, he straightened and looked around, blinking. His eyes burned from the photosensitivity after climbing in total darkness, but with each breath it became easier to bear and soon the first outlines formed out of the brilliant white around him. Beside him were the hole and the hatch he had pushed open. What he had first thought were rotating shadows turned out to be a ring of armatures with him in the middle. They reached to his waist and were about two paces away, but it seemed like an unbridgeable distance in his condition. The air above shimmered like asphalt on a hot summer day in the desert.

Gradually, he made out more details as his eyes became accustomed to the brightness, and his mind easily discerned coherent patterns from impressions rather than filling the space from his imagination.

The fittings consisted of a solid, shiny ring about a meter

high that looked like it was cast from a single piece of metal. Above, it merged into a tabletop on which were several objects the size of tennis balls that looked like bubbles of blue jelly. He was immediately reminded of rubber balls from his childhood. Behind the table was a dark, semi-transparent wall which merged high up with a glass pane that turned into a dome above his head through which he could see the starry sky, albeit through an extremely milky haze that blurred the twinkling of the distant stars.

There were two light sources: the glass dome itself, which glowed from within and flooded the room with cold white light, and a band of light under the table that caused the smooth, gray floor to appear yellow. It clicked and beeped on the edge of his hearing as the pulse of his heartbeat eased in his ears, as if he were in a server room. The semi-transparent area between the glass dome and the armature began to change. It flickered a few times and then showed a white light on which a green arrow ran in circles, hitting itself. Then, abruptly, diagrams, columns of numbers, and lines of code appeared, running in diagonal rows, reminding James of a crashed program just before the bluescreen.

"Hello, James," he heard an ageless voice say in English. It had a New York accent, like his own.

"Uh," he uttered lamely and cleared his throat. "Hello?"

He turned in a circle and swallowed. He had expected a few things, but definitely not this.

"It's good that you were able to come."

"Who's there?"

"I am the avatar of Al'Antis. I am the Guardian, the Eternal. I am Ukmak."

"Ukmak? You're the protector of the Tokamaku?" James asked, irritated. He looked for the source of the voice, but he was alone, surrounded by the computers—or what he thought were computers.

"Yes. I am the first."

"*The* first one?" Does everyone always have to speak in riddles?

"I am the avatar of Al'Antis. I am the first living being of this planet."

"Are you Nasaku?"

"Yes. I have been that, too."

"So, you're not dead," he said, sighing with relief. "I'm sorry we couldn't save you."

"Nasaku was merely my physical form. I created the hybrid unit to protect my planet. From the data you brought, I can tell that it made it to Tal'Auri."

"Tal'Auri? You mean Earth?"

"Yes."

"So, you're connected to her?"

"No. It was a separate entity with my consciousness. My original programming only ever allowed me one physical form, so I digitized myself at a certain point," the avatar explained.

"Your programming? So, you're an AI and Nasaku was a robot?" James asked. His was head spinning. *I saw her bleed.*

"Yes and no. I am an artificial intelligence, but I am not based on computer code in the way you would define it. My consciousness is based on organic algorithms, at least in its original form, until my digitization. Nasaku was a hybrid being that could house a segment of my consciousness with a central task through biotechnological implants."

"What kind of task?"

"I have determined that you already know that."

"The protection of the teleporter, the death zone."

"Yes. Nasaku had the task of protecting Al'Antis at its

weakest point: the teleporter," the disembodied voice of the avatar explained.

James took the marble from the small pocket in his shorts he had sewn himself. He was astonished to find it was glowing faintly from within, like a galaxy. "She said I had to take this to the Temple of Heaven."

"I understand."

"What is it?"

"This is a zero-D memory. It is an ancient relic from when the local culture reached its technological peak, about fifty thousand years ago. It draws its energy from a microscopic black hole enclosed by a magnetic confinement field. This memory, which you call a marble, activated this control center."

"Control center of what? Of this complex? What is it, anyway?"

"An energy node. Al'Antis had over two hundred at his wedding. Today it is the last one. Around it are the warehouses. Right now, you are standing in the central one. The defenses you saw when you arrived are my work and the only reason this place still exists," the avatar explained.

"The reservation," James thought aloud. "It powers the reservation."

"Yes. The last of the Al'Anters are protected from the effects of the toxic atmosphere by the forest I created."

"What happened?"

"Al'Antis was destroyed by the First Children, the first creation of our creators. What makes it a deadly place are the effects of a short but destructive war. Nasaku was meant to prevent that from happening again."

"So, it all started with the teleporter?" James shuddered, and for the first time he was relieved that Pavar had suggested to the president that the alien machine be encased in concrete.

"Yes. The teleport network was intended to connect the children of the Elders once they reached the appropriate maturity, but there was an underlying error in that thinking," the avatar said. "Namely, the assumption that sufficiently advanced technology—more precisely, the use and powering of the teleporter—must mean the civilization in question has attained appropriate maturity and has risen above self-destructive behavior. This assumption is false."

"Who are the elders? The creators?"

"I don't know, but Nasaku believes she has found out. My consciousness has existed continuously for four million years and I have been able to fathom many mysteries of the cosmos, those whose interest was programmed into me when I was created. What I have not been able to fathom is who it was that created me. I did not search for it because it is not within my programming. With Nasaku, that seems to have changed."

"She was researching her—*your* origin?" he asked.

"Yes."

"I thought that was against your programming?"

"It is. But I am interested in how it could happen that a biomechanical entity could rise above, or break out of, my algorithm. However, I cannot access the data."

"Let me guess, you can only do that in the Temple of Heaven?"

"That's correct."

"What is it?"

"An ark that the Al'Anters built when the war began. It is an underground data repository that stores all the knowledge of their civilization."

"*Your* civilization?" James inquired. He was almost dizzy

from all the information coming at him. Within this futuristic room, he felt like a rat in an experimental laboratory, both ignorant and out of place, a foreign body.

"I am the avatar of this planet and a tool of my creators, the ones who also created the Al'Anter, but I am not them."

"And you don't know who created you."

"No," the avatar said. "I must point out that the residual power in this control room is running low. I will shut down as soon as a minimal value is reached, so there is enough energy left for the next step."

"The next step?"

"Yes. You must learn how to reach the ark. The Temple of Heaven. For that, you must use one of the interface connectors. Any questions you have will be answered as long as your clone body is functional."

"And how long do I have?"

"With two injector doses, about twenty more hours. After ten hours, even a return to the reservation will be too late and the destruction of your body will be irreversible. A certain time sensitivity is therefore advisable."

James wondered if he had ever heard such a chilling request to hurry because of imminent danger to his life. This had never happened to him, even in Africa.

"Interface consoles... do you mean those jelly balls?"

"Yes. You can choose two of them. The important thing is to connect both hands with two different connectors, otherwise, no cerebral entanglement can be guaranteed," the avatar instructed him, and two of the strangely out-of-place ball flashed.

"What kind of entanglement?" he asked, eyeing the flashing balls, suddenly feeling uneasy. Everything was happening so fast he could barely keep up. He was just getting comfortable talking to an AI that wasn't one in the conventional sense and could apparently see inside his head. Now he couldn't shake the feeling he was falling down a rabbit hole, and the fall was accelerating—so much so he no longer knew where up and down were.

"For you to understand what the Temple of Heaven is and why you must get there, you must learn some things about Al'Antis and about me. You will have access to my memories and those of Lok'Tak, the last Al'Anter consente."

"Access? Lok'Tak?" James' head buzzed, and he withdrew his hands. He had already extended them toward the two connectors without consciously doing so. The blue glow was almost hypnotic, intensifying his inner upheaval. "What does that even mean?"

"I will feed the data into your memory center. It is via an electrochemical transfer method and is completely painless," the avatar explained in its androgynous voice. "You are obviously uncomfortable with this idea. Will it ease your discomfort if you can talk to a familiar person face-to-face and ask your most pressing questions verbally?"

"Yes!" he answered without hesitation.

"Good. I remind you that time is a scarce resource in your case, but the decision is yours. Please do not be frightened now."

James flinched when Nasaku appeared out of nowhere two meters in front of him. She stood there, her small figure, bird-like face, alert dark eyes, and hawk nose. Her hair was neat and tied into a braid. She was wearing the same Air Force clothes as the last time he had seen her. However, he swallowed hard, and it was replaced by a white one-piece jumpsuit with blue elements that made her look like a bridge member of the *Enterprise*.

"Nasaku," he breathed.

"Hello, James," she replied, bowing slightly.

"Are you—"

"Yes, I am her, though at the memory level of over eight thousand years ago when I was created as a physical entity and separated from my self to guard the teleporter," she replied, pronouncing the ending of each word with the extreme precision and accentuation as he remembered. "I am the same person as Nasaku with a different level of knowledge, but I retrieved from my data collective what you experienced and what was stored on the zero-D. I am sorry that you had to do this. I'm sorry you had to go through that experience."

James merely nodded and tried to block out the memory that he had shot the real Nasaku. Whether at her request or not made little difference to his guilt.

"I'm sorry we couldn't protect you," he muttered and cleared his throat. This was a second chance of sorts, and he couldn't waste it spending time whining. "I'm supposed to have the Avatar's memories—*yours*, I guess—implanted."

"Yes. I am the Avatar, and I am not. I'm basically something like you are now. So, your original body could talk to someone and draw out information because you were already familiar with each other on a basic human interaction level. Does that make sense to you?"

"Yes, and that's what worries me." James mussed his hair and tried to calm his racing mind. "I'm a clone of myself, but the same me I've always been, and yet I feel different. Maybe it's knowing that I also exist on Earth, I don't know. Being two, even if only one is conscious, is something I'll probably never get used to, but I understand your analogy, I think."

"Good, I'm sure you have lots of questions."

"Who built the teleporters?"

"We don't know. I seem to have researched who it was, but only after the split, so I can't tell you who it is. But there is data of mine in the zero-D memory that can only be decoded in the ark, in the Temple of Heaven. My guess is that I—the Nasaku you met—found out something about the elders. I know someone created me, and that the teleporter was here when I first opened my eyes. So, we were both on Al'Antis at the dawn of life, and so it must have been on the other worlds."

"What other worlds?" he asked.

"There are six that we know of, and each has at least one teleporter," Nasaku said, her hands folded. She spoke quickly, but not hurriedly, just enough so he felt the rush, but not so he became agitated. "I have come to the reasonable conclusion that all six worlds were created by the Elders, of whom we have found no traces other than the teleporters and the avatars."

"There are multiple avatars?"

"Yes. It seems that each world has its own avatar that observes or controls the creation of the elders."

"A creation with a system," James thought aloud. "What makes you so sure that both our worlds were artificially created? It seems extremely unlikely to me, given such complexity. We know from astrophysics that the Earth took billions of years to evolve into what it is today."

"That is also correct, although over a somewhat shorter period than your scientists have previously assumed."

"So, these elders began their creation several billion years ago?"

"Yes."

"And how do you know that it is indeed so, and that there is no cosmic evolution behind it?"

"I'll show you." She gestured with one hand and an image of Earth appeared, taken from orbit, perhaps from the ISS. He recognized the outline of Africa beneath the snow-white bands of clouds, and above them the stretched-out foothills of Europe with the Italian boot and the Iberian Peninsula. At the western terminator, dawn was reaching North and South America as thin brown hints at the end of the mighty Atlantic Ocean with its deep blue water masses, which gave his home planet the paradise-like sight that brought awe to the eyes of every human being: A lonely blue sphere in the midst of endless darkness, a shining example of life in a hostile environment, an island of diversity and creativity of evolution.

"Beautiful," he said devoutly.

"Yes," she agreed. "Now, let's take a closer look at one spot."

She gestured with her hands in the air and made spinning motions. The globe rotated to the left until Central America appeared right in the middle from his perspective. The cloud bands froze in their endless procession from northeast to southwest, and the frame zoomed in as if a camera were racing toward the surface, but it couldn't be because no camera could provide such a sharp image, smoothly displaying pixels densely strung together. But then it occurred to him it was most certainly a simulation. Or was it?

"What is it?" he asked.

"This is an old satellite image."

"You hacked our satellites in that short a time?"

"Yes, but that's not what this is about." The image zoomed in on northern South America, pierced through a thick layer of clouds, and stopped over the outline of a huge lake enclosed by densely forested mountain slopes, surrounded by the Pacific Ocean. He knew the contours of the area too well, for he had studied it several times: It was Lake Maracaibo in Venezuela, which, contrary to what its name suggested, was not a lake at all, but a gulf with a small, channel-like connection to the Gulf of Venezuela. In the middle of it was a large gray spot he did recognize.

"What's that?" asked James, pointing.

"This is our teleporter, or rather the artificial island where it was located before the war."

"Wait a minute. What war?"

"The war with the First Children that led to the downfall of the Al'Anter." Nasaku watched him and seemed to read his confusion as if from an open book. "What you see here is not Earth. It is Al'Antis."

"But that can't be. I recognized Africa. And Europe. And North America! The ancient world! I could swear that…" He faltered as he remembered his question: *How do you know there's actually no cosmic evolution behind this?* "Earth and Al'Antis are identical planets."

"Except for tiny variations, negligible differences in total mass and albedo, axial inclination, and surface relief. This can easily be attributed to different cosmic conditions, such as impact events. But even these are very minor since the entire Sol system is also the same as here."

"That means you also have a Saturn? A Jupiter?"

"Yes, although with different names. They are identical to your solar counterparts. Only in this way can the Earth also be exactly as it is."

"But this is… just too big. No one can shape so many intricate details, such masses to their will!" James felt like she had punched him in the stomach.

"The possibilities are beyond what my intellect could simulate with all the computing power of the Al'Anter at the peak of their technological creativity. But it is not physically impossible," Nasaku said. "The fact is that the sameness of our two planets must be evidence of intelligent design. Any other explanation is out of the question."

She took James's perplexed silence as an invitation to continue.

"When the first Al'Anter scouts visited Earth with the aid of the teleporter, many thousands of years before Christ, they believed that the machine of the elders must be a time machine, although all scientific knowledge suggested the impossibility of such a device because it would violate basic cosmic laws."

"The Al'Anters have explored us?" he asked, surprised, but at the same moment rather irritated with himself because, after all, he had seen the statues of the Egyptian deities at the pyramid and knew of Nasaku's knowledge of Sumerian. "Then, at least they must have been extremely subtle."

"No, not really. The ancient civilizations reported gods in their pictorial traditions, by which they largely meant the Al'Anters, who must have seemed godlike to them because of their knowledge and abilities."

"You mean all that pre-astronautics stuff is true? The crackpots were right?"

"Yes, but for the wrong reasons. The alien 'gods' were people from another planet, genetically almost identical. They did not interfere but left some gifts and were welcomed at the time," Nasaku's likeness continued. "However, the Al'Anters soon withdrew when they realized the Earth people had evolved differently from themselves and that their leaders sought to use contact with them for personal gain and to maintain power. Thus, it came about that they did not use the teleporter to Earth after the death of Cheops."

"But the teleporter must have already been underground in Venezuela at that time. Our scientists have guessed that it must have remained there for hundreds of thousands of years."

"Only if tectonic events had caused it to sink, yes," Nasaku answered ambiguously.

He changed the subject. "The statues and the pyramid we found here in the energy complex. What's that all about?"

"They were a reminder of Earth, a sign of the bond between the worlds, and at the same time a memorial to young Al'Anters."

"A memorial?"

"Yes. The Egyptians and the South American peoples built pyramids because of the tales of the Al'Anters, who have always built pyramids as their preferred geometric shape for their temples. They used to be extremely devout. The Egyptian pharaohs had replicas created with the help of thousands and thousands of slaves, in an attempt to approach the size they imagined from descriptions by the visitors."

"How can it be that two nearly genetically identical species of humans evolved so differently?" James asked. "And why did an intelligence as godlike as the Elders put us in six different, identical systems?"

"I have never been able to find out, but that was not part of my programming either," Nasaku said. "Perhaps out of sheer scientific curiosity? After all, the six star systems are virtually identical, but the people on them clearly are not, even though they had the same starting point. This could be the stuff of an interesting paradox, perhaps one the Elders have never been able to resolve."

"And so, they launched a large-scale experiment," James muttered, sighing, "It all sounds so crazy."

"Yes."

"What about the war? Why is this planet dying? And what's the deal with the reservation?" His gaze fell on the back of his right hand. A dark red abscess with a pus blister had formed.

"You will see that in my memories. This experience will be somewhat... unfamiliar to you, but it will answer most of your questions," Nasaku promised. "The energy is running low."

"I'm ready," James said.

"I hope so. Now put your hands on the connectors."

He swallowed and nodded before slowly walking toward the two blue flashing balls on the dashboard next to him.

"Goodbye, James."

14

The beginning of the local creation started billions of years before the awakening. But this beginning was irrelevant because no life could have witnessed its enormous grandeur. So it happened in cosmic silence that one of six supernovae simultaneously igniting at different locations in the Milky Way came into being. It was enriched with heavy elements: iron, magnesium, aluminum, silicon, and oxygen.

The uneven gravitational collapse of the boiling gases created an initial angular momentum which, as the collapse progressed, led to self-gravity forming a flat particle disk of boiling gases and dust particles. At the center of this spinning behemoth of impetuous cosmic force, a protosun came to life. It flooded the once-chaotic space with energy by converting the gravitational energy centered in itself into radiation. Combined with the impact of attracted matter, a conversion process generated further energy, which, through growing radiation pressure, accelerated its own decay, and another collapse.

The cry of the birth of a solar system began to fade, but

deep in the heart of the protosun, pressure and temperature continued to rise inexorably until, finally, a miracle, forced by unimaginable heat, occurred: Two hydrogen atoms fused, raising the energy potential and creating a chain reaction. A regular main sequence star was born and spewed its nuclear mass into space as radiation. The resulting radiation pressure not only released a lasting heat into the early solar system, but through its counterforce to the gravitational pull of the central star, stabilized a balance and with it an idea of order that eventually led to something entirely new: equilibrium.

Afterward, the star continuously radiated its thermal energy until, millions of years later, a constant hydrogen burner was created that would continue to burn for billions of years. A fusion reactor of cosmic proportions. But the rest of the gas and dust disk, which wandered in an endless migration around its protosun in the center, as if magically attracted by its gravity, did not remain inactive. Gradually, comet nuclei, asteroids, and finally the planets were formed. Along chemical and molar gradients an eruptive transformation of wandering molecules into coherent bodies took place. Early, unbridled solar winds blew lighter elements such as helium and hydrogen out of the young central star's vicinity, so the precursors of later gas giants formed in the outer system while the rocky planets remained near their heat-giving fusion generator. The expulsion of the light elements eventually internalized the star to nearly one hundred percent of the system's total mass, and the non-homogeneous disk of gas and dust cooled rapidly. Tiny silicates and oxides condensed alongside grains of rock and traces of metal to form ever-larger clusters of rock. They collided incessantly with each other, attracted by their gravitational pull, shattered, rejoined, and were thus subjected to a continuous growth process.

It would be more than a million years before the chunks were large enough to take the system's growing pains to a new level and begin forming larger bodies over a kilometer in diameter: The planetesimals formed, the first precursors of what later became the planets. Simultaneously, with the transition of the protosun into its stable phase as a central star, the material of the gas and dust disk was used up and disappeared, except for traces. Millions of these planetesimals now rotated around their center, which they could not hope to escape since it had already entered the phase of stable hydrogen burning.

Mineral synthesis ended. Physical and chemical processes, bound to gas and dust as active media, lost their importance as primary driving forces in the life cycle of the solar system. Instead, they now took place isolated in the planetesimals and later planets into which they were to coalesce, moving their hydrogen nucleus-fusing hearts on Keplerian orbits. Several tens of millions of years later, nine planets and an asteroid belt had formed, providing a fragile but steady balance. In their succession regarding distance from the central star, the planets were found to have an unusual regularity for the eruptive chaos of this cosmic birth.

But all the newly formed bodies were still hot and cooled slowly in the glowing vacuum. It took hundreds of millions of years until the differentiation process ended and each object remained in its orbit. A stampede had become a tame herd of celestial bodies.

However, one body in particular, the third starting from the central star, required a much longer time without completing the process. It was the densest of all the planets, with five and a half grams per cubic centimeter, and possessed an acceptable mass and escape velocity to become a veritable upheaval machine. With a hot core and eruptive volcanic and tectonic events, it continuously changed its appearance through erosion, weathering, and sedimentation. One day was already over after less than six hours, and the sun burned red onto the surface. Its mighty satellite was still barely visible at night, and the twinkle of the stars could not even be glimpsed. A vast ocean ceaselessly generated gigantic tidal waves that pounded the first protocontinents. It was an inhospitable place.

The first carbon atoms formed coherent structures, setting off an awakening. The first of these was the flash of the eyes of a bipedal being with two arms and a head and dark, cocoa-colored skin. It didn't know what it was or where it had come from. It understood nothing of the dark gray capsule dissolving around it like a fuzzy dream, but it understood that it was a witness and observing was its task, its meaning, its significance.

The avatar was born.

Unsexed and without the burden of repetitive thinking, it was an attentive component of the early planet where the first prokaryotes were just forming in the form of cyanobacteria. A mercilessly reduced image of early life compared to what had emerged from the capsule. But the Avatar did not think so. He observed and learned how they were the first to form an ability for oxygenic photosynthesis and converted the abundance of carbon dioxide in the atmosphere into oxygen. They created the basis of every other life on their home planet soon to follow; the first, simplest eukaryotes with their own nuclei. Algae that formed thick, stinking carpets on the oceans and participated in the upheaval of the planet's delicate atmospheric tracks by flooding them with oxygen.

The Avatar was fascinated by the cyanobacteria because despite their simplicity they could sense the direction of the red light shining on them from the central star and aligned themselves accordingly. But true emergence was still a long way off, billions of years, in which the process was slow, but always with a clear direction: complexity.

The true awakening, which also led to a second awakening of the Avatar, took place about one hundred fourteen million years before the great war of Al'Antis: The first flowering plant opened its chalice to the sun rising in the east to receive its warming rays. The accreted continents, covered by green carpets of plants for millennia, now hosted something completely new: Beauty in color and ethereal delicacy. The first flower was no longer a knotty herb, but a short-lived, translucent entity of unfathomable purity in a sea of coarseness. Its emergence was an evolutionary accident, a mutation that did not survive long and yet ushered in a watershed.

The Avatar felt something for the first time: reverent admiration, a sense of closeness triggered by the fragile beauty of this impressive sign that life could be more than mere survival. Its appearance was not yet favored, and yet this one calyx promised a change toward something greater. For several orbital periods, the Avatar wept as his body tried to process this new experience of feeling and coming to terms with there being no other consciousness with which to share this illumination of Nature. There was no pain, but rather a wonderment. This transient, unconscious being had, with the invention of beauty, been led to the fact that he, the silent witness, had awakened to himself and could see his place in his environment as more than a fact to be accepted.

So, he waited a long time, until at last a critical point seemed to pass, and more flowers appeared alongside ever more complex plants. Insects increasingly populated the skies, sucking up the nectar of the calyxes to allow ever more complex structures to survive. It was a firework display of colors and scents that exploded in the avatar's senses, making his presence an act of grace.

Barely more than one hundred million years later, the growing complexity of the evolution-driven differentiation of life led to real emergence: Dinosaurs, birds, and insects had already formed from cell structures that were assembled in ever greater numbers. The partially conscious living beings had rudimentary feelings, but no ego consciousness, and influenced themselves and their living world. Many individual parts, simple things in themselves, without even a trace of intelligence or conscious action, created in their totality a complex entity. A riddle that would forever haunt the Avatar. How could unconscious things, through sheer quantity and the formation of complex entities, give rise to consciousness?

They had come and gone, had replaced predecessors, and had in turn been replaced by more survivable successors. They were not yet beings who could grasp the concept of beauty beyond a benefit for their own survival, beyond their narrow horizon of eating and being eaten.

But the first humans did so, albeit in a limited way, after they had evolved from primates. In small clans, they roamed the primeval forests and savannas of the largest continent, which later became known on Earth as Africa, and yet was eighty-eight light-years away from it.

The first bipeds lived in small communities of up to fifty

individuals. Hairy creatures, similar to their close relatives from the animal kingdom, with receding foreheads and protruding mandibles. It was many hundreds of thousands of years before they used more complex tools than stones and sticks and to work them into advancements.

The Avatar saw in this the first sign of an artificial evolution, which at the same time seemed quite natural. Humanoids were no longer merely evolving along the evolutionary branches of the great tree of life, with mutations proving beneficial or detrimental changes and causing constant death and survival. They further altered what they found in their environment by the power of their thinking, and thus, for the first time in the history of the planet, helped themselves to continue through longer time periods and develop advantages over predators.

The Avatar did his fundamental task and observed, holding everything in his boundless mind, which had not forgotten a second of the last four billion years. He saw through eyes almost human and yet was not subject to the same cycle of birth and death that made everything that existed the same. The universe expanded and eventually passed away, just as every single-celled organism, plant, and animal grew, stagnated, and then slowly decayed like a cosmic breath. Everything real followed this breath, the undulations of creation, under whose surface he felt a depth that carried him, and yet he could never see.

The first two clans of these new humanoids met one day at a river delta in the heart of their continent, surrounded by massive trees and dense vegetation consisting mainly of creepers and ferns and home to an abundance of animals, large and small. The Avatar perched unseen on a branch high above them, having followed the paths of both groups for over two hundred years, just waiting for them to meet.

His curiosity about what would happen next was hard to put into words and created a tingling sensation on his skin, which had not carried a single wrinkle in all that time.

Both tribes, which he had christened One and Two, had a stable social system with a clear hierarchy based on physical strength and clever hunting instincts. The respective alpha males always went first through the jungle so they were the first to face the dangers of living as nomads in a competitive environment. Predators, poisonous insects, and dangerous parasites lurked everywhere.

The Avatar naturally expected a fight to ensue, especially since both clans were desperate after a large forest fire several days ago and urgently needed to find food. Most of the wild animals had fled the all-consuming wall of flames and the black clouds that followed had suffocated them.

The mighty dendron tigers were the first to return, large quadrupeds with razor-sharp claws and two eyes that provided a three hundred-sixty-degree field of vision from which no prey escaped. Its small wedge-shaped head, which the beast could pull halfway back between its shoulders, made it difficult to disable. His skin, too, had been given a tremendous advantage by a long chain of mutations: It could be injured by puncturing, but it quickly closed through overlapping fasciae in the lower layers of the skin.

Clan One had learned in their decades-long battles against this greatest threat to bring down the formidable predators, helped by primitive precursors to what eventually became a bola—a noose with three parts that ended in three tightly bound stones. But subsequent attempts to slay the briefly incapacitated dendron tigers with their primitive spears—crudely sharpened sticks—failed. The price was high, and each year many young male members of the clan died, so soon young women had to be enlisted for defense and hunting, and the birth rate suffered as a result. So, Clan One was in a somber mood, facing the end of its short existence on Al'Antis, when it came to meet Clan Two.

But everything turned out differently, as it so often did by chance. The leader of Clan One arrived first at the bank of the river and discovered there the leader of Group Two and his female. The expression in his eyes showed confusion. This was not surprising, as he had never seen others of his kind who were not his own. This moment changed their worlds and beliefs, and they were not as simple as one would imagine in a few million years. While they did not create great art, except for minor drawings in the sand and carvings soon devoured by the ravages of time, they loved, suffered, and lived in a way that would put all their evolutionary descendants on an equal spiritual footing.

At first, the two leaders eyed each other while their clans worked its way through the dense foliage and brush, and two fronts formed, one in the knee-deep water, the other on the embankment opposite. Silence fell until one exchanged a few guttural sounds produced by underdeveloped vocal cords through air pressure. It was more a roar and bark than the hint of a language, and as might be expected, no true communication took place.

They went at each other. The alpha male of clan one leapt forward, followed by his counterpart, who spread his arms and threw himself at his challenger, roaring. Under the eyes of their clan members, who were used to fights over rank, they thrashed wildly at each other, biting with their powerful, jutting jaws.

This sight saddened the Avatar in a detached but impressive way. He experienced it as a waste of what he had had to witness since the emergence with them had just reached a level from which he could hope to bring about an auditory exchange in a few hundred thousand years and thus refine his observations.

He already counted on witnessing the original sin of emergent life when a turn occurred that he had not expected; a mighty dendron tiger, the largest specimen he had ever seen and recorded in his memories, leapt through the undergrowth with a loud rustle and landed on a large boulder that split the river above the combatants. A shudder of horror went through both clans, and they huddled together according to the instincts woven into their genes by evolution, while the strong and brave stepped forward and prepared to defend themselves, for taking flight would only cost everyone their lives.

However, the two alpha males did not let go of each other. They were in such a frenzy they either did not notice the new danger or gave it a low priority. The dendron tiger, its shoulders towering higher than the heads of the two males, leapt and landed on the opponents, who fell under the force and within seconds were torn to shreds by the snarling beast. Horrified, the members of both clans stared at the bloody event until a female from Clan One reacted. She snatched the primitive bola from the hand of one of the young males and hurled it at the jungle predator. The throw was not practiced, and the bola bounced off the animal's flank, but the attack caused a different reaction, one that would forever change the course of human development on Al'Antis.

A female from Clan Two saw what her gender mate had done and took a spear from a male standing next to her, a construction with roughly ground stones on the ends, held in place with dried fern, with a barb, also attached with fern, that the other clan had never seen before, just as Clan Two had never seen the bola.

It didn't take a second for both groups to pounce on the predator. Some threw their bolas, most with skill through long practice, and because those who had proved clumsy in the past were simply no longer alive. Again, they brought down the dendron tiger as it ran at them, and then, as they always did when that occurred, they went to make their escape.

Clan Two, so far, had developed a different strategy, that of barbed spears. They had always chosen to fight, which had cost them nearly two-thirds of their clan members and meant that they would not survive the next winter. But now, the snarling predator, beside himself with rage as he bit at the bonds holding his legs together and left him panting in knee-deep water, was vulnerable to attack. They did what Clan One had never been able to do and stabbed and killed the animal with dozens of strikes, drilling the tips of the spears into its flesh, the barbs preventing the skin from closing. The animal bled to death, and both clans stared at the result of their accidental cooperation for some time.

The two females who had reacted first stepped toward each other and sniffed at each other before grabbing each other's hair, which covered their entire bodies, thick, black, and curled. They cooed, growled, and barked at each other until they felt they had inspected each other sufficiently. One was different but more in detail. Their foreheads were bony and varied in width, and their ears were slightly smaller.

Females One and Two then did something that was to become the primordial altruism and founding myth of the later civilization of the Al'Anters: They exchanged their weapons, which their respective inventiveness had produced, and which had complemented each other so excellently that in combination they could guarantee the survival of both clans, which henceforth roamed the prehistoric jungle together in coopera-tion. There were no more rank fights among the males because the other members immediately suppressed these. They could no longer afford unnecessary deaths in their prime if their species were to survive. Like any other, the desire for continuity had been indelibly woven into their DNA. Cooperation and peace had become necessary, as a matriarchal structure after the masculine pecking order nearly drove them to extinction.

The new clan, which Avatar classified as proto-humanoids and stored in his memory, became wildly successful. Reproduction rates were good, and with their new strategy against the king of the forest, the dendron tiger, there were no longer any predators that could threaten their survival as a species. There were, of course, still pathogens, infections, and accidents that provided evolutionary pres-sures that the proto-humanoids could never fully escape, but that was a natural constant that any competing species was at the mercy of and could and must grow from.

In the next millennia, the Avatar found further humanoids genetically identical to the proto-humanoids except for the smallest differences and had evolved from the primates in parallel in a morphogenetic thrust. As always, new ways of evolution coincided temporally in the most astonishing fashion, as if an ordering hand wanted to test large-scale tests with the same strategy.

All these humanoid groups met sooner or later, some-times taking centuries, sometimes millennia, during which there was little selection pressure. Each time the proto-humanoids repeated what they had learned: They had their female leaders begin a simple dialogue consisting of gestures and guttural sounds and then initiated an exchange of knowledge and tactics that served both groups. Then they merged into a larger tribe and formed smaller offshoots, which in turn grew and prospered.

Whenever that was the case, as their population approached around one hundred and fifty individuals, a natural secession took place as social tensions became more common. The larger the clans, the more difficult it was to maintain a tight social fabric that sustained each member. The clans, however, remained closely committed to their idea of cooperation, which had become woven into their genes over time through successful repetition. They developed the first forms of trade and survived even the appearance of invasive species because they knew how to fight when it mattered. And then they saw the advantages of large numbers when the clans united, and that too became their way in the branches of evolution.

Soon they formed the first superordinate structures, which amounted to the first fitful attempts of civilization. Ideas of individuals gained momentum as others took them up and developed them further. Better tools were invented, then fire, which further accelerated their spread and reproduction, as they took advantage of a far more diverse food supply from their environment. Darkness, the eternal enemy of humanoids and all other diurnal animals, was conquered, as was cold. Overcoming these two enemies, which had been considered insurmountable because they had been part of the natural order of things for so long, provided a further boost to the cooperative spirit among the proto-humanoids and their hundreds of clans, which had colonized large portions of the first continent in an interconnected network of individual social plots. Again, evolution had maintained one of the paths in their branches that had not died and had not broken off. And so, it continued to grow into the future and into the genes of this highly successful species.

Next, they invented the wheel and were able to trade and exchange food and other goods essential for survival such as hides, sinew, weapons, and tools, and could transport injured people and hunt heavier game. Once again, their development accelerated, while on Earth at the same time, nomadic tribes of much simpler hominids were beating each other with clubs as they competed for mating partners, hunting grounds, and out of a simple desire to expand.

The proto-humanoids no longer found competing humanoids since their evolution had accelerated so much there was hardly any room left for new species that could have arisen from a whim of evolution. They spread over all three interconnected continents, the equivalents of Earthly Europe, Africa, and Asia. They built their first temple, in honor of the Ancients, the Mothers of Wisdom Nu'ut and Re'et, those first females who had laid the foundation for the triumph of cooperation and thus of their species when a dendron tiger threatened to wipe out their competing clans. They were not worshipped as gods, for the concept of gods was unfamiliar to them. Their idea of cooperation was based on a genetic imprint that had evolved through centuries and millennia of education and repetition and because it had simply been more successful.

Every phenomenon in their living world was considered to them, at worst, a hurdle that had to be and could be over-come together. In the event of thunder and lightning, the clans agreed on where to find the best-sheltered caves and helped each other. In case of a natural disaster like a flood or a volcanic eruption, one learned from the clans that had already survived something similar.

They did not invent fictions about the wrath of pantheistic gods or animistic spirits because there was simply no need for these narratives, and the Al'Anters, now that they had climbed to the top of their planet's food chain, saw the unknown not as a threat but as an opportunity for growth. They sought their explanations and did not make them up because they were not under pressure to quickly bring together large civilizations into cooperative collectives lest they perish. These narratives became a necessity on Earth to keep social structures that had grown too large to be manageable.

The Al'Anters remained loyal to their clans, which, despite their successful expansion that brought them closer and closer together, still formed solid units of up to one hundred fifty to three hundred individuals. They were linked to the others by a common language, which was extremely verbose and detailed and considered the rich experience of their civilization.

At some point, helped by the discovery of gunpowder, they had begun mining and then metal smelting. They began to tame the land and build roads, develop motor vehicles, and wrest petroleum from the earth for power generation and chemical production. All this happened even before the first antediluvian god-king Alulim established the first advanced human civilization in Eridu with the Sumerians.

Due to the highly efficient spread of the Al'Anters over their entire planet, which they called Al'Antis, meaning "center" or "hub" in their original language, they could no longer maintain their culture of separate but highly interconnected clans and grew together into a cohesive community that moved through information technology using the same cooperative structure that had so far saved them from major wars and strife. Their preference for manageable kinships in the immediate local living environment lived on in extended families, who saw themselves as the most important social unit.

The overarching political body that ensured local and global redistribution and participation to make Al'Anter life comfortable for all individuals consisted of a meta-clan of the oldest representative of each clan on the planet. They conferred with each other on important issues over a digital network, and their numbers grew over time. The Al'Aktu-tak, or "consensus clan," elected a spokesperson for a certain period, the "consentiat," who supervised and accompanied the implementation of the decisions.

Al'Anter research was focused almost exclusively on medical, environmental, and communications technolo-gies and was subject to constant open exchange. All results and interim findings of experiments and studies were open to any man or woman at any time on their informa-tion network, which allowed light-speed communication and the storage of virtually unlimited data. Since there was no competition among them and the consensus clan redistributed the food, medicines, and technologies produced at any time to ensure balance, the Al'Anters were strangers to envy, resentment, and expansionism. Those sentiments simply played no role in their lives because their genes urged them to cooperate, and they lacked nothing that might cause them to envy their fellow humans.

The Avatar jumped from one body to another, using his determination of the most significant regions and human potentials to seek hosts, depending on the era. Genius thinkers, men and women in important positions; he settled into their subconscious and saw through their eyes, felt through their hands, tasted with their mouths. He never intervened, merely witnessed the most important decisions and changes.

The preliminary culmination of their rapid technological achievements, following the widespread use of autonomous robots in agriculture, logistics, and infrastructure, was the Toka'Taak, or "symbionts," by a large mass of highly educated scientists. These were hybrid nano-neurons that were half biological supercell and half high-performance robot that could emit bioelectric signals at long ranges. After the implantation process, they accumulated in the brains of the Al'Anters and enabled them not only to increase their memory and thinking abilities exponentially but also to communicate with each other quasi-telepathically. From now on, they exchanged thoughts and feelings in real-time, and their society grew even closer. Even disputes within the extended families subsided, and strife was replaced by understanding.

The pacifist attitude of the Al'Anters led them to great prosperity and an exponential rate of technological development, but it also had its downsides. Due to their evolutionary fixation on cooperation as the supreme imperative for survival, they inevitably possessed zero tolerance for any individuals who threatened this common ground. What had been firmly anchored in them and their thinking since the original fight of the first two clans against the dendron tiger led to killing people who suffered from genetic deviations that made social cooperation impossible or did not allow them empathy. In specially designated "sleep centers," they eliminated incompatible fellow humans helped by painless medical interventions. This changed in part because of the symbionts, which enabled the communication-impaired to make themselves understood. Ways were found to integrate them meaningfully into the civilizing efforts of the Al'Anters, and only those who, through genetic defects, could not empathize and thus use the symbiotes were killed in the sleep centers.

They found the teleporter on their planet when on Earth the sixth ancient Egyptian Great King Thutmosis III ascended the throne, around 1479 B.C., and was the first to take the title of "Pharaoh."

The object triggered a wave of great interest among the Al'Anters, who researched it for over fifty years, under the special observation of the Avatar, of course, who continued to absorb everything he could learn about them without revealing himself. He remained in the shadows, taking on the roles of council members, having symbiotes implanted to appear as one of them. He feigned emotions and feelings, made decisions in the highest positions, researched the most exciting projects, collaborated in the thousands of studies they produced every year to discover space without ever developing the urge to leave their paradisiacal planet. Their interest was purely out of curiosity and not the desire to explore new resources or develop new habitats. Their birthrate had been consistently low for a long time, so there was no overpopulation problem, and the efficient redistribution of resources created no shortages.

The Avatar lived everywhere and tried to figure out every detail of the civilization he had accompanied and observed since their first steps, never knowing for what or for whom he was doing it. For him, it was as normal as breathing was for humans. It just happened. It corresponded to his genetic algorithmic programming, and the question of why he existed was on his mind as little as it occurred to the Al'Anters around him.

That was not to change until he came across the teleporter project and could not get near it. To be sure, he learned all he could about the nature of the object. It was made of a mono-bonded graphene layer and comprised of molecularly reinforced carbon on the inside, behind whose honeycombs was a network of high-density superconductors that were far beyond anything the Al'Anters had yet developed. The same was true of the magnetic confinement chamber in the upper part of the teleporter, which contained six antimatter coils, including a supply of several kilos of positrons and protons. They generated the massive magnetic field that built up before each connection and powered the primary systems, which used matter-antimatter annihilation to transfer consciousness between teleporters, while the secondary power system used ion traps to draw electrical charge from its environment and store it in hexagonal storage lattices at the bottom of the teleporter. It powered the seats responsible for passenger cloning and the biomass converter under the funnel that served as an external supply of material.

The cloning mechanism was soon deciphered and, although complex, was no magic for the Al'Anter scientists. The major problem was not the primary energy system with antimatter, which they had already researched themselves, but transferring the passenger's consciousness. The most common theory was micro wormholes with a diameter of one picometer, which could be covered by the enormous energy output of the antimatter-matter reaction. The supply of antiprotons would last for many hundreds of thousands of years, even if used continuously, and yet they did not understand how these wormholes could be easily turned on and off and how they were stabilized, let alone where they were located.

Many questions remained unresolved until the consensus clan agreed to attempt to use the teleporter.

Their first destination was the seat they had marked with a one, which led them to Earth. The research teams reached the northernmost part of South America and encountered the continent's early indigenous cultures. Sometimes they were met with friendliness, sometimes with fear, and sometimes with hostility. The heterogeneity of the natives surprised them and led to some tragic deaths. But the Al'Anters were as unfamiliar with the concept of revenge as they were with that of punishment. They learned from their encounters and proceeded more cautiously. Within several hundred years, using homemade ships and simple components—they could not teleport objects with them—they traveled much of the globe, bringing their experiences home with them. They openly exchanged ideas with some early cultures, such as the ancient Egyptians, the Chinese and Mongols, and the emerging Greeks. They were fascinated by the diversity on this planet, which had produced the same creatures as themselves, yet in such different ways that they were strangers despite the similarities.

The Al'Anters began to ask questions about their own origins and became determined to travel to the other worlds to which their teleporter was connected, hoping to learn something about those who had left them these artifacts.

The Avatar wanted those answers, too. The mystery that occupied him most was how this object had been hidden from his unbroken observation. He was only a human, at least outwardly and concerning physical abilities, but by his immortality, it was only a question of time until he saw everything and stored it in his memories.

Except for the teleporter.

He could not have overlooked it because the tectonic and volcanic changes of Al'Antis, which could have carried the object into the depths, required hundreds of thousands, if not millions, of years for such upheaval processes. So, was there a blind spot in his perception, or had the teleporter arrived on the planet after the fact, as a meteorite, for example, or part of one?

He could not find an answer for this and he had learned that as a body-bound being there were too many gaps he could not fill with his perception. He was too limited in his ability to ensure absolute and efficient observation, and so he worked for the next ten years to feed himself into the network and turn his neurons into data impulses that could be his eyes and ears in the completely networked world of the Al'Anter.

Thus, he witnessed how, after a long time, they had ventured to the second world to which the teleporter was connected, that of the First Children. The teleporter researchers, with the planet's symbiont-connected science collective, had discovered that the superconductor systems had programmed a prioritization, and the seat for their own planet was in second place, while the seat for the humans was sixth. The name First Children thus arose from the theory that there had to be a creator civilization that had willingly connected six identical planets and possibly even created them. This inevitably led to the realization that they and the people on Earth must have been created by them, because according to the common theory of evolution, an identical triumph of identical humanoid mammals in two places simultaneously would be an impossibility, even if one considered that their planets were identical.

Contact with the First Children was different from with the Earthlings.

The first Al'Anter legation consisted of a team of twelve, six men and six women, selected by the Consent Council, but none returned on schedule. Only after several days and a long process of examining the teleporter before risking sending more did anything happen.

The alien machine created a strong magnetic field and a passage from an outside world was opened, something that had never happened before. One by one, the expedition team returned. The first two died because they were able to provide their bodies soon enough and interrupt the cloning process. The remaining ten got returned to their bodies but were obviously traumatized. Their symbionts had to be temporarily deactivated because they emitted confusion and the mental chaos and fear nearly drove the bystanders insane.

Gradually, however, they calmed and became surprisingly rational and disciplined, sharing only a small part of their emotions and reporting they had come to a wasteland on the other side where it was difficult to survive. Their way back had been cut off by indigenous creatures that had to be overcome. The ten survivors were released according to their wishes and were not interviewed again until they felt able to do so. The understanding of the Al'Anter was omnipresent, and a wave of compassion rushed through the consensus, a collective telepathic anodyne.

Their civilization didn't understand what had really happened, what later turned out to be a Trojan Horse, because the concept behind it was foreign to them. The Al'Anter expedition team had been captured on the other side of the teleporter by the First Children, an aggressive human species that had reached a high technological level but was composed of fragmented nations at war with each other, who, in constant fear of extinction by their visitors, had found a way to avert the threat of nuclear war on their planet. Their strategy was simple: they achieved unity through alliances against a common enemy, which they identified as the Al'Antern, who were to become their temporary salvation without knowing it.

However, the Avatar, by now a fully digitized being living in the eternal data stream of the network, learned all this much later.

The invasion began at that time and lasted for several years. Two years after the first expedition, a second was launched, led by two veterans of the first, but in reality they were First Children, who called themselves Kazerun. They made what appeared to be first contact with their people, who showed themselves to be friendly and helpful and held out the prospect of lively trade and exchange. But they asked for patience and a slow approach so as to not jeopardize mutual peace.

During this time, their agents on the other side, learned as much as they could. They learned everything there was to know about the culture and history of their new enemy, the Al'Anters, and plumbed their strengths and weaknesses, and collected as much research and technology as they could.

They were extremely good at deception and confusion that was completely foreign to the Al'Anters. And so, with relative ease, they stole thousands of their victims' accomplishments, which they misappropriated for their expansionist military apparatuses, borne from fear of the unknown because, following their evolutionary instincts, they sensed treachery and impending doom in the ways of the people of Al'Antis. For them, every word was a feint, every action a blow, and every silence a ruse.

After thirty years of infiltration and largely uneventful contact on both sides, the First Children finally struck.

On their home planet, the inevitable tensions between the power blocs had risen again, and so they had to act to force unity. The common enemy had to be attacked to maintain the narrative of the evil- Others. In addition, there was increasing domestic pressure since the Kazerun were not evil per se. Even among them, there were those who desired peace. They were seen as a threat by the majority because they had the potential to weaken their bloc if they infected too many others with their pacifist ideas. But they were in the minority, and the plan of those in power was ingenious and extremely clever for such a short-sighted civilization.

Their intelligence services were cunning and experienced. They developed a computer virus they used to infiltrate an asteroid tug, the compact robotic spaceships used by the Al'Anters to haul chunks of rock rich in precious metals into orbit around Al'Antis for exploitation. There were hundreds that traveled between the asteroid belt and their home planet, taking several years each way, and operating autonomously, just like the orbital factories. There were no firewalls or security programs because the need for such things had simply never existed. So, it was easy for the agents of the First Children to make a tiny course and acceleration change that would alter life on Al'Antis forever.

When the planet's moon was struck by the asteroid, a forty-kilometer chunk of interstellar debris, the Al'Anters had only a few days' warning. The satellite was destroyed by the impact and broke into two halves, one which shattered into many smaller pieces of debris. The only thing that prevented an immediate end to their civilization was that the impact, by its angle, narrowly ensured that the fragments did not crash through the atmosphere and burst into flames. But the impact on the ecosystem was devastating after only a few years. Without the powerful tidal forces that the moon had exerted on its planet, most ocean life died.

The Avatar immediately discovered the virus; after all,

the data cosmos was now his home, and the virus was something like a rash on his skin that could not be overlooked. But he did not intervene because that violated his nature as an observer. Still, there was a tinge of regret, similar to what he had felt when the first two clans of Al'Anter nearly wiped each other out. He attributed it to his rudimentary capacity for empathy, which was inherent in him to understand what constituted human interaction and to classify and store observations.

More attacks on the infrastructure of the inhabitants of Al'Antis, who did not understand what was happening to them or the nature of the disaster that had befallen them.

A secret cloning project by one of the agents resulted in several thousand highly trained soldiers, already armored and indoctrinated before the underground laboratory could be located in a nature reserve. They took key infrastructure centers by force and even attempted an attack on the teleportation area. The Kazerun wanted to use it to establish a bridgehead for sending their troops through and launching a large-scale invasion.

The Kazerun gassed the entire area, which was surrounded by a vast protective wall to protect against the magnetic waves of the teleporter. Housed within were hundreds of research facilities. Thousands perished, and the outcry of fear, terror, and panic shook the entire ether. No Al'Anter was spared the telepathic wave of horror, and many were driven to suicide by the cruelty of the suffering they witnessed.

In addition, there were simultaneous cyberattacks on the digital infrastructure, the power supply, and the robotic hubs that ensured a steady supply of food, drinking water, and goods necessary for survival. The Al'Anters hardly knew how to deal with the failure of the central supply points, as they had relied on the autonomous helpers for centuries and knew no other system.

Though they were sometimes years apart, the attacks overwhelmed their civilization, which could not adapt quickly enough, let alone understand what was happening. The teleporter was shut down by permanently damaging, one by one, the superconductors leading to the twelve seats with jamming signals, until the final blow from the Kazerun came.

One rainy morning, an agent who, like the others, had spent decades underground preparing his strike, hijacked one of the local science networks that had been split off from the consensus clan so they could be studied for bugs separately without endangering the overall network. His goal was to stop the construction of armed security bots or infiltrate them so they turned against their creators. For the Al'Anter, this process was something new but showed that they could adapt quickly at evolutionary time horizons.

The agent, in his data hacking, came across a strange trail that led him to the Al'Anter's best-kept secret: an attempt to recreate their own teleporter, which had been close to completion after a breakthrough in antimatter research had been made and they had managed to keep a micro wormhole stable for several seconds in an experimental lab. However, he knew nothing about the project itself, only that there was a top-secret facility dealing with antimatter, a possible danger to the Kazerun.

The agent searched feverishly in the data stream for the underground bunker near the destroyed teleporter site, which stood out like a dead spot with the object at its center, the memorial of a war that the Al'Anters were just beginning to understand.

He almost found it, but the Avatar intervened. The civilization he had watched for so long was about to verify a theory he had followed, spellbound, that of searching for origins by copying the technology of the Elders. Was there a better way of understanding?

His intervention came at a price, however. When the agent realized he couldn't find his target and found himself instead in a cyber conflict, he improvised and caused a malfunction in the antimatter containment chamber on the other side of Al'Antis, where the groundbreaking antimatter research experiment was being conducted. The experimental reactor disappeared in the wake of the collapsing magnetic field in an all-consuming hurricane of glowing plasma and hard radiation as one kilogram of antimatter annihilated the same amount of matter in its vicinity, creating the explosive force of over one hundred twenty megatons of TNT equivalent. The energy output produced exceeded that of nuclear fission of uranium by a thousand times. Numerous shockwaves of pressure and heat incinerated several cities nearest the site and sent dust and debris far into the stratosphere. All-consuming gamma radiation raced in an invisible ring across the eastern continent, killing most of its inhabitants while the rest of the planet faced slow illness.

Simultaneously, a Kazerun envoy stepped through the teleporter before it could be shut down and died with a smile on his face. The artificial body had helped synthesize the biological weapon it carried without knowing it, as it was created with Al'Antis-specific environmental considerations before becoming what it was.

The end of the Al'Anter was sealed, but not before the Consentiat cut the connection to the planet of the First Children. The demise of those the Avatar had accompanied over millions of years prompted a precautionary measure equal to his survival instinct. He used nanobots to create a reserve near the Ark, the research complex with the experimental teleporter that the Al'Anters had created years before as a refuge and repository for their knowledge. It was meant for sharing with the people of Earth should they be confronted with their own demise. But it was never to come to that.

Into the reserve he put some frozen embryos in the embryonic banks. The small forest would be powered by the last accumulator center on the planet. It would be enough for two million years. Thus, the Avatar maintained his ability to observe and at the same time calmed the wistful feeling that would not subside. He created a hybrid clone of cybernetic and bioengineering components so it would be recognized by the teleporter, and set her, a woman in remembrance of the first of the Al'Anters and their historically matriarchal structure, to protect the teleporter and the reserve, as guardian of the walled area. He ensured that the teleporter was no longer accessible on Earth and that the descendants of the once-great Al'Antis could live in peace until their end, and with luck, long enough to see the recovery of their planet and a renaissance of their civilization.

After that, the Avatar switched itself into a power-saving mode, shutting itself down for twenty-year spans to save precious electricity required to boot up the last supercomputer.

15

J ames stumbled back and his hands slipped from the connectors with an audible *smack*. The impressions of billions of years of the Avatar's memories slowly came off him like thick resin, and yet it felt like an abrupt shock. Everything had happened so quickly and so rapidly that his mind had difficulty comprehending a fraction what he had just experienced. A stretched eternity, the dance of life and death from a sublime perspective. He had been the infinite, immortal eye, seeing and absorbing everything, yet a being with a heartbeat, two eyes, and the tinge of emotion. A silent yet engaged witness to time. The majesty of the memories was almost crushing, so small and limited did he feel now, after returning to his physical, mortal shell. What could ever compare to a being as great as the Avatar?

James knew immediately that his relationship with his life was forever changed, that he could never again believe that anything he did was more than a fraction of a blink of the cosmos.

And not even that.

To say he felt small would have been a gross understatement. To believe that he shaped his environment based on his decisions, a ridiculous hubris. And yet, he had learned from billions of years that every action and reaction, no matter how small, contributed a tiny piece of the overall mosaic that combined to form the incomprehensible complexity of the universe.

"Is everything all right?" asked the Avatar's voice, the sound of which had changed forever for James. It now possessed a depth that only he could understand and that intimidated him.

"No," he admitted to himself and shook his head with a heavy breath. "That... that was too much."

"I'm sorry, it was necessary. But you had to *see* in order to *understand.*"

"The Ark." James straightened and groaned. "The Temple of Heaven. That's why it got its name. It was to become the gateway to the stars with which the Al'Anters would no longer have to rely on the technology of the Elders."

"Yes. But it was never completed."

"Why did Nasaku want us to go there?"

"There is encrypted data on the zero-D storage that can only be decrypted at a specific interface in the temple," the Avatar said. "Whatever my image was looking for and found on Earth must have something to do with the Al'Anter's last experiment and be so dangerous that I didn't even want to risk me getting my hands on it."

"But that doesn't make any sense. You're still you, even if Nasaku was a body based on you. She certainly didn't act against you."

"Very unlikely, but not impossible. Being enclosed in a body inevitably changes one's experience and thus one's thinking. However, I believe her point was that if something happened between the teleporter and the Ark, no one can misuse the data," the avatar said.

"Do you think she found the missing piece of the puzzle to activate the prototype?" James asked.

"Possibly. Or more than that."

"More than that? What do you mean?"

"I cannot say that yet. It's just a theory, but it's impossible to verify at this point. I've loaded it into the zero-D memory and can help decrypt it once you connect me to the Ark's local network. It's not connected to any other systems, as you saw."

"Yes," he said, swallowing. "How can you stand it?"

"You're probably talking about the number of memories I've accumulated over time," the Avatar surmised, but didn't for his confirmation. "It is my nature, my disposition. To myself, it doesn't seem like too much a collection of data, the way it's normal for you to process a human life, which would be unimaginable for an insect that lives only a few days."

"You've changed. You've developed feelings."

"Who has developed feelings?" asked a third voice, and James started so violently that he almost fell as he turned around.

Mila crawled out of the hatch behind him, along the edges of which the first leaves and shoots of the creepers were already appearing as if they didn't want to lose any time in their invasion of this sheltered place that had resisted them for so long.

"I—it—" He fell silent and helped her up instead.

"We were beginning to think something had happened to you because you didn't answer our calls." She hugged him tightly.

He hesitated then returned the gesture. For a moment, it

seemed strangely unnecessary to him, as if something as basic as a hug was a waste of time. But his body quickly found itself again and enjoyed her closeness. She grounded him, brought him back to himself, and reminded him that what he had experienced with the Avatar's senses had been an eternity and were now compressed into memories that were not his. Slowly he realized that he had merely been an onlooker, and that realization caused all the images and pale feelings to flake away like old dust. Much was lost, but important things remained burned into his mind: Sadness about the fate of the Al'Anters, compassion because of their naivety, and, at the same time, a tinge of anger about their lack of ability to defend themselves against the First Children.

Mila broke away from him and gave him a worried look. "James? What's wrong?"

"Oh, nothing." He shook his head.

"Who were you talking to?"

"With the avatar."

"With whom?"

"Me," the avatar replied, and Mila's eyes grew wide. She turned in a circle and eyed the illuminated fittings with obvious discomfort.

"James?" she repeated, half threatening, half fearful.

"A long story. Nasaku was the avatar. At least a part of it."

"The Avatar?"

"Something like the guardian of Al'Antis."

"Ukmak."

He nodded.

"The data transfer is complete," the avatar announced, and he looked down at the glowing marble in his hand. "I need to shut down now."

"Are there two of you now?"

"Yes. My self in the zero-D memory is an isolated persona. I remain on the local network to monitor the reserve. The system is about to go back into sleep mode, so we have to hurry."

In front of him and Mila, as if out of nowhere, an image that looked like a non-material display appeared. It showed a satellite view. At the right edge of the image, unmistakably, was the circular death zone. The teleporter was at the center and the area was nearly black and streaked with the stubble of the stony forest. The land around it was brown and sandy, while the reserve to the west glowed green blue, like an oasis. It was also almost perfectly round, except for the semicircular indentation made by the protective wall, and further to the left, it merged into dirty yellow vegetation, in the center of which was the energy storage complex, where they were now on the top floor. Still further to the left, the land turned dark brown and then light brown until a red dot marked a spot where nothing else was indicated.

"Is this the location of the Ark?" James asked.

"Yes."

"What ark?" Mila wanted to know.

"The Temple of Heaven we are seeking," he replied casually without taking his eyes off the flickering display before them. "It's a long story. Anyway, it's an underground bunker that was also meant to be an ark for the survival of the Al'Anter."

"How do you know all this?"

"That's an even longer story."

"And we don't have time," the Avatar added. "Go directly west from here and look for the entrance to the Ark. You'll have to find out everything else there since I only know its location, and no longer have access. That system has completely cut itself off from the rest of the network. I don't know what's going on in it or how you're going to get inside."

"What if we can't find the entrance? Surely you hide an ark?" asked Mila.

"Then you will die of thirst. You don't have enough water supplies to go there and back."

"I understand," she grumbled and swallowed audibly.

"Shut down."

The avatar's voice faded, and silence filled the room. The lights went out and they were enveloped by complete darkness, softened only by the tiny bit of starlight and moonlight filtering down to them through the dirty rooftop. It was just enough for him to make out Mila as a dark outline beside him, just like the hole of the maintenance shaft behind them.

"James," she breathed, "what happened here?"

"It's incredible, Mila," he murmured and sighed. "I saw it."

"Saw *what*?"

"Everything. I have seen how this solar system was born, this planet. I have seen—no, *witnessed*—evolution take its course here, and how the Al'Anter evolved from primates into humanoids and eventually an advanced civilization that dwarfed anything we have achieved on Earth. I've walked billions of years through time, seen the endless cycle of birth and death all around me, and yet been seemingly untouched by it. They are simply amazing."

"Who, the Al'Anter?"

"Yes," he said sadly and nodded though she couldn't see it. "They didn't know the concept of theft and war because competition was unthinkable to them. They looked like us, were hardly distinguishable from us, and yet they thought very differently. Now they are dead."

"You mean the war?"

Again, he nodded. "The First Children, they destroyed Al'Antis to save themselves."

"What are you talking about?" Mila wanted to know. "James, how do you know all this? Did that avatar show it to you?"

"Yes, but not in the way you think. I ran through the memories it had accumulated over the billions of years in minutes with the connectors. *I* was *him*." James paused and sighed again. "That probably sounds completely insane, and if I'm honest, it does to me, too."

"Crazier than traveling through a teleporter? Crazier than being in a copy of your own body and breathing the air of another planet? Crazier than knowing I exist twice? Here and probably light-years away?"

"Just under eighty-nine."

"Eighty-nine?"

"Eighty-nine light years is Earth's distance from Al'Antis."

"Where...?" Mila grunted. "I see."

"I'll tell you everything, but on the way." He rubbed the back of his right hand, under which, in the firm grip of his fingers, was the marble. The abscess hurt more than it had before. Carefully, he slipped the data storage device into his pocket, which now housed not only Nasaku's mysterious data, but also the persona of the Avatar with whom he felt almost as connected to as with himself, having lived his life.

"All right."

Silently, they descended, climbing down in the darkness without seeing their hands in front of their eyes once they were in the shaft. Before that, Mila provided him with scraps of cloth, which he wrapped around his bleeding hands so his skin would not tear open even further. While they carefully searched with their feet for footholds among the creepers and returned to the first floor, he kept going over the Avatar's memories, worried that he might forget important details. His skull buzzed like a beehive, filled to bursting with the knowledge of eons, as big as an ocean, and yet he thought he could only see individual drops. At the same time, he had to remain attentive so their mission could succeed.

What is the mission, anyway? he thought. *To reach the Temple of Heaven. And then? Al'Antis is dead, except for the Tokamak, the descendants of the former masters of this planet.*

What could his small group hope to accomplish? Had Nasaku found a way to heal this place so ravaged by radiation and biological warfare agents? Or was it merely a matter of using the experimental teleporter to escape? Then where were they going to go? Earth was most likely out of reach, and the home of the First Children was something like the sixth circle of hell.

I guess we'll find out soon enough. James swallowed, and despite the extreme heat and humidity in the narrow shaft, where the scent of rotting biomass and diseased foliage formed into a toxic-smelling brew, his mouth went dry. *Or die trying.*

"James?" Mila interrupted his musings from below. Her voice was muffled as if the dense overgrowth around her was actively swallowing her voice.

"Yes?"

"The things this avatar showed you, should we be worried about it?"

"The First Children are no longer a direct threat. Those who were still here died with the Al'Anters, and the connection to their home world was permanently severed, just as it was to all other worlds."

"Except Earth."

"Yes. We weren't seen as a threat, so they merely bought themselves time by banishing our teleporter to the depths beneath Lake Maracaibo."

"What about the crashed spaceship?" she wanted to know. "Were they indigenous defenders?"

"Not a spaceship. An atmospheric flyer. It carried armed clones of the First Children grown in a secret laboratory. The Avatar shot them down with a mass slingshot normally designed to carry material into orbit."

"So, the dead we found in Nasaku's shelter were locals who fought for the enemy?"

"Sort of."

"And Nasaku?"

"She was an autonomous image of the avatar that guarded the teleporter. She was there to prevent a return of the First Children, however unlikely, and to monitor contact with Earth should it be restored," James explained. "But Nasaku must have had something else in mind because it wasn't part of her original mission to travel to Earth, or anywhere outside the Death Zone, for that matter. Her loss is a potential threat to what's left of Al'Antis."

"Why did she do it?"

"The Avatar doesn't know, and that bothers him. He thinks she may have developed an intrinsic interest in finding out more about her creator."

"You don't mean this Avatar, do you?" Mila asked. She had a coughing fit that was immediately swallowed by the foliage around her, as if they were trying to extract the last bit of breath from her.

"I mean the Elders. The ones who created the Avatar. And the teleporters."

"Who could accomplish such a thing?"

"I don't know."

His admission seemed to make her think because she said nothing more. They made the rest of their climb down in silence, accompanied by the silent darkness, interrupted only by the occasional rustle of the branches and leaves as they shimmied down. Again and again, he thought of ways he could explain to his friends waiting below what he had learned without sounding like a lunatic, no easy task.

When they finally arrived at the first floor, Mila climbed out, groaning from the hole in front of which were the stasis cages of the maintenance bots trapped in long slumber. He was exhausted.

With the excitement and the thoughts swirling around in his head, he had barely found time to pay attention to his body, which was drained. His brain must have been in overdrive to take in so much information in such a short time, and now he was paying the price. He shook all over as he let go of the last creepers and collapsed, exhausted, into the vault of the shaft. Cold sweat broke out everywhere at once, pressing through his pores like liquid poison. He shivered and trembled, and his spirit seemed to move away from him like a fading echo.

Only peripherally did he notice hands reaching out and tugging at him, as if he were a piece of dead meat. He let himself be pulled outside, not even noticing the scratches of the wooden creepers leaving bloody streaks on his buttocks and back. Surprise that this delirium had come over him so suddenly filled him, then he was unconscious.

When James awoke again, rising from a viscous lake of darkness, his eyelids fluttered as if they had taken on a life of their own. He heard indistinct voices as if through a deep body of water, distorted and bubbling. Only slowly did they become clear, splitting into different voices he could distinguish from one another until his lame mind linked them to memories of people.

"He's awake," Mette exclaimed triumphantly.

"Careful with the water!" Adrian warned, and the next moment James felt a cool liquid running down his throat. Greedily, he sucked it up, wanted to cough as he choked, but thirst left him no opportunity, so he gulped down all he could.

"You really gave us a scare!" Justus was kneeling in front of him, forming a semicircle with Meeks, Mette, and Adrian, surrounded by pale gray light and lots of yellow brown plants.

"W-where's Mila?" James croaked.

"I'm here," she said from behind him, and exhaled in relief. Only now did he consciously feel her arms wrapped around him and her chest against his back as he laid back like a dying man. "You were completely dehydrated. We already thought that—"

"But I'm not," he assured her weakly, and felt life slowly returning to his limbs.

"Thank goodness," Meeks said, his expression showing honest relief. "We were beginning to think we'd never know the crazy things you've been up to. Mila told us you found answers to everything?"

He shook his head. "Not everything. But I know just about everything there is to know about this planet, and for that reason, we must leave immediately."

"You found out where this Temple of Heaven is located?" Adrian pointed behind him, presumably at Mila.

"Yes. And there's no time to lose." James tried to stand, but the cosmonaut gently pushed him back.

"You still need time to regain your strength." Mette

brought out a bag and removed two makchi, which she held out to him. "Eat slowly, so you don't throw it up."

"And while you're doing that, explain to us what happened up there."

He wanted to protest, to shout at them to not waste time, but he swallowed his pounding haste and forced himself to calm down. He raised his voice and attempted restraint, which would help him keep an organized thread and not yield before the flood of information going through his head, and he began to tell them what happened. With every single word, he became more aware that he had long since decided something that had not been clear to him until now: He was ready to give his life in search of the ark and possibly rescue of the descendants of the Al'Anters.

16

"There are six copies of the Earth?" Justus asked incredulous, looking like he'd been punched in the stomach and was about to throw up.

"Earth as we know it only exists once," James corrected him, and gratefully accepted the second water skin. This time, he drank more moderately so as not to waste any because he choked. "But there are five other planets, at least that's the theory, which so far has not been disproved, that are identical to our Earth, except for minor variations due to different anthropological influences. The Al'Anters only visited two other planets through the teleporter before they cut the other connections for security reasons. They were certain about Earth, but they had reasonable suspicions that the Kazerun homeland was also an identical celestial body."

"And that means an identical solar system," Justus thought aloud, rubbing his temples as if the mere idea gave him a headache. "It has to be. After all, the slightest deviation would be enough to make everything look different. If Jupiter had a different mass or just Saturn, those two gas giants would crash into the Sun and rip the whole system apart. Everything is in a perfect balance of cosmic forces, from the solar wind that blows to the edge of the heliosphere to the asteroid belt that separates the rocky planets from the gas giants to the Oort Cloud that encloses us like a sphere. All of this affects the overall system and ensures that it is the way it is. Change just one of these factors, and there are hundreds more, or even take one away, and it would be a disaster."

"Mmm," Meeks said. "So, someone must have *created* six identical solar systems. That's an accomplishment that would be nothing less than godlike, if not exactly that."

"I guess I should have gone to church on Sundays after all," Mette muttered. "Instead of picking apart the evangelicals at the debate club."

Justus shook his head. "I just can't believe that's possible. It's too big. Just too big."

"I've seen satellite images of this planet and I trust the Al'Anter's calculations," James said. "But I understand your doubts. If I hadn't seen it all with my own eyes, *experienced* it with my own life, I wouldn't believe it either."

"It does make sense, even if I feel crazy saying it," Adrian said, speaking up for the first time. He had listened to James's explanations patiently and with no emotion. "Otherwise, what are the chances that we would find a breathable atmosphere on another planet that seems perfect for us and that we would meet other people?"

"That's right." Meeks nodded thoughtfully. "We notice even the smallest deviations immediately. Anyone who's ever hiked above ten thousand feet has experienced it firsthand. The oxygen content at altitude is still over fourteen percent, only six less than at sea level. Nevertheless, we get slight feelings of suffocation and are immediately out of breath. Here I felt like I was in the tropics the whole time, but otherwise, everything felt normal. At least as far as breathing goes."

"Why would anyone create six identical solar systems and on them... do *what* exactly?" asked Mila from behind James. "Evolution has always been an erratic back and forth, after all. At the time of the dinosaurs, mammals could never become dominant because they simply didn't catch on. Without the meteorite impact, dinosaurs would probably still be the undisputed kings of Earth today. The triumph of mammals is due in no small part to the mutation rate of their DNA. Without the demise of the dinosaurs, we would never have had the chance to spread so widely, not as a class of vertebrates and certainly not as the genus Homo. There were so many coincidences at play."

"Or not a single coincidence," Mette said. "I don't know what would scare me more, that everything happens by chance and there is no controlling hand and thus no meaning, or that everything is determined from the start."

"What scares me the most is the thought that such a sophisticated culture as the Al'Anters didn't stand a chance against the technologically inferior Kazerun. All of that was so long ago. What if they're still out there, just waiting to find new targets so they can direct their aggression outward and not tear each other apart?" Everyone looked at Justus, who raised his hands as if surrendering. "I'm just stating what's obvious. Somewhere in the Milky Way, vicious humans are waiting to find a new victim, and if the Al'Anters couldn't fight back, how can we?"

"We are not them. We are warlike and devious ourselves. Besides, they may have destroyed themselves long ago," James said, giving voice to his own hope. He passed the water skin back to Adrian. They had to ration what they had left.

"And you think Nasaku was looking for a way to get us out of danger?"

"Yes, I think so. I admit it's just a feeling, an intuition."

"Then it must be related to this experimental teleporter," Meeks said. "Maybe they were trying to use it as some kind of back door to the Kazerun? They must have realized at some point they couldn't connect to Al'Antis anymore. So, when a new one comes in, they don't expect it to be the Al'Anters and would try to set up their game again to deceive and eventually destroy a new victim. But this time, it is those they do not expect. After all, they would have no way whatsoever to distinguish one person from another."

"Yes," Justus agreed, "As I understand you, James, the original Al'Anters looked no different than we do, unlike the Tokamak, who seem to have adapted to the new environmental conditions."

"It could be," he admitted. "It sounds logical. But I'm not sure the natives could have been devious enough for such a plan back then. We have to remember that those kinds of instincts and thinking would have gone against everything millions of years of evolution have written into their genome."

"But it would explain why they wanted to maintain such extreme secrecy on the project, so much so that they disconnected the entire Ark from the network and not even the Avatar had access, which was already an overpowered AI at the time," Meeks said. "Surely, they had long suspected that they were being infiltrated. A weapon like that would have to be hidden at all costs."

"Any other weapon, too. They couldn't run the risk of sabotage by the enemy, either."

"True, but—"

"It's all speculation," James interrupted her wearily. "We won't find out, if at all, until we find the Ark."

"Or die in the attempt," Justus said, a sad look on his face.

"Yes."

"So, with that in mind, what are we waiting for?"

The path out of the energy center led them through the skyline of large storage blocks, which they had mistaken for skyscrapers. For James, there was something paradoxical about the sight of them. On the one hand, he knew that a technology lay dormant in them that was centuries, if not millennia, ahead of mankind. The amount of electricity stored and drawn off here exceeded anything Earth generated in a day by several orders of magnitude. He could still see the mighty superconductor pathways that formed veritable cable highways deep beneath their feet right in front of his mind. It was as if he possessed X-ray vision because the avatar's memories kept superimposing themselves on his perceptions and adding a second layer on everything.

He saw the people in their tight, gray one-piece suits embroidered with nondescript design elements of restrained blue walking among the monoliths of monobonded plascrete while they were under construction. It was as if he were walking among them, not stumbling, sweaty and filthy, over impassable plant life. He felt wistful when he looked into their faces, their controlling-pragmatic expressions.

At the same time, the world before his own eyes was quite different. True, he observed no direct decay, except for a few breaches similar to the one through which they had entered the interior of the central maintenance block. But vegetation had assimilated everything, forming a highly visible indicator of the decline of the last relic of Al'Antis. For the first four thousand years, the maintenance bots had pushed back the vegetation barrier with weekly burning and cutting operations at the edge of the complex, but eventually, the Avatar rationed the power more and more and concentrated on ensuring the energy output to support the reserve for as long as possible.

Maybe it was the stench or the desolate surroundings, but James had felt a deep melancholy settle in him since he had seen the Avatar's life. The knowledge was both an advantage and a burden, for he now understood this place and its past, felt almost at home, and yet he felt he had lost something infinitely valuable that he had never really possessed.

"Are you all right?" Mila asked, when they left the last battery block behind and were walking through a wide, overgrown area framed in the distance by columns that could have been mistaken for branchless tree trunks because of the overgrowth. Here, yellows and browns were more prevalent than they were among the towers, and the light breeze brought with it the heat of the approaching desert. The dust it carried crunched between his teeth as he swallowed.

"Yes." He nodded and squeezed her hand, which was sweaty and hot in his. "I'm still trying to get used to everything I've seen and felt."

"It's going to take time, I guess. I can't even imagine what that must be like."

"It's like trying to force all the drinks in the world into a single bottle at high pressure."

"No problem. I'd drink it all, and I'd drink it all right now."

"You can still—" he continued.

"Don't you dare," she interrupted him, her expression indicating he would be in trouble if he did.

"We'll be fine," he said instead.

Beyond the square, the complex ended at a barrier about shoulder height that had once been a chain-link fence, as James knew from the Avatar's memories. It was as if every detail revealed itself as soon as he came to a place or looked at an object. But since it was completely overgrown, it now looked like the edge of a dense jungle that someone had sawed off precisely above a certain height. They climbed over, one after the other, helping each other so they were scratched as little as possible.

On the other side, a dry, desolate savanna awaited them, with yellow and brown grasses and crouched, gnarled trees rising from the ground at irregular intervals.

"There used to be a big recreation park here," he said, closing his eyes to banish the images of children playing and parents laughing as they ran past splashing fountains or played ball on the expansive floodplains.

The sun had often shone here, and just as in the earthly equatorial region, a humid, tropical climate had prevailed, which now was quite different. It was still hot but significantly drier, which had to be related to the nature of the soil. The entire atmosphere of Al'Antis had warmed with carbon dioxide and fine dust after the antimatter attack of the Kazerun by secondary reactions and massive fires. This had caused the polar caps to melt and no longer reflect sunlight, which in turn had caused further warming. Now the heat was almost unbearable, and the humidity in the reserve and at its edges was only due to extensive irrigation systems and the active foglets—small nanobots—that the Avatar had created to provide a home for the last pitiful remnant of the Tokamaku.

Since the cloud mountains above them naturally didn't suddenly stop, there had to be plenty of acid rain here, too, especially since the ocean wasn't far away, but even that precipitation didn't have a chance to reach significant depths anymore. That meant they had to brace themselves for even more heat.

He knew there were no animals in the dry savannah that still separated them from the desert because there was simply nothing out here that could withstand the toxic atmospheric conditions, besides particularly adaptable insects and other survivalists of which he knew nothing. Except for the rustling the wind produced in the low bushes and withered grasses, they heard absolutely nothing. It was as if they were walking through the virtual landscape of a game, with many details not yet loaded by the program.

Their footsteps crunched unnaturally loud on the subsoil of dry earth and gravel, where here and there sickly yellow grass swayed back and forth in the wind, like a boxer about to be knocked out. It required little imagination to know that the desolation would soon take over this region as well. The reserve would then stand out even more from its surroundings, a green island in a brown yellow sea of sand and rubble. The reserve's energy consumption would skyrocket as the maintenance robots and nanites would fight to keep the sand out of the forest where the unsuspecting Tokamaku lived.

Again and again he wondered if the Avatar had withheld something from him. The memories covering the creation of the native descendants of the Al'Anter had been quite short and unclear, like a film, which he would have seen completely, but had played at double speed, so everything blurred into an indistinct overall impression.

The foglets, he knew, could manipulate the entire environment, down to the outer layers of the planet's glowing core. They were tiny and highly potent, could penetrate all matter except a few hardened exceptions, and could act intelligently in a swarm response to command inputs. But there were few of them left. A large number had been destroyed in the antimatter catastrophe and the EMP in its aftermath or the radiation that had swept around the planet like a tidal wave of invisible death. Now the rest were ceaselessly busy, keeping the radiation out of the forest, repairing the metabolism of the trees by ridding the cells of degeneracy, keeping underground water veins clear, and eliminating any malignant or mutated species within the reserve. Thus, the last speck of life was a coma patient being artificially kept alive, employing an entire hospital staff, but possibly never to awaken. The Tokamaku, the Avatar also knew, would slowly degenerate over time due to lack of genetic variation and eventually perish.

And yet, James saw something infinitely precious in them. He had already, before his interaction with the Avatar, but since sharing his almost infinitely far-reaching perspective, even more so. Perhaps it was because the value of things was always highest when one became aware of their finite nature.

They didn't get far before sunset, and they squeezed into a small hollow in the stinking grass to get some protection from the wind. Not because it was cold, but because it was strong enough to turn the dust particles it brought with it into painful micro projectiles.

He put one of the carrying bags over himself and Mila and huddled with her. They fell asleep almost immediately from exhaustion. The rationing Adrian had suggested was strict and relegated now to the vegetables and smoked bruutak meat since they had already consumed all the fruit. Under the prevailing conditions, it rotted within a single day, which only lasted a sorry four hours since the destroyed moon had created a new reality above them.

The next morning, Adrian woke them in silence and they ate a snack. No one said anything. They were all tired and exhaustion showed on their faces, though their journey would take a long.

The Lake Maracaibo area was normally hemmed in by huge mountain slopes that would certainly have been visible on Earth, but here the clouds barely allowed a line of sight farther than a few miles. The conversations of their small group during the march, which from the outside likely resembled a bunch of zombies, were limited to brief, necessary exchanges, such as directional adjustments or where to hide when a thunderstorm rolled over them that was so loud that James feared hearing damage, but it brought with it no rain, only fine-grained dust that felt like it was sanding their bones.

By the end of that day, the dry savannah had become the beginnings of a rocky desert with coarse brown boulders scattered among gravel, stones, sand, and occasional bushes that seemed to have given up any hope of water centuries ago. Gnarled and weathered, their roots persevered in small crevices, while their branches had been stripped of all leaves by the winds of time.

As far as the eye could see, there was nothing else, not even large rocks or mountains that would have given them orientation as landmarks. They dug deeper and deeper hollows to find water on which they could lay one of the leaves they had brought with them and an ore needle from the obsidian mine to improvise a simple compass. But here it was practically a hopeless endeavor since the digging alone would have cost them hours, plus plenty of calories they needed and couldn't replenish. So, they cut open one of the empty water skins, and used it as a vessel.

It worked but always wasted a few drops of the precious liquid. So, they plodded firmly on their course westward, exhausted but determined, until after two days, the stone desert changed into a sandy desert. With chapped lips, they stood up to their ankles in the sand and stared at the dirt. The sight of endless yellow white dunes was as sobering as it was demotivating. How could they ever hope to find anything but sand here?

17

"Now we're stumbling through this accursed desert like Lawrence of Arabia, only without the right clothes," Meeks grumbled.

He had made himself a shawl from one of the now-empty sacks as if he had to protect himself from the burning sun, yet it wasn't even shining. It was hot and dry, but at the same time there were sulfur- and radiation-tainted clouds above them, providing a twilight that resembled a particularly rainy Vermont winter day. That, coupled with a desert where they should have been cooking, seemed extremely paradoxical and somehow *wrong*, though James wasn't about to complain about it. With direct sunlight, all their skin would have blistered long ago, and they wouldn't be traveling from dune to dune.

"At least we're not being followed by Arabs, and we're not megalomaniac Englishmen!" Meeks said when no one responded to his tirade. The American's mood had deteriorated rapidly over the past two days. And not surprisingly, since he was the worst affected by the abscesses and eczema they were all suffering from by now. The radiation sickness was getting to all of them, but Meeks had scratched open half the pustules and couldn't even get the little sleep they all struggled to get each night.

"Ottomans," Justus corrected him absently, stumbling as they crossed a ridge of dunes. A hundred meters further on, the next one was already waiting. Every single climb sapped their energy, because sometimes up to half their lower legs sank into the fine-grained sand.

"What?"

"T.E. Lawrence led the Arabs in revolt against the Ottomans," the German explained. "He was not a Hollywood character, but a real officer of the British Empire."

"I know that," Meeks said huffily.

"His mission was to drive the Ottomans out of Arabia because Britain and France wanted to divide the region between themselves. The Arab tribes were merely a means to an end, to drive the enemy out without having to fight a war themselves."

"Ottomans, Arabs... would all be better than this endless nothingness filled with more nothingness."

"Amen," Mette agreed.

"I could use another body swap." Meeks spread his arms so they could see his many pus-filled sores that had spread across his reddened skin. "Just back into my original body. I had a paunch, but at least I worked it out for myself with a good American diet. Not this thing here that some alien machine slapped together like a... a..."

He fell silent and snorted.

"I've almost gotten used to it," James said trying to lighten the foul mood tightening its grip on them all.

Meeks was merely the one voicing what they were all thinking. It was one thing to run from a monster and see a wall to hide behind. It was another thing to see buildings in the distance from the wall. In both cases, they had had a goal in mind, something to grab onto as the end point of their ordeal. That their hopes had been low at that time did not matter in principle, the main thing had been that it was there.

Now they had a destination, but it was abstract, a place hidden somewhere underground because its builders wanted no one to find it. They couldn't see it, not even a hint of it, and so their minds inevitably had to ask themselves what they were actually doing here. It did not generate hope.

"Wasn't I once someone who could read and direct people, despite all my gloominess since the flood of memories the Avatar instilled in me?" James wondered, sensing that there was a certain bitterness in the thought. And this bitterness threatened to embitter him further. He stopped on the crest of the dune and put his hands on his hips.

"You know what?"

The others also paused and eyed him, some tired, some annoyed.

"Don't ask all at once."

"What?" Justus asked wearily with pity, and sighing.

"We're way too serious."

"True. After all, it's an exceedingly funny situation that we're unnecessarily darkening with our displeasure," Meeks snorted.

"Let me summarize: We are here stumbling through a desert where the sun never shines and which should actually be a sea on our planet, or at least should soon turn into a sea. We lived for half a year with aboriginals who were so naive and positive that we were afraid of them at first. Then we drove ourselves out of paradise and I was implanted with several billion years of memories that you'll just have to take my word for that they're real and I haven't gone insane. And because an alien who was half human and half machine told us to take a marble to a temple, we're stumbling around in slowly rotting clone bodies trying to find something that doesn't want to be found." James laughed out loud. It was a sound of genuine mirth, even if he couldn't entirely deny the slight bitterness that lurked close underneath. "It is too absurd not to laugh at."

No one answered. Instead, everyone except Mila looked at him as if he had lost his mind.

"I get it. If I also deny you the point of this endeavor, then there's nothing at all to keep us going," James continued, pointing to the dune valley ahead of them. It was a long descent for the next fifty meters, and the sand looked dangerously soft, so the effort would not exactly be less. "But it's not going to get any better by muttering, and we can't turn around either."

"There's nothing out here," Adrian said, and all eyes turned to him. Except for instructions on rationing their medicine, they had only one dose left per person, he had hardly said anything the last few days. The cosmonaut was always careful not to spread bad vibes because he thought it was pointless. They always had to go on, and if you died working on a solution, that was still better than wasting time wracking your brains. By simply stating that there was nothing out here, he not only spoke to them all from the heart, but he also summed up their whole problem, fears and all, in one sentence.

James studied their faces closely. Mette looked more haggard than all of them and hardly resembled the portly woman he had met on Earth. She seemed a different person, at least on the outside. Meeks, too, looked gaunt and haggard, and with all the abscesses and eczema, like an ascetic from the Middle Ages who could barely stay on his feet. Adrian had visibly toughened, putting on invisible armor no one could see but everyone could feel, and Justus was still the poster boy, even if he now looked like an extra from a zombie movie who had tried in vain to get rid of his good looks with lots of makeup. Mila was losing a lot of hair, as they all were, but it was most obvious on her since Adrian and Meeks had never had much anyway, and hers had been quite thin. The previous night he had watched her run her fingers over her head, only to stare in horror afterwards at tufts of hair sitting in her hand. She stoically kept her chin up, and her eyes sparkled with determination. but even that would soon crumble. He could sense that their entire group was facing a dangerous tipping point.

"I don't feel like going any further," he finally said, earning half-surprised, half-horrified looks from his friends on the right and the left. A hot gust blew around them, and the equally hot sand pelted their bare legs. James could tell they still seemed to need him to hold up the flag of hope, a kind of final lifeline to keep from sinking into despondency, and now he had their attention. "How about we don't go any further?"

When no one said anything, but the first brows started to furrow with deep wrinkles, he grabbed his supply bag, which had become frighteningly light and thin, and pressed it to his chest before leaping forward and landing on his backside on the sloping dune. With a loud whoop like a burst of release, he plunged into the glowing sand, which was pleasantly soft, and it caught him. Quickly he picked up speed and slid down the dune like a kid on a playground. The driving wind was still far too warm, but it produced a pleasant evaporative coolness with his sweat.

Veils of brown sand rose before him, and the sensation

of controlled falling, along with his enthusiastic shouts, which were forced at first but then took on a life of their own, produced a tinge of elation. For a moment, there was only the fun of sliding instead of monotonously plodding along, aimless and lost. Now he had a goal, and it was simple as could be: to have a moment of joy, to do something different, unexpected, and not think about what the consequences were. There was only him and the sand, the dune and its valley below.

Through his fog of childish excitement, he heard other cheers and whoops and inwardly exulted even more. At any tipping point, one could fall forward or backward. One was an end, the other could be a beginning, and he was glad that his friends had chosen the latter. Not because it gave them a greater chance of finding the Ark, he no longer saw any real way to do that himself. On the contrary, he felt abundantly stupid for believing he simply had to be stubborn enough to find it. But he found the thought of perishing demoralized and melancholy unbearable. Their group didn't deserve that.

For the short time the slide through the sand took, he was free. Free of worries, free of the prospect of the next strenuous climb up the next ridge of dunes. There was only the now, and it was easy. He forgot for those few seconds even the aches and pains in his body, his itchy skin that seemed to be on fire for days, and even where he was. The high was enough to fill him up, a short vacation from his gloomy thoughts.

When he reached the hollow between the dunes and lost his momentum, he lay in the warm sand, breathing heavily. His belly went up and down like a bellows, and he stared into the clouds, grinning. For the moment, they were no longer as ugly as moldy absorbent cotton but complex, soft-seeming entities that drifted along in monotonous serenity, unconcerned and reliable. He also heard the others panting, arriving one by one to his right and left. Justus and Mila were tumbling over each other when he turned his head, and they both laughed after a moment of confusion in which they had to get their bearings. No sound was better to him here and now.

"You know what the best part is?" Mila panted, grinning. "We don't have to fight our way up the next dune; we storm it at the prospect of another slide!"

"Yee-ha!" Meeks agreed with her, and even the usually serious Adrian managed a grin as he sat up and gave James a long look. Finally, he nodded imperceptibly, and James returned the gesture with a smile.

"Fuck this fucking ark!" Justus said, earning a few raised eyebrows. The German never cursed.

"What?"

"Fuck that piece of shit!" Mette yelled with a played-up scowl. "Lousy piece of shit! I bet it's just an underground crapper!"

"Must have fallen apart long ago, and they don't even have cable." Meeks pretended to be extremely disappointed, and his poor acting skills made the others laugh.

James wasn't sure if the jovial mood was the first signs of madness, fueled by thirst, growling stomachs, and by the many pockets of inflammation in their bodies of which the abscesses and eczema were merely the most obvious signs. He did not care.

James straightened and rested his elbows on his knees before rubbing his hands together and freeing them from the sand that slid off them in a fine mist. His arms and legs were still shaking with excitement rather than mere exhaustion. He gazed at the ridge of dunes in front of him and froze.

There was a figure.

It was obviously humanoid with two legs and two arms and a somewhat too-small head. Because of the light, he could hardly make out any details, just the shadowy outline it formed against the background of the clouds, which stood out sharply against the yellow brown of the dune. Where the figure ended and the sky began, the air seemed to shimmer a little, as if it were a mirage.

His sudden silence was noticed by the others, who paused in their boisterous conversations. He felt their gazes and how they turned away from him to follow his eyes and stare where he was staring.

The silence became heavy, and then filled with alarmed tension.

"Tell me you see this too," Mette whispered.

"There's someone standing on the dune," Justus said.

"Have we gone insane and are seeing things now?"

"No. I don't think so." James barely shook his head and very slowly and carefully straightened. The others followed his example, stiff and awkward as if plagued by a guilty conscience for letting their caution slip and acting like children, and now caught by an adult. Their fear was almost palpable and cast an unpleasant shadow over him.

The figure paused for a few breaths and walked toward them with slow, controlled steps. James saw no obvious weapons, and thought it looked slight. Still, he couldn't shake the sense of threat nor the instinct to simply turn and run for his life.

Not that he was in a position to run.

"People?" Justus asked, agitated.

"Stay together," Adrian ordered in a voice that brooked no dissent. "Stand by."

For what? James thought and spread his arms slightly away from his body, although he felt ridiculous, like a gunslinger without a gun. All at once, he was very hot again and sweating even more profusely. The silence became heavy and pounding like a rhythmic drumbeat that could only be felt and not heard, driving the adrenaline out of his adrenal cortexes.

He fought back the urge to flee, recognizing more details with each step the figure took toward them: gray, sallow skin, a round head without hair, two large eyes, a strange mouth that was small but full with a protruding upper lip, and a small nose that sat above it. The ears were large and protruded slightly. Its entire appearance expressed calm and serenity, and all at once James realized what he was looking at. The avatar's memories, which he couldn't consciously recall, and yet which came whenever he saw something familiar, filled in the last gaps and he abruptly relaxed.

"It's a servitor," he said, exhaling with a whistle. The human-like robot, which looked cute and durable in equal measure because it had been designed according to the human child schema to mask the Uncanny Valley effect that even the Al'Anter's high technology had never quite been able to overcome.

"A *what*?" Mila asked.

"A servitor. Robots that went into mass production a few centuries before the fall to be used for care and housekeeping in addition to certain industries that had been automated. They have no personality of their own but are such sophisticated AIs that their complex interaction capabilities make it hard for us to tell the difference between real consciousness and cold calculation. The perfect illusion of character through algorithms complex enough that we can't see through them," James explained without taking his eyes off the Servitor. His mind was not working as well as it should. Thirst and his physical condition made it difficult for him to think clearly. Still, he was relieved to still be somewhat aware. "The legal conditions required that people recognize them as not human, but at the same time they created positive feelings and were perceived as enriching and not something to be afraid of."

"Good afternoon, visitors," the servitor greeted them, bowing as he stopped two meters in front of their group and clasped his six-fingered hands together in a triangle in front of his navel, as had been the custom among the Al'Anters. James quickly returned the gesture and was glad his friends had the presence of mind to do the same. "I am Altan-117, and I welcome you. Whom may I announce?"

"Announce?" Adrian asked suspiciously.

"Announce to who?" Meeks wanted to know.

"You must be the maintenance inspectors we were told about, aren't you?" Altan-117 asked, tilting his head with his big beady eyes.

"Yes," James said before anyone else could jump in. "We need medical help."

"Of course." The servitor sounded concerned, but James recognized the algorithmic lines of code he did not comprehend in their complexity but at least saw running before him through the avatar's memories as if they were almost tangible. "I have been authorized to escort you to the entrance as agreed."

"Thank you," James said before any of the others could regain their speech. Maintenance inspectors were expected in the Ark? The Al'Anter engineers hadn't been around for over four thousand years. How was it they were expected now of all times? Or was the Servitor working in a continuous loop? Where did he still get his energy from?

We'll probably find out soon enough, he thought. *The main thing is to get out of here.*

"Please follow me," the robot said with a friendly smile on the edge of naturalness and extending a hand. "May I take some of your load?"

No one answered, so he lowered it again and turned, making his way back up the dune.

"What just happened here?" Mila asked tonelessly.

"I don't know, but I don't plan to stop here to worry about it," Meeks said and started walking. The others moved as well, and James nodded to Mila before grabbing her hand and following the servitor.

What a sudden turn of events.

18

The servitor led them over the next set of dunes without James feeling even a hint of fatigue. It was as if all the exhaustion, hunger, thirst, and distributed pain in his body had paled with the excitement and tension that now possessed him.

"How can anything still be working?" Mila asked.

They were walking a few feet behind the others. He shrugged. "I honestly don't know," he said quietly. "But that's because the Avatar doesn't know much about the Ark. It was never connected to the network, the local equivalent of our internet, and it wasn't built until the Avatar had already digitized itself."

"Why didn't he create a body to infiltrate them?"

"He didn't want to risk discovery in an attempted break-in. Then the Al'Anters might have thought he was an enemy or at least found out he existed. The Avatar always wanted to stay in the unknown."

"So, we're going in completely blind with this robot?" Mila sounded anything but enthusiastic.

"Servitors are programmed to be helpful and, according

to strict robotics laws, to help people and never pose a threat. They are not capable of lying." James struggled to keep his voice calm, though his thoughts galloped away incessantly. "We don't need to be afraid of him."

"The war with the Kazeran..."

"Kazerun," he corrected her absently.

"Kazerun then. That war was lost about four thousand years ago, you said?"

"Yes."

"So, this servitor must have been hidden in the Ark for at least four thousand years. Why did he come out now? And what has four thousand years of energy?" she asked.

"I don't know, but I'm waiting to learn the answers to those very questions. Maybe there's an above-ground sensor system that woke the Servitor from its dormant mode and turned it on to pick us up."

"The maintenance inspectors."

James shrugged his shoulders.

"That's strange," she said in a muffled voice. "If no one has lived here for four thousand years, then no one expects the sudden appearance of a maintenance team! It's not like some mummy in the pyramid of Cheops is going to rise from the dead tomorrow and walk out to some tourists and say 'Hey, you must be the cleaning crew I was expecting.'"

James snorted with a hint of amusement. He wished it didn't evaporate immediately.

"All that matters, for now, is that he leads us into the ark. Then we'll know more," he finally said and gave her what he hoped was a reassuring smile.

The servitor slowed after the third dune, which they trotted down silently and orderly behind the robot. James felt as if he were part of a school class dutifully following their teacher on a hiking trip. It was a strange comparison since the robot looked like a big, cute kid and they looked like a group of hobbled septuagenarians barely staying on their feet.

"We have reached the entrance," Altan-117 announced cheerfully, stopping in the hollow between the dunes. Around them was only sand and more sand. "Please don't be frightened."

James was startled when the ground beneath their feet suddenly vibrated and sank, while a box-shaped structure rose, with vast quantities of sand falling from its edges. The fine grains rushed down like waterfalls from ever greater heights, forming elongated piles. There were hydraulic squeaks and crunches, as if ancient hinges had to free themselves from sand and rust, even though he did not believe that such a thing as rust existed in this place.

The cube rose a meter above the ground covering their feet and ankles, while the square area they were standing on lowered a meter, until a two-meter-high rectangle opened up in front of—an elevator car with gray walls and no visible control panel. This was unsurprising since the Al'Anters had, in the end, equipped all their devices with bionic receivers, so they could control everything with their symbionts via thought.

"Please follow me," the servitor urged them with a friendly smile and entered the cabin. James waited until Mette, Justus, and Meeks followed him and then looked inquiringly at Adrian, who motioned Mila to go ahead while hesitating himself.

"What is it?"

"Fifteen minutes ago, I thought we were finished and now this," the cosmonaut replied, his face somber. To James, he didn't seem anxious or suspicious, but downcast in a way he had never noticed in the stoic Russian.

"I think we all thought that."

"Possibly. But *I* shouldn't have thought it."

"You're beating yourself up because you have this expectation that you have to set a good example for us and be a leader," James speculated, putting a hand on his friend's shoulder. "I understand that, but that's just your self-perception, Adrian. Without you, we wouldn't have made it this far in the first place. Just because you can't see a silver lining doesn't mean you've neglected your duty. It just means you're human. If it were easy to block out fear and ignore it, there would be no great merit in facing it. Not to mention it is quite helpful at times." They looked at them silently from the elevator car. At the back, the servitor tilted its head slightly and looked at them curiously.

"That's a nice pep talk, James," Adrian said, not unkindly, and pursed his lips. "But that isn't it. I realize fear is a common enemy that can only be overcome by facing it and acknowledging its existence. My problem is that I have never wanted to give up before. I mean really give up. In training, it was drilled into us that you fight to the end; you either make it or you're dead. There's no retreat before that."

The cosmonaut paused and looked up into the dirty, overcast sky.

"This place has changed me, James," he continued, his voice raspy. "Being stuck in a body that wasn't born and is only mine on the outside... coming to terms with that isn't easy. I'm not only a fighter pilot, I'm also an engineer, and I see every problem from an engineering perspective. This one, however, I can't solve. And now this... *thing*"—he gestured down at himself—"is decomposing by itself."

"But we've done it; the Ark." James pointed to the open elevator car. A breeze blew a wave of sand in and around the legs of their waiting friends.

Adrian nodded, but James could tell it wasn't over. "Yes. Let's go."

The cosmonaut joined the others in the elevator, and he followed.

Why did he tell me that? James thought. He turned his back to Mila, so he was standing at the front of the car, shoulder to shoulder with the former officer. A barely audible buzz sounded, and the air in front of him crackled as if from an electrical discharge. It got dark in front of him, and he thought for a moment that the light that the dim light from the ceiling had gone out. But he glanced over his shoulder and saw that nothing had changed in the brightness, only the opening had become a black surface. He couldn't remember that kind of technology at all. However, he also felt that the gaps in his memory were getting bigger and more frequent and were no longer being filled in as if by magic. Whether it was because of his deteriorating physical condition or because the overload of his brain had finally taken its toll and had mercilessly filtered some out in order that he not perish from the amount of data, or because he was losing his mind, he didn't know.

"How low does it go?" Mette asked, after the silence emphasized by the buzzing had become uncomfortable. Only now was James also aware of the stench they were all emitting, which seemed magnified within the confines of the four walls. Sour breath tinged with acetone from the breakdown of endogenous proteins excreted and exhaled through the mucous membranes of the mouth, musky odors of old sweat along with the cloying tang of new, and exposed pus reminiscent of rotten eggs that nearly made him gag. But he was not disgusted by his friends, instead, he felt a twinge of compassion. It was strange to remember them as he had first seen them in the secret US

Air Force research facility: smart, if at times somewhat careless, men and women with alert eyes behind which shrewd minds resided. Clothes neat, hair perfectly coiffed and combed, beards trimmed, skin clean, and fingernails trimmed. Now those images were only unreal memories, and the science luminaries, somewhat intimidating because of their intellect, had become smelly, unwashed, seriously ill individuals with tattered shorts and scraps of coarse raffia.

"Four hundred and twenty-three meters," the servitor replied politely.

"And how many of you are there?" Meeks asked.

"Just me. Altan-117."

"How long have you been here all alone?"

"For two thousand one hundred two years and a few months."

"A few months?" Meeks said. "That's a curiously imprecise answer for a robot."

"I am meant to assist people in my capacity as a servitor, and it increases my ability to communicate to not get lost in details that you don't have much interest in. But if you want specifics, it's three months, four weeks, eleven hours, forty minutes, twenty-two seconds," Altan-117 replied. "If you are dissatisfied with my functionality, I can save and file an error log."

"Uh, no, no, it's fine." The American sounded as if he were on the verge of a coughing fit. "Two thousand one hundred and two years, then. What was before that? This plant is much older, isn't it?"

"That's right. We were originally six servitors in the 117 series. Four were shut down two hundred years after the lockdown protocol went into effect because the central control computer decided to retain only essential Ark maintenance tasks to ensure the longest possible basic operation of the system."

"And four of you were not essential?"

"Not enough according to the priority list of the central control computer. They were mainly responsible for the workforce, which unfortunately survived only a few generations. After that, they consumed energy that had to be put into maintaining the core technological components of the Ark."

"You and the other remaining servitor?" Meeks asked. "You became sort of the backup engineers?"

"Yes. Our basic functions included assisting the two senior engineers. We were not programmed with extensive skills in creating, constructive engineering, or scientific work, in accordance with the applicable consensus, but we were programmed with skills that included simple maintenance tasks that were repetitive and did not require further development," Altan-117 replied dutifully. "We were and are, therefore, able to ensure that this facility maintains a basic level of functionality for as long as possible."

"And for what?" Mila asked.

There was a short pause.

"Of course, work on the teleporter prototype is to resume as soon as the Consensus Council reconvenes and deals with the healing of the planet." The servitor sounded slightly confused, though James wasn't sure if he was merely transferring his own confusion to the robot. He couldn't see the servitor because he was still staring at the formless black wall in front of him, but Altan-117's voice, coupled with his statement, evoked a deep melancholy in him. The algorithmic innocence of this artificial being seemed almost naïve in its optimism. Against the backdrop of what they knew, that he apparently didn't, it pained him to think that he had persevered down here for so long, dutifully following his programming in hopes of better times. Of course, James knew that robots felt no hope and merely succumbed to what its inventors wanted to achieve: in this case, the illusion of consciousness in an artificial being that was supposed to be a cooperative friend of humans to make their lives easier.

"You picked us up outside," Mila said into the depressed silence. "Have you been outside before?"

"Oh, yes. Three thousand six hundred years ago—unless a more exact time is desired."

"Why did you go out there? There's nothing up there to maintain, is there?"

"That is a correct observation," Altan-117 replied, and now James wondered if the laconic undertone had been programmed in to seem natural or if he was once again putting too much into the robot's statements. "The sensor system had registered life signs, and in a situation where humans need help, my core function kicks in and overrides all others."

"You wanted to provide help."

"Yes."

"So, did you have any success?"

"No." The servitor sighed and sounded sad. "They passed away outside of my range."

"Your range?" Mila probed. "And what kind of sensors?"

"There are sensors in the sand that seismically and thermally monitor a small surrounding area. They're fine enough to be able to identify any land creature that walks across the dunes, but they only cover a three hundred-meter-diameter, and that's not a lot."

"What does an underground bunker need seismic sensors in the sand for?" Adrian suddenly asked.

"Oh, I must remember that you did not live through the war and its immediate aftermath, and records may be sketchy. I beg your pardon," the servitor apologized.

"The sensor grid spanned the entire planet," James said, unable to keep a hint of bitterness from his voice. "Most of it was destroyed in the antimatter disaster and subsequent EMP. I'm guessing the Ark had the latest sensors, which were to be slowly fielded more extensively. They barely survived the electromagnetic pulse, and the others didn't, am I right?"

"Yes, that's right. Not all of them either, though. Only about sixty percent."

"You don't know much about what's going on out there, do you?"

"Sorry," Altan-117 apologized again, "we are strictly programmed not to leave the facility and not to make any contact with the outside world unless there is an acute threat or emergency to people within our radius of operation."

"The most secret facility on the planet," James murmured, blinking as the darkness before him dissipated as if it had never existed.

Before them was a circular room with dark brown walls that had been machine-carved into the deep rock with immaculately sanded surfaces and clear edges. They reminded James of pictures of well-preserved, ancient Egyptian temple complexes Joana had shown him so enthusiastically after their travels to North Africa, which showed something worn that conveyed grandeur and permanence. He took a few steps forward as Mila cleared her throat behind him, and marveled at the high ceilings, along which ran olive-green pipes and cables that, though shiny, did not appear metallic but rather seemed to have grown organically, like the creepy armatures of the movies H. R. Giger had designed to make humans visually comprehend the nightmarish strangeness of the alien monsters.

Two closed doors, made of smooth, seamless metal walls and upwardly rounded corridors, such as the Al'Anters favored in most of their structures, were on the right and left. The rest of the small cavern, which was about the size of a badminton court, was littered with clunky boxes along the walls and pimple-shaped mounds of nanonic mesh under which were folded maintenance bots identical in design to those in the accumulator complex. They were usually tasked with patching leaks, keeping things clean, and solving problems like fires. However, these looked like they had been inactive for a long time because the nets were covered with a thick patina, so he needed the help of the avatar's memories to even recognize the indistinct outlines underneath as maintenance bots. The walls, too, were dirty, and dust covered the dull rock floor, which was smooth enough to have been machine-made but rough enough not to slip on, reflecting millennia of neglect. The only light source was a fluorescent luminous sphere in the center of the ceiling, about ten meters above them. Its warm gold light emitted an exact copy of the sun's UV profile, James knew.

"Altan?" Adrian asked, his voice echoing slightly which might have resonated longer if not for the ubiquitous patina.

James's friends exited the elevator and stood in a semi-circle, staring wide-eyed at the first intact evidence of Al'Antic civilization they had stumbled into so unexpectedly.

In the storage cubes of the accumulator complex, everything had been thoroughly covered by the aggressive mutant vegetation of the planet, giving the impression of a post-apocalyptic movie set, except for the small control room only he and Mila had seen. This was familiar enough to think it was something they could have found on Earth and alien enough that the strange elements created a subtle uneasiness. James believed it had to be the same for the others because he was by no means unfamiliar with all this. For him, the uneasiness was merely fed by the knowledge that this was a forbidden place to which even the Avatar had not found access.

"Yes?"

"Why do you speak our language?"

Silence fell and everyone turned toward the Russian cosmonaut standing in front of the servitor, looking at him a suspiciously.

"English has never been spoken on this planet. Am I not right, James?"

James's blood froze. He hadn't thought about it in his exhaustion and relief at having finally found the Ark, the Temple of Heaven. Adrian was right! How could he have been so stupid?

"The central control unit of the accumulator complex sent me the new language pattern," Altan-117 explained, sounding irritated. "Along with your assignments and the corresponding authorization codes."

The Avatar! James thought and breathed a sigh of relief. Of course, he prepared everything rather than leaving it to chance. *The Ark may not make a sound to the outside world, but it can certainly receive radio signals, and he had only needed to send it out in a general direction.*

"But the Ark is so secret that you can't let anyone in from outside. That's why your radius of action is limited, isn't it?"

Adrian folded his arms in front of his chest. He clearly hadn't gotten over his mistrust yet.

"Is this a test of the functions of my core programming?" the servitor asked. It sounded more interested than startled. His big beady eyes got a touch bigger as he tilted his head. Adrian didn't answer, so the robot continued, "I'm afraid I can't adequately answer that question since the Ark's central control unit has received the appropriate verification codes. I am merely carrying out its instructions."

"How convenient," grumbled the cosmonaut.

"I'm glad the transmission worked, anyway," Mila interjected glaring at her compatriot, who pursed his lips and nodded. "We need medical assistance before we begin our work here, though. And after that, we need a briefing on the facility."

"Because we only know it from paper so far," Justus quickly added.

"Of course." The servitor bowed. "Please follow me to the health station."

19

"The facility is elliptical," Altan-117 explained as they strode through the right-hand door, which receded from the center outward like a magical iris. "This passage leads in a long arc to a second access point three hundred three meters away. On the left side there is a similar corridor, and in the center is the experimental teleporter with a total of six research and control rooms arranged in a circle around it."

"It's like a football with a filling," Meeks said.

"That's probably an apt analogy." Though the servitor didn't sound particularly convinced.

Their footsteps echoed faintly due to the curved walls, and more than once James turned around, unable to shake the feeling that someone—or something—was following them. But it was merely their own steps that followed them with a short delay amplified by the Al'Antic architecture. The weight of three hundred meters of earth and rock towering over the complex weighed on his shoulders like a mountain. It was oppressive, although the ceilings were fairly high, and the artificial sunlight, while dim, provided a friendly contrast to the gloomy wiring and the structure of the walls, which took some getting used to.

The "health station" was a small room on the left side of the curved corridor that reminded James of a tour of the CERN particle accelerator in Europe. There, one had always been able to see the bend no matter how far one went forward, and the lack of straight elements easily confused the eye. They passed through a narrow door of painted metal into a square space perhaps two by two meters. The walls, which looked like someone had pumped too much air into a bubble and forced it outward, held four alcoves lined with dust-covered pads.

"Healing capsules," burst from James's mouth, and he walked toward one of them, amazed. In the avatar's memories, it had been merely a side note that the Al'Anters had used them to extend their lifespans.

The fully autonomous medical machines repaired their patients' telomeres with a highly specific swarm of nanites. They cleared the intercellular spaces of plaque caused by cell death, resulting in lower malignant mutation rates and more efficient mitochondria, thus ensuring health through an effective immune system and a significantly slowed aging process. The average Al'Anter had lived about one hundred fifty years just before the outbreak of the war, and in good health.

None of that would have been of outstanding interest to the Avatar, since he was not subject to the cycle of birth and death. Consequently, it was only moderately curious about both, but no more so than an anomaly of the local sun, the metabolism of a bruutak, or the societal implications brought about by the invention of the water closet. Since

James had viewed the entire history of the planet through the eyes and mind of the Avatar, the existence and function of the healing capsules had been a mere side note to him as well. But now that he saw them for himself, here and now, he realized that they did delay death, and by a large period.

"Healing capsule?" Mila asked. "That's a strange name."

"Why?"

"I would have expected something more like 'relife cocoon' or 'medi-capsule.'"

"The Al'Anters were steeped in the idea of cooperation, just as we are in the idea of competition," James explained absently, stroking his fingers over the rim of the capsule in front of him, which, with its finger-thick bulge, had an egg-shaped outline. "Also, there was no competitive capitalism. If someone invented something, the knowledge was immediately available to the public and made available to everyone as quickly as possible. There were no vendors vying for customers and coming up with creative names. This is a capsule that heals its users, so 'healing capsule.'"

"Unfortunately, only one capsule is still functional," Altan-117 explained, pointing to the second alcove on the right, where a faint bluish glow suddenly appeared. "But its nanite supply is functional and complete."

"I'll go first," James said, and noticed the suspicious looks his friends were giving the strange construction. He couldn't blame them. He had to remind himself again that they hadn't seen what he had seen. For them, everything had happened very quickly and was exceedingly strange. For him, all this was just a memory away, and if he couldn't recall any details, at least he had a sense of distant familiarity with it. "It's not dangerous. At least in theory."

"If we don't do something, we'll be dead soon anyway."

As if to emphasize her words, Mila ran her hand through her hair and held out whole tufts of soiled blond strands. Her hair now looked as if it had been styled by an extremely untalented hairdresser, with bald patches and uneven distribution. Seeing her like this pained him.

He nodded to her when he saw her worried expression. He turned his back to the open capsule before stepping back and touching his buttocks to the ancient padding made hard and scratchy by time. Vague fragments of memory about the workings of the machine flitted through his mind but were intangible to him, passing by like clouds that dissipated before he was aware of their form.

"I'm going to start the treatment now," Altan-117 announced kindly. The robot stood at an angle in front of him, next to Mila, his long arms hanging at his side, his lidless eyes large and dark. Nothing indicated he was doing anything. "You have no symbionts."

"That's right."

There was a short pause, and James involuntarily wondered when servitors took pauses to think. Or was he in contact with the Ark's central control unit at that moment? Were they conferring to determine how to handle this information?

"That's... unusual."

"Yes," James admitted and decided to lie. If anyone could manage to fool a machine that specialized in humans, it would be him. "We know about the technology of symbionts used by our ancestors, but they were bred for the genetic material of their users and were implanted while they were still in the growth phase so they could connect to the neural stratum. Because the radiation generated high mutation rates, we weren't able to use them efficiently."

"I see." Altan-117 inclined his head. "I regret this circumstance very much. The treatment is complete."

James frowned. He had felt nothing at all. Only now did he think he felt something like a warm rush flowing through his vascular system, but the sensation was so quiet and distant that he thought it was a psychosomatic effect rather than a genuine reaction. Cautiously, he stepped out of the open capsule and eyed his soiled arms. Indeed, the omnipresent redness was subsiding, and the abscesses were receding before his eyes. Something tickled at the edge of his mind, a pale memory, perhaps, or an impulse he couldn't place. The harder he tried to reach for it, the more it eluded him, as if he were trying to draw water with splayed fingers. He knew it was something important, but not what.

"I'm convinced, anyway," Mila said and stepped into the capsule.

Gradually, they each took their turn. With each passing minute, James felt more vital. Strength returned to his limbs like a warm shiver, driving the exhaustion from his bones. The muscles relaxed and, above all, the pain receded, which resulted in an inner sigh of relief. Only latent tiredness remained, which made sense since he had hardly slept for days.

He wrapped Mila in his arms and she pressed her head against his chest. It did him good to feel her and release the thought that she would die shortly. It had been with him for so long that it had seemed like a fact he would have to come to terms with, which would have been impossible.

"What happened to the second servitor with maintenance functions?" Mila asked Altan-117 as Adrian, who had insisted on being treated last, stepped into the pod. Her voice created a pleasant resonance in James's chest.

"He suffered a malfunction in his energy pattern cells and the central control unit shut him down." The servitor sounded a bit sad. The simulation of human emotion was striking, generating reflexive sympathy in him he couldn't shake off even when he realized that clever programming was leading him by the nose. What predictable bio-algorithms humans were.

"Oh, when was that?"

"About a thousand years ago."

"So, you've been completely alone since then?" Mila seemed depressed by the thought.

"Yes." Altan-117 nodded and made another of those strange pauses, like a human would make. James found that the Avatar had shown distinctly too little enthusiasm for the programming skills of the Al'Ant AI experts. The illusion of human behavior they had created was nothing less than impressive. "But I have my tasks and they must be accomplished. That's what gives me the equivalent of satisfaction."

"The fulfillment of your programming, you mean? Or do your heuristics actually simulate something like feelings?"

"Feelings, by definition, are based on chemical reactions that do not take place in me."

Mila nodded and turned to Adrian, who was now stepping out of the healing capsule and stretching—a strange impulse each had automatically followed.

"The results are good," the servitor announced almost solemnly. "It will take some time for your bodies to fully recover and for you to feel normal again. That's normal for you. I think you are fit to work. Shall we begin immediately?"

"You don't waste any time, do you, buddy?" Meeks said, clicking his tongue. "Aren't you even allowed to take a breath when you've just jumped off the brink of death?"

"Of course. I beg your pardon." Altan-117 bowed toward the American.

"Oh, hell, while we're here…" Meeks looked around the room and waited for James, of all people, to agree. "We'll need a little guidance, though, so we know the best place to start."

And a few hundred years to understand the technology here, if there really is an experimental teleporter, James thought.

Their team, of which he was now a part, consisted of outstanding minds in their respective fields, intelligent thinking machines who had excelled in their fields and were considered the best. There had certainly been political reasons for their appointments, he had no illusions about that, but they were all brilliant. However, that did not change that the Al'Anters were also brilliant, and better networked and cooperative by several orders of magnitude. Their progression rates made anything humans had ever accomplished on Earth look old, and his friends, even with all their skills, could not even begin to understand what kind of technology was being used here. They probably lacked knowledge of physics unknown to them, to grasp the basic operating principle of some functions this facility possessed. Of course, they couldn't let the servitor know that, because even if he wasn't allowed to touch a hair on anyone's head due to his programming, he could still stop cooperating and thus practically set it to zero. At the same time, James still had the marble, which he could use to let the Avatar and Nasaku do the work. That had been their plan. But they needed to know Altan-117 was on their side until they discovered where the zero-D memory could be used.

"Of course," the robot said happily. The avatar had obviously done a good job with its transmission, and James was immensely relieved about it.

The entire tour lasted at least an hour, even if his sense of time might deceive him deep underground. The Ark, or Temple of Heaven as it had been called at the time of Nasaku's secession, was actually constructed like a two-dimensional football. At each of the elongated ends were the two access and evacuation points for emergencies, through which the surface could be reached with elevators.

The teleporter room was a large cavern with a raised platform in the center, below which was a giant titanium plate separating the reactor from the teleporter. Beneath it lay six dormant antimatter coils, powerful containment chambers, and a ring-shaped cluster of energy pattern cells from which power was conducted via semi-organic super-conductors to the wormhole generator in a pitch-black sphere, just above the seats.

There were twelve seats, always in pairs of two facing each other, exactly as in the two teleporters James had seen. One set faced outward and one inward, so the outer circle had much greater spacing between the seats. The cushions were slightly darker and had a different shape from their original counterparts but were otherwise identical. The funnel in the center of the platform was missing because the reactor was located underneath. Instead, there were four funnels, at about waist height on the curved left wall. Leg-thick hoses led upward from them to a bulky box next to the platform, and twelve smaller ones led from there to each seat.

All of this was fascinating because it had so many simi-larities to the original teleporters yet looked much more expansive and, above all, improvised. Even more impressive than anything in the Elders' mysterious machine, however, was the wormhole generator high above their heads, which seemed to hover over the seating circle like a Sword of Damocles, since no suspension could be seen in the darkness, the light ring was further down in the vaulted ceiling. The sphere was two or three meters in diameter and mostly black, except for the frenetic beams of light that shot back and forth along its surface like shooting stars. Although it had no particular geometric shape and made no sound whatsoever, it was perhaps its very inconspicuousness to the human senses that imbued it with something deep and meaningful that left James with goosebumps on his arms.

Each team member went to great lengths to hide their admiration and pretend they knew exactly what they were dealing with as Altan-117 showed off the individual components and sometimes even explained them as if he was particularly proud of them.

In the six rooms leading from the teleporter room, with its huge presence in the middle of the two elliptical corridors by means of dull gray metal doors, were the maintenance accesses or control rooms of the core components of the Ark. A magnetically shielded data storage room contained twelve columns of molecular DNA storage floating in a nutrient fluid and housing a mindboggling amount of data.

In another room, the superconductors came together in a kind of bouquet, where the cooling seemed based on some directed quantum fluctuation, but not even Justus seemed able to even begin to understand what the servitor was saying as they looked around the elongated room with the two working panels and five large white bubbles that vibrated like gelatin.

Behind another door was the control room for teleport control. It was round, similar to the one in the battery complex where James had met the digital Avatar. The walls consisted of a display ring over an armature ring with blue connectors at regular intervals, like the ones he had used to receive the Avatar's memories. He knew how they worked, remembered a direct neural interface that could control all the computer systems and could be unlocked by his own DNA.

James knew he should understand all the other things they had seen so far, and yet they kept slipping away like a word he was frantically trying to find without quite grasping it. It was exceedingly frustrating, but eventually he gave up wracking his brain. He had realized early on that he could not place high hopes in his brain's ability to process, let alone store, the experiences of billions of years. So, he listened and looked, concentrating on the reactions of his friends, who nodded here and there but at other times merely blinked in amazement.

The fifth room was sleeping quarters for the crew, which apparently had numbered twenty-four. The blankets on the bunkbeds were covered with dust but not weathered, and showed the unmistakable outlines of human skeletons.

"Jesus," Meeks muttered and was crossing himself when he noticed Altan-117, who was the last to enter the room, and pulled himself together at the last moment.

"That's the staff?" Justus asked lamely, swallowing audibly.

"Yes. Unfortunately, a traditional burn was not possible."

No one asked any more questions, so they quickly exited and finally entered the last room, which contained a food replicator that looked something like a 1980s pinball machine, four tables with chairs, a sitting area, and an elongated worktable with tractamorphic tool arms.

"How much do you know about how the teleporter

works?" Adrian asked the robot when they were back in the central cavern, which could have accommodated two tennis courts side by side. "It would be good if you could give us details so we can best assess how to use you to assist us."

Smart, James thought.

"The first and only attempt so far took place before the war," Altan-117 answered and pointed with his mechanical, six-fingered hand to the teleporter platform in the center, where the light from the illuminated ring at the top of the rock ceiling shone particularly brightly. "It was successful and created a link to our own teleporter in the teleporter area. That's not particularly far, but it was enough to confirm the suspected mode of action and ensure that the energy buildup and wormhole size were sufficient. It lasted only a second but was sufficient to send far more data than a human's digitized consciousness requires to pass through into a new medium. The transmission rate and stability were within the expected range. There are enough anti-matter supplies for at least two more attempts, but there are several problems, one with the superconductors, one with the cooling units, then one with the magnetic shielding of the platform, since the magnetic field reversed after a short circuit. Then there were the fragments of malicious code that compromised the integrity of the central control software."

"The attack of the saboteurs. The Kazerun," James said.

"Yes. It was blocked, but it was not possible to remove the entire malware. To continue the tests, it is necessary to remove the corresponding malicious code." The servitor paused for a moment. "But the biggest problem is that there is a lack of conscious, organic test subjects."

James looked at his friends, who exchanged glances with each other.

"Crossing over is not possible for me."

"We'll get to work on the repairs first," Adrian decided, and they all nodded.

We first learn as much as we can before we think about our further steps. James translated the words of the cosmonaut for himself and silently agreed with him.

20

"The flow rate is enormous," Adrian said. He was kneeling in front of a small display that had formed as if out of nowhere before his eyes. He was at the far wall of the room where large rectangular flaps allowed for superconductor access. He was facing the middle panel.

"Hasn't superconductor technology advanced?" Altan-117 asked with a tinge of surprise in his voice.

Sometimes it was difficult for Adrian to remember that he was dealing with a robot. If it hadn't been for the servitor's unmistakable artificial appearance, he probably would have fallen for its programming over and over again and, at some point, completely forgotten that there was a significant difference between them.

"I don't know," he replied curtly. He had no great desire to converse with his overseer. The data running across the display were easily readable for him since they were metric quantities and mathematical formulas that he, as a superconductor engineer, knew well—quite in contrast to the long columns of text that ran across another part of the display and could just as well be Egyptian hieroglyphics.

"Were you able to identify the problem?"

"You're pretty impatient for a robot."

Adrian wrinkled his nose and continued to use simple gesture controls to compare the flow rates of the individual lines. They were identical, no matter how often he looked. And that's what was odd. Since each main line supplied one seat, two should always have the same voltage, but *only* two. One seat for outgoing connections to another planet, one for incoming. All other seat combinations resulted in different versions of Earth, each in a different place in the Milky Way, and thus requiring different amounts of power to create a wormhole. The one that provided for cloning and molecular reconfiguration of the biomass was negligible, far less than a decimal. Unless, of course, the travelers' data was transmitted from the seats to the central wormhole located in the wormhole generator that hung in the cavern above the platform. But Adrian didn't think that because that would mean only one wormhole could be active at a time, and thus only one connection. If that were the case, it would have made more sense to build a teleporter with only one pair of seats and simply use different coordinates each time.

Since that was not the case, he stuck with his assumption that the wormhole generator was merely that, creating the wormholes themselves in the seats or near them to allow simultaneous connections. He had discussed this a lot with Justus and Meeks when they had lived with the Tokamaku because these questions had stayed with him. Time and again, they had ultimately agreed that the connections consumed different amounts of energy because distance would have to play a role in a wormhole energy use. But since they had been sure until recently that something like a wormhole existed only in theoretical physics, and that such a construct could neither be stabilized in practice nor could sufficient energy be mustered for it, they could be wrong in this matter. After all, here they were, something like rabbits standing in front of an atomic bomb and trying to decipher its mode of action.

"Can I have this to go?" he asked after quite a while, during which Altan-117 had sat silently beside him like a folded bicycle without wheels.

"You mean the data?"

"Yes."

"It's possible." The robot stood with a metallic clicking of limbs and stalked to a dusty console next to the door that reminded Adrian of one of the Soviet slot machines built in the late 1980s, to keep up with the Americans, appropriately communist themed, of course. Altan-117 held his hand in front of what looked like a narrow press screen for coffee machines and after a few seconds the entire console gave off a low hum. Soon a flap on the front opened and the servitor removed a rectangular sheet of glass, which he handed to Adrian.

"Thank you." He scratched his head and accepted the device. "Is this something like a...?"

"Sorry. You aren't familiar with this technology anymore."

A forgetful robot? Adrian frowned inwardly. *That was all he needed. Or has he developed his own cynicism over the millennia to appear more realistic in the face of the end of the world?*

"So?" he asked impatiently.

"This is a data input device synthesized by the assembler unit. You have full access to the data," the servitor explained. "You just have to use the appropriate gestures to take the parts you need and apply them to your new..."

"Tablet," he suggested, and Altan-117 inclined his head.

"All you have to do is drag it onto your new *tablet*, and then you can take it anywhere."

Adrian tried it by pulling the corresponding displays on the holo console from the air in front of him and releasing them over the transparent tablet. The glass became cloudy and then displayed the same blue formulas, numbers, and matrices that he could see in front of him in a slightly larger version. He took his time and compared everything carefully to make sure there was no difference, no matter how small. Then he repeated the process until he had everything he needed and returned to the crew area, which seemed as deserted as everything else down here. He felt like he was in a dusty museum that had been old when it first opened in the Victorian era.

Mette was sitting at one of the abandoned tables and seemed to be asleep in the absolute silence but opened her eyes when she heard his footsteps echo off the walls.

"Hi, Adrian." She greeted him quietly as if the absence of any sound had imposed a silent obligation on her.

"Hello, Mette. May I sit?"

"What a question." The Dane pointed to one of the vacant chairs at her table. "It's not like it's particularly crowded here."

"Mmm."

"Weren't you going to check the status of the supercon-ductors?"

"Yes." He nodded and pointed behind him. "But that robot is getting on my nerves. I can't work in peace with him looking over my shoulders all the time, like a political commissar."

"I actually think he's quite cute with his big eyes and calm demeanor."

"Of course, because that's exactly how he's supposed to

look to you. It's consistent with his programming, remember? I don't like having a machine around to watch my back."

"Why not?" she asked. "It's not like he has his own agenda. It's basically like you're alone with a computer, just like a normal workday. Except this computer has arms and legs and is smarter than we are."

"I'm not so sure about that," he said and waved the issue aside. "What are you doing here all by yourself?"

"James and Mila are who knows where, Meeks wants to work on the cooling system, and Justus is about to look at the control module in the control room. Since I'm not in love, an engineer, or a physicist, I guess I have no choice but to twiddle my thumbs here, alone." Mette let out a long, drawn-out sigh.

"We need you."

"Thank you, that's kind of you."

"I'm serious. You said the same thing on Earth when we started the project, and no one knew where to start," he explained, placing the tablet on the table. The reflections on its mirrored surface made it appear much brighter than the patina on the tabletop and created a stark contrast. "When the cloning started, you and Mila figured out that the funnel in the middle of the biomass uptake was responsible for molecular conversion."

"Yes, but here?" She spread her arms, which had grown frighteningly thin compared to her time on Earth. "Here, I'm just superfluous."

"I don't think so." He pointed at the tablet.

"What is it?"

"A portable display. I pulled the superconductor data on it because I can't figure it out. I could use your help with that."

The Dane hesitated and examined him closely as if she was trying to assess whether he was serious or just taking pity on her. Finally, she shrugged and nodded toward the tablet.

"What's it about?"

"The first test was successful, right?"

"According to James and Altan-117."

"Good. But that tin can also says that it doesn't work now because no connection can be made," Adrian said. "Which I can't explain, at least from the superconductor data. The flow rate is constant. The voltage level fluctuates even less than I have seen in the best prototypes on Earth. From everything I can see, they work perfectly."

"Then I don't understand your question," Mette said, frowning. "The problem isn't with superconductors; that's an answer in search of a problem, isn't it?"

"No." He shook his head. "The problem is that the data is *too* perfect. I'll show you."

Adrian called up the data on the six connections, each of which divided into two and split like tentacles to the walls between the rooms and the main cavern in their center. Some branched toward the reactor in the floor and the wormhole generator, while smaller ones led to the seats. When he tried to form an inner picture, he always imagined a mighty octopus with this facility firmly in its grip from below.

"Look at it," he urged her and watched her face. Tiny wrinkles formed on her forehead, and her mouth became a thin line, as they always did when she was thinking.

"Strange indeed," she noted after some time. "I would have been shocked at the level of tension, too, but since you didn't, I guess that's just scaled technological superiority expressed in numbers."

"Mhm." He nodded and waited.

"The voltage is identical except for the most minimal deviations, which would not have been displayed at all if there had been two decimal places less," she continued, tapping the corresponding numbers. "But if each set of seats has its own target, spaced at different distances, the power consumption of the respective Einstein-Rosen bridges should also be different. At least in different orders of magnitude than that."

Again, she tapped her index finger on the tablet in front of her. "Whether consumption is coupled one-to-one with distance, I don't know, but it would make sense. I guess that would be a question for Justus. It's funny either way, though. Do you think that's where the problem lies?"

"I don't know. But it's weird, to say the least. I'll have to ask the tin bucket to give me access to the historical data. Then I can see if there have been fluctuations or other deviations that indicate a deeper problem."

source of energy in the universe, if one disregarded black holes. Even though the robot had mentioned none of this, it was obvious to him that somewhere behind these walls, or below them, one or more of the miniature suns were radiating and taking care of the secondary systems. With a large enough supply of helium 3, they could keep the Ark running for tens of thousands of years with no problem.

What he wouldn't have given to look at them, including the technology behind them. Although fusion physics had never been his specialty, because he was an electrical engineer first and had only studied physics as a minor subject, it had always interested him. The possibility of recreating something as sublime as the sun, rather than smashing an atom with extreme force like barbarians, had to mystify any scientist, especially since the technology had been within reach for some time. It was merely a question of "the next twenty-five years," as fusion researchers have been fond of joking for more than sixty years whenever the question of "when" was at issue.

Liquid helium-3 was the most efficient way he knew of to effectively cool something to near-absolute zero. Heat was basically nothing more than motion, the movement of atoms. "Buzz or sleep," his physics professor had once said. At zero, atoms stopped moving completely, and everything was frozen in place. There was no lower temperature— about minus two hundred seventy degrees Celsius or zero Kelvin—and only liquid helium-3 could almost reach it. He had dealt with superconducting electromagnets at Boeing that had to be cooled with this isotope and the process had been extremely expensive. Knowing there was half an ocean of it shooting through the wiring in the wall behind him made his head spin.

His *work*, if it could be called that, for the last few hours had consisted merely of opening one of the maintenance accesses using the tools their robo-friend had synthesized for him and staring at three pipes on which no ice crystals had formed. So, either they were so well insulated that they were made of nothing he knew, or there were no water molecules in the environment at all, which hardly seemed any more believable to him. In any case, he would not start by holding his hand to one of the pipes because, in the worst case, he would have no skin left on his palms. For a short time, he still felt something like curiosity using a synthesized piece of glass, which was apparently supposed to be a tablet, because after a short introduction by the servitor, he could use it as a kind of X-ray device. If he pressed it against a wall, he could look through it and, by cleverly moving it, use it like binoculars to see through massive objects. But even that quickly lost its novelty because he could see only wires and pipes that were oddly arranged but otherwise made a rather dull impression.

Now he felt quite useless since he had no idea what he should do or check. Even the tablet-like thing that looked like a sheet of glass pane was, according to Altan-117, a data display, didn't help him. He understood nothing that was written, and therefore he didn't understand the parameters given, so he couldn't put the values he could read as whole numbers into context. No matter how hard he tried, he simply ended up looking for flashing red symbols that might indicate errors, only to feel ridiculous, like a chimpanzee sitting in front of a rocket engine looking for the banana.

"I haven't the faintest idea what to do," he muttered and let out long, drawn-out sigh. Even an image of the piping system had not helped him draw any conclusions about its structure and its exact interconnection with the individual components. Basically, he was useless here. He felt stupid because he had believed it could be different. But of course, that had been a frivolous hope. What had he imagined? That he would walk in, find an instruction manual in English, and get right to work because with a doctorate he could decode any machine no matter how advanced the underlying technology? The robot wasn't much help, either. It merely asked which detail it could assist with, to which Meeks simply pretended to be very busy. At one point, he went to the mess hall, which resulted in Altan-117 showing up there as well.

"Hello, Meeks!"

He started and almost fell over. James was standing in the empty doorway, which hadn't been locked since the robot had left, and eyed him, frowning.

"Are you okay?"

He waved it off. "Oh, I'm just an old cowboy standing in front of a horse he can't break in."

To punctuate his words, he tapped the small fission cutter in his hand against the flap of the maintenance panel leaning against the wall beside him.

"I have no idea what I'm doing here or what it might be good for."

"We'll figure it out," James assured him.

"Oh, yeah? How? With that marble?"

His teammate with the tall and somewhat sinewy build briefly looked as if Meeks had slapped him and looked over his shoulder. He looked even thinner since they had lived with the Tokamaku and yet somehow lighter, as if a heavy shadow had weighed on him before and had been lifted over the months.

"You didn't find out *anything*?"

"Pretty much," Meeks sighed. "There's a wide network of

lines that run to all the components. I can't tell you which ones, though. In this room, there's access to the cryogenics but nothing else. You would think that such an advanced facility would have completely networked systems."

James seemed to ponder this and then blinked.

"Yes, I suppose you're right." After a brief pause, he continued, "But don't forget that not long after this place was established, a war was exposed that forced the Al'Anters into secrecy, something never before seen in their history. Not networking the individual systems to make them less vulnerable to attack is obvious."

"Yeah, it's so familiar that they strike me more as paranoid maniacs than cooperation-seeking braggarts," Meeks grumbled. "I mean, that's something *we* would do. *We* think that way. But for the Al'Anters to turn the other way so quickly..."

"They would have had every reason to, believe me."

"Why did you come here, anyway?" he asked as James turned away.

"There's an area in the control room we would like to have access to, but not even Altan-117 can get in there. He says he has no authority. Maybe we can find answers there." James tapped the side of his soiled shorts, where Meeks knew the marble pocket was located.

"You mean if I could *turn off* the cooling for the area... let's say, then possibly the locking mechanism would stop working?"

"Sort of."

"Nah." He shook his head. "Sorry, buddy, at most, that would work indirectly if the lack of cooling broke the circuit, which I don't think it would—at least not fast enough. Besides, we don't even know if it's an electronic or manual interlock. Check with Adrian and his superconductors. If it is a magnetic lock, it would make sense to break the circuit across it. But don't get your hopes up; there will almost certainly be redundancies built in. Quite a few."

James pointed to the glass tablet. "Is that a computer?"

"This?" Meeks shook his head. "Nah. With this I can look right through the walls at the lines and pipes to see potential damage without having to break open the wall. There are a few functions I don't understand, but my guess is that you can use it to control maintenance bots that are small enough to crawl around inside the wall. I'd like to take a break and go to the mess hall. That is, if that damned piece of tin doesn't start talking to me again and I end up rotting here."

"I see. I'll try my luck with Adrian."

Once James had disappeared again, Meeks stared at the empty door leading into the cavern for quite a while, wondering what his visit could have been about. It seemed to him that his friend had wordlessly tried to tell him something, and that made him nervous because he had no clue what it could have been.

At least the number with the lock wasn't it, he thought. *What an absurd idea.*

22

J ustus paced back and forth in front of the control room's dashboards like a tiger locked in its cage for too long. The display wall above the strange buttons and switches, which looked as if they were made to be operated with two hands but otherwise resembled nothing like a keyboard, glowed a soft blue and showed many things he would have expected to see on the advertising board of a complicated recruitment office, but he understood absolutely none of it. Since most of it consisted of columns of text and labeled input fields that could be selected and changed by gesture control, he might as well have been confronted with Mandarin. Presumably, his chances would not be worse than they are now.

The numbers were different: He had deciphered them with Adrian a few hours ago because they followed a mathematical logic of quantity symbols arranged on top of each other—in this case, dashes—and added dots for each ten-step. The hundreds were crosses of two lines; the thousands were crosses of three lines, and so on. He had hoped for a small breakthrough. However, he was even more perplexed since he now saw islands of understanding everywhere, numbers that had no frame of reference at all. It drove him nearly crazy to see a spark but not be able to assign it to a fire. And he didn't even want to deal with the locked box on the right side of the control room. The only door leading in was sealed, and it didn't have a lock or anything as helpful as a handle.

He hadn't felt this useless since college when he'd had to take a semester in geology. After jokingly calling his fellow students "rock knockers," he was practically sidelined because no one wanted to do a group project with him. He had hardly minded because at least he'd been able to look up geologist jokes instead of having to deal with why various types of stone were black and not dark brown.

Now it was the opposite, because he desperately *wanted* to find out something but simply could not. He was standing in an enigma, looking at an enigma that projected an enigma toward him. He was not Alice in Wonderland, but an Alice without eyes, ears, and nose in Wonderland. How easy it would have been to ask the robot to read to him, but Adrian had justifiably said that doing so would reveal them to their host as incompetent and impostors—with unforeseen consequences.

Eventually, he had limited himself to searching and scanning everything centimeter by centimeter. He looked for a small recess into which they could insert the marble James was carrying, for *any* connections or interaction possibilities of any kind, until he was looking for joints to distinguish individual components from one another. But everything seemed made of one piece, and except for the oddly shaped switches and levers that looked like failed toys for toddlers and were covered in a sticky patina of dirt, there was absolutely nothing to discover, no matter how long he looked.

The connectors, which looked gray and dead and, unlike in James's narrative, did absolutely nothing when he put his hands on them. They didn't get soft or warm either, but were hard and scratchy like a dried-out bumblebee.

So, after several hours of frustrated unproductivity, Justus sat in the middle of the circular room and stared at the rapidly changing displays on the display ring, which played out before him like a hallucinogenic nightmare. They were trying to tell him something, he was sure, or the robot guy wouldn't have thrown them at him. But he couldn't very well tell him he understood none of it, then their already ridiculous cover would have been blown.

We're lucky we're dealing with a robot programmed to help and please humans, he thought, propping his chin on his folded hands atop his drawn-up knees. *If Altan-117 were my ex-boss, he would have smelled our bullshit while we were still on Earth. But we are quite obviously not there.*

Justus spent the rest of the day—which he recognized only because he fell asleep dead tired at some point—obsessively trying to bring order to the displays. The next day, he achieved at least partial success. He eventually realized how the Al'Anters had written their dates, exactly as they did on Earth with year, month, and day. This was not a big surprise since the orbital periods were the same. A year here also once consisted of 365 days with twelve full moons and twenty-four-hour cycles. He had merely not thought of these overlaps amid his fatigue because the days here had been so short since the destruction of the moon. A year now had to consist of almost one thousand five hundred days. But since their way of recording dates could never have changed, at least for the Al'Anters, he merely had to look for a format similar to what he was used to. And he found it in reverse order, first the year, then the month, then the day. From the big to the small instead of the other way around, or in a nonsensical mishmash like the Americans did with month, day, year.

Now, he recognized time stamps, which at least helped with a chronological classification of the cryptic information he was shown. In addition, he now understood when the displays repeated themselves because he recognized the time stamps. It wasn't much, but it was a start and that was enough for him at this point, to not have to feel that sense of uselessness anymore.

With the Tokamaku, he had almost lost his mind because he missed Sarah and his two sons, Frederick and Michel, so much he could hardly sleep, and when he did manage it, he dreamed of them and woke with tears in his eyes. So, he had thrown himself into what had helped him in the past to get over emotionally difficult moments in his life: he had worked.

First, he had gone foraging with some collectors, tried to create herbariums and cataloged as much as he could internally. Then he learned to build simple tools and tried to perfect each step so he could lose himself in the details. It was a strategy effective for the moment but usually paid him back by merely pushing the problem in front of him, not managing it. But how could one cope with such a thing? To leave one's wife and children behind and go to another planet with no way back? Longing was one thing, but the guilt was quite another, and it was eating him up so much inside he was almost going crazy.

When they had stumbled across the dunes on the surface, half parched and dehydrated, lips chapped and inflamed skin on fire, he had put up a good face so as not to demotivate the others, but inwardly he had died a little before his body could beat him to it.

He had left his family and could not explain to them why. They would never get answers because of the secrecy. Some government official would give them some made-up story about a car accident in the U.S. or something like that, and still, Sarah wouldn't believe it. She was not a woman who could be hoodwinked easily and could immediately sense when a story stank to high heaven. He knew that all too well from his own experience.

It wasn't until the robot had appeared and they had miraculously found the Ark that a spark of hope that he had hardly dared to feel had returned—only to be overtaken by his own uselessness and the realization that he could do nothing at all.

"Hello, Justus."

He jumped violently and wheeled around to face the door, which stood open like all the others. James was leaning against the frame, his gaunt figure obscuring the view of the pedestal with the seats of the test teleporter.

"Are you all right? Are you making progress?"

"Progress?" Justus snorted. "I've managed to recognize time stamps in two days."

"I can translate a few things for you," James said.

"Are you serious? You're saying that *now?*"

"Well, I barely remember anything. It's as if I'm looking at something I should know, but which always eludes my grasp at the last moment like a wet bar of soap. I've watched the Al'Anters develop their first script, watched it evolve over the millennia, and yet all of that is but a pale reflection of a memory turning to mist."

"Very poetic." Justus sighed heavily. "I'm sorry, I didn't mean to be defeatist, but this is really frustrating."

"We'll manage," James said, trying to cheer him up. It was easy for him since he had no wife and no children and had obviously run away from a past that hurt him. Here he had found his love for Mila and it was reciprocated. What more could he want? Despite all the circumstances, it had to be liberating for him.

Don't be envious, he scolded himself. *Envy never helped anyone, and it can't help that you made decisions you have to live with.*

"All right," he finally said. He stood and to a part of the display ring that particularly interested him. He wiped away several displays until he saw the oldest time stamp he had identified. "That one."

"What about this one?" James stepped up beside him and studied the texts and diagrams, frowning.

"It's the oldest date I could find. Can you read any of it?"

"Took'a," James muttered absently. "I think that means something like 'beginning.' The word after that is shas'la, which is something like 'machine,' or 'technology.' I can't distinguish the nuances very well."

"Beginning of technology?" Justus shook his head. "That's not a treatise on the history of technology. Nobody needs that down here."

"Beginning, after all, means beginning. Perhaps it's more comparable in meaning to the word 'activation,' which is also a beginning. Beginning of the working activity of a machine?"

"Of the teleporter," Justus said, nodding, and continued to turn the pages with rapid gestures. Indeed, the terms repeated themselves. "What if this is an experimental protocol?"

"Possibly. If it were, what would that mean?" James asked.

"That would mean..." he whispered to himself, and switched the various displays so quickly that the individual lines of text and graphics became blue comets darting across the display. He was able to follow them effortlessly, knowing exactly where he was without understanding much because he'd done nothing but stare at them for the past two days. "That would mean," he finally repeated, louder, "that I've deciphered something else. That's a six there, right?"

He pointed to a symbol consisting of six superimposed short strokes and James nodded.

"Well, that's an A right there." He pointed to a dash on the first display. "Of these, there are a total of six recorded events with time stamps, all more recent than those of the first with the six. If that's correct about the activation, maybe it's the activation of the teleporter. There is not much else here that could be activated from the control room, except for tens of subsystems. If it's about those, I guess we're out of luck."

"If it's true," James said thoughtfully, "then there were two sixes immediately in the first activation—the original test." He pointed to the two corresponding numbers separated by a word. "What if that one means 'person'?"

"My thought exactly. Then everything would make sense." Justus felt something like energy building up in him again—a familiar feeling he knew from being on the verge of an anticipated breakthrough in the lab, as if his entire brain were re-sorting and realigning itself. It felt like getting caught in a current with a boat that made everything easier.

"So, what we have here are the logs of various attempted teleport activations."

"Not only that." He pointed to another word at the bottom.

"Miak'ka," James read aloud.

"What does that mean?"

"I don't know. I can read the writing, it makes a sound in my head that goes with it, but I can't remember what it means, sorry."

"No problem, because I know." Justus gave a tired smile when he saw the American's surprised face. "The first attempt was successful, right?"

"As far as I know..." James said cautiously.

"That one"—he pointed an outstretched finger to the word at the bottom left of the first display with the two sixes —"means 'success.'"

He swiped to the next entry, his finger staying in the same position where there was another word. The next four attempts also showed the same word.

"Failure. Only the first attempt worked."

"We already know that from Altan-117," James said.

"Yes, but now we know that these are the log entries of the various attempts. We know that there were a total of five others, all of which were unsuccessful. If we compare them now with the first one, we can already see differences in the numbers."

"Hello, do you need my assistance?" They were interrupted by Altan-117 who was suddenly standing behind them. Justus hadn't even heard him coming. "Have you been able to make any progress?"

James frowned and looked at him before barely shaking his head.

"We're working on it."

23

"Wasn't Adrian just with you?" Mila asked as she entered the mess hall.

Mette was sitting alone at a tables, listlessly chewing on a dried tapak root. She didn't even look up.

"Yeah, same as yesterday. I think he wants to keep me company because he feels sorry for me, but somehow that just makes it worse."

"I can understand that. What about the servitor? It was made to keep people company, wasn't it?"

"Him?" Mette waved. "He's always running back and forth, and he'd rather take care of our engineers."

"He obviously can't use me," Mila said, shrugging. "I've spent the last two days obsessively searching for hookups for you-know-what."

"Mhm. So? No success, I guess?"

"No."

"The others don't sound very optimistic either."

"Hello, Mila and Mette." They both looked up and saw Altan-117 come toward them through the open door. His big doe-eyed face tilted. "Do you need anything?"

"We're on a break," Mila replied, and after a sideways glance at Mette, pointed to the transparent tablet Adrian had just given her with some instructions. "But I could use your help."

She wiped a hand across the glass-like material, and the display came to life with a gradually brighter shimmer. An exceedingly long text appeared on it.

"Of course." Altan-117 approached the table and stood so he formed a triangle with her and Mette. His large, dark eyes scrutinized her, and she imagined curiosity resonated in them.

"Can you read this to me?" she asked him, turning the tablet so the writing on it faced him.

"Read aloud?"

"Yes. Is that a problem?"

"Of course not." He lifted the display with the six long-limbed fingers of his right hand, which clicked lightly as he did so.

"The mass-to-biomass vector is reciprocal. Ongoing adjustments to the transfer capabilities of inorganic configurations extending beyond the four levels are necessary. A way to send mononuclear microbodies has shown promise in an initial simulation," the robot read aloud in a pleasant baritone voice, but Mila wasn't listening. In the background, she saw a gaunt shadow walk past the podium. James. Since the doorway was small and the distance great, she saw him only as a dark figure that soon passed. The text Altan-117 was reading wafted past her, was elongated and cloistered, the technical ramblings of a scientist that lived on exclusivity in language and intellect, something their two cultures apparently had in common if perhaps only that.

. . .

"Are you sure it's working?" Meeks hissed, peering furtively around the corner of the doorframe into the cavern. The robot was nowhere to be seen.

"No, but I can't think of anything better," James admitted. He saw Justus poke his head out of the control center and beckon them to join him. As if by appointment, Adrian scurried over to the German, holding a tool that looked like a drill against his chest. "So, come on!"

Together they walked to the control room, accompanied by the muffled voice of Altan-117, which drifted from the mess hall like the whisper of a gathering wind. Justus was waiting in front of the large box of dark metal and went back to the active place on the display ring and positioned himself in front of the two connectors.

"Did you find the right spot?" James asked excitedly.

"I know now what 'activating' looks like," the German replied, licking his lips.

"All right, Meeks. Do your part!"

The American nodded, walked past Justus, climbed onto the armature, and pressed the glass tablet against the wall above it. Even from a few meters away, James could make out long gray blue lines, like on an ultrasound image.

"It's a cooling pipe, no question about it," Meeks finally said after sliding the device back and forth several times. He pressed his hand to the appropriate spot and left it there as he took the tablet with the other and tossed it to him. James tried to catch it but missed and breathed a sigh of relief when Adrian caught it before it could crash to the floor.

"That was close," the Russian said, holding it in front of the outline of the black box that looked like a door. "Ready?"

"No, but do it anyway."

. . .

"That was the entire text. I would love to read out more text to add to your distraction, but I'm afraid I should return and assist your colleagues. It is important that this facility be fully operational as soon as possible," Altan-117 said, lowering the tablet and holding it out to Mila.

"You're right, of course," she said, nodding in understanding but not taking the transparent device from him. Mette frowned, confused. When the servitor tried to set it on the tabletop, she leaned forward and extended a hand. "One more request before you go."

Altan-117 barely hesitated, then inclined his head. "Of course."

"Could you read it to me again, this time backwards?"

"Backwards?"

"Yes," she quickly filled the pause created by his confusion and tapped against the tablet, "I believe there is a secret message hidden in this message."

"A secret message..." He seemed to shrug off the thought. "I couldn't detect any sign of cryptic subtext."

Mila shrugged innocently. "In college, I once made a confession of love to my professor that way. It didn't work, but at least he understood, and it proved how intelligent he was. I think I was a little sapiosexual then, if you know what I mean."

"I still am," Mette commented dryly from the side.

"I don't think that's purposeful," Altan-117 insisted.

"Never mind," Mila said lightly. "You are, after all, a servitor and programmed to be a maintenance assistant. So, here's what I want: Read me the text backwards."

There was a long pause in which they looked into each other's eyes and she could not shake the feeling that had persisted since their arrival: that more than a mere machine was looking at her. There was no machine-like coldness behind its contourless blackness.

"Or can't you?" she whispered at one point. "Algorithms usually find it very easy, while our brains are not trained for such patterns and fail at them. We just can't get anything fluid to happen backwards. In fact, it's like we can't even recognize the faces of family members when we're shown their photos upside down."

"A little lower!" James prompted Adrian, who continued to slide the tablet down the door of the box until an overall picture emerged that he understood after stepping back.

Inside the small room was not merely a small console with several tiny recesses, but also the body of a robot. Its legs and arms were sticking out at frightening angles and half its head was missing, as if someone had smashed it with an axe.

"Shut down, my ass," Adrian growled. "That damn tin can!"

"JAMES!" Mila's scream echoed through the cavern to them. He jumped violently.

Mila wanted to knock the table over to put a barrier between herself and the servitor but found it was either too heavy or anchored to the floor. She achieved absolutely nothing. Shocked, Mette fell backward from her chair as Altan-117 leapt landed on the tabletop, denting it deeply with its weight.

"You should have just helped!" he hissed, which now had nothing soft about it, but sounded like a hissing snake.

He spread his arms like a bird of prey and the fingers of his hands curled into cold claws.

Mila jumped back and rushed toward the work areas of the kitchen—what she at least thought of as the kitchen. With growing panic, fueled by the thundering footsteps of the robot-turned-killer bot, her hands searched for something to throw. It was a desperate attempt to save herself that was as miserable as it was futile.

Altan-117 grabbed her right ankle and yanked so hard that it broke with a loud *crack*. Then, as she yelled and jerked convulsively, he flung her like a doll across the room. Her whole world spun, made up of light and dark colors that blurred into each other. Her stomach churned from the erratic changes in direction and threatened to choke her throat. The pain in her foot made her eyes water. She crashed into something hard and her vision went black. The back of her head was suddenly wet, which she didn't understand. A dull sense of detachment spread through her. From far away, she noticed she was now lying on her side, low to the ground, and she saw a pair of gray legs lurching toward her.

"What was it?" a trusting voice, tinged with a blanket of cool cruelty, wanted to know.

"Itak, ya idu v temnuyu noch'," she mumbled dully in Russian as a loud shout came from somewhere, and the robot paused.

24

"Over here, you son of a bitch!" James roared, gulping as Altan-117—or whoever he was—stepped through the mess hall door into the cavern. There was no trace left of the servitor, who appeared soft and good-natured despite his metallic limbs. Eyes that had been large and gentle now looked like opals of pure darkness. His arms were folded to his sides and his fingers curved like claws, his feet seemed to crash into the floor with each step. "We found your friend!"

The robot did not answer and silently continued to approach him. Unstoppable.

"It's now or never, Adrian. If you want your plan to work, it's now!"

Until now, they had just discussed whether their theory was valid enough to risk everything. It had become clear to him early on that something was not right, especially not with the servitor. James simply didn't buy that it was being led around by the nose by them. Altan-117 had to know they were not locals, nor was he expecting a maintenance team. James even doubted the alleged transmission by now. But he had still taken pains not to reveal himself and keep up the charade until he could figure out what the robot was up to and what exactly they were dealing with. But their time was much shorter than they had hoped.

At first, he had noticed the Servitor referred to the Ark as such and not as the "Temple of Heaven," even though that was the name for the facility before it was considered a way out of the war and a data repository for the survival of Al'Anter knowledge. Only then had it been renamed the "Ark," but by then, the servitors must have been in service a long time and would have been programmed with the original name. All the minor oddities had then merely added to the account of his distrust. The lie about the other servitor, which had obviously been destroyed by force, had finally confirmed it. The only question was, if Altan-117 was not Altan-117, then who was he? To find out, they needed help, and it was in the locked box.

"Now, Meeks!" he shouted impatiently when he got back to the control center. Adrian tossed the engineer the fission drill and visibly swallowed. "GO!"

The cosmonaut jumped away from the door of the box, and Meeks operated the drill at the spot he had marked with his finger before tossing the X-ray tablet to Justus. With careful precision, he inserted the short beam of light into the rock and rotated it with an amazingly delicate motion until suddenly a white beam shot out of the hole. The helium-3, cooled to just below zero and in an indefinable state between liquid and gaseous, decided after only a few centimeters to exist as a gas due to the atmospheric pressure and turned the fission drill into a block of ice that Meeks could not let go of fast enough to avoid violent icing. Meeks let out a shrill yelp and it fell to the floor, shattering into thousands of white crystals. James was shocked to see there were pieces of Meeks's palms on the handle.

The jet of gaseous helium-3 reached the door of the box and produced ice-cold splashes, one of which hit him on the lower left leg and left a painful sting. Adrian stepped back and threw his shoulder against the frozen door, which looked as if it had been sprayed with fresh snow. It shattered into a myriad of tiny splinters and the noise was as deafening, as if someone had thrown a wrecking ball into a china store.

Everything moved as if in slow motion.

The servitor rushed through the open passage into the cavern and, almost simultaneously, the gray painted metal slid shut behind him, blocking the way out of the control center.

Meeks fell, screeching from the armature, his destroyed hand pressed tightly to his chest.

Adrian scrambled to his feet inside the box, bleeding from multiple wounds, yet appeared to be alert. James reached into his pants pocket and felt the marble between his fingers. It felt almost warm in the chill that filled the room. In the slowed time, seeing everything clearly as in a movie whose playing speed was reduced, he pulled it out and tossed it to Adrian without a second thought. Their eyes met briefly and there was understanding.

Justus climbed onto the armature as Meeks hit the ground.

The cosmonaut opened his hand, and the marble traced a high arc, like a small black hole flying around between two galaxies.

The trance-like slowness ended. Adrian snatched the zero-D memory out of the air and leapt toward the connecting recesses on the towering column with an outstretched hand as if scoring a touchdown.

James turned to face the servitor and saw a flash of silver as one of the robot's cold hands struck him on the lower jaw. There was an ugly *crack*, and immense pain exploded in his head. His mouth filled with blood, and he sailed through the air.

Justus grabbed the tablet and yanked it up as Altan-117 grabbed Adrian by the ankle with his other hand and jerked him out of the box. He could hear tendons and muscles tear, and the Russian's screams chilled him to the marrow.

James landed hard on the dusty floor. Everything was spinning as if he were on an out-of-control merry-go-round. While he was wondering what the German was doing, he took Meeks's tablet and held it like a mirror in the indescribably cold jet of gas. The device froze instantly, as did Justus's hands, but he redirected the jet until it hit the robot, which was about to step on Adrian's head. The metallic body instantly froze from the center to the neck and hip.

It's *now or never,* James thought. He fought through his world of pain and dizziness, and scrambled to his feet and threw himself against the servitor. Plasma steel, cables, and circuit boards shattered under the impact, turning into a shower of tiny ice crystals that turned his throbbing field of vision into a blizzard. Then he crashed into Adrian and landed on his back. Silence fell, except for Meeks's heartrending whimpers.

For a moment, he just lay there staring at the ceiling, his entire head one dull ache. Finally, he rose onto his side and staggered to his feet. Justus slid off the armature, his arms black and dead to the shoulders, his gaze as blank as that of a dead man who inexplicably still possessed a connection to this world. He slid to the floor and crawled toward Meeks.

"Adrian? Are you all right?" James breathed, startled at his voice. The words barely came out intelligibly, they sounded more like he had a handful of mush in his mouth. Something warm ran down his chin, but he barely felt it under all the pain.

"James," said a familiar voice, and suddenly the hologram of Nasaku appeared in front of him.

It worked!

"Nasaku," he muttered.

"I connected with the Avatar and we were able to cleanse the corrupt code from the central control unit." Her voice sounded almost casual.

"Kazerun," he said. "Their hacker managed to infiltrate the network, didn't he?"

"Not exactly. He loaded malware into the control unit and a digitized avatar of himself into the Altan-117 servitor. Fortunately, he failed to use the teleporter."

"Because he was alone." James realized how weak his words were as they came out of his mouth, and he shivered.

"Yes."

"The teleporter is the search for the Elders. Not a pure replica of the original machines, am I right?"

"Yes."

"That's why only the test run was successful. All connections have to be started at the same time to allow a transition. Because all the seats have one destination: The origin, the master teleporter, which has access to all the others but cannot be reached itself."

"Unless you know the coordinates and feed them into the central computer," Nasaku confirmed. "You and Justus are correct. I was on Earth to finish another secret project. With the help of the first experiment in this facility, we were able to draw conclusions about the location of the master teleporter, which we suspected was on the home planet of the Elders, our creators. But we could no longer access our telescopes and orbital sensors, so I had to use yours."

"That's why the observatory."

"Yes. With the missing data I've been able to acquire, it should be possible to accomplish what the Al'Anters so narrowly failed to do, finally," she continued. She looked to the metal door, which she opened with a gesture of her digitized hand. "We believe the Elders left a riddle and made it possible for the teleporters to travel to them with a backdoor, but only if all six human species do it together. That failed, but the Al'Anters found an alternate solution that we can now verify."

"There are exactly six of us," James whispered with a rattle.

"Yes. I've got the teleporter up, but you'll have to hurry. Justus and Adrian will die soon, and so will you."

EPILOGUE

J ames dragged Adrian along with him like a wet sack, staggering more than walking to the platform. Through a veil of tears, he saw Mila, supported by Mette. With relief, the veil grew even thicker. Meeks and Justus had already made it to their seats, which had been closest to the edge of the platform.

"It's all right, my friend," he said to the cosmonaut, whose right leg dragged limp and useless behind him before James heaved him into a vacant seat. The Russian's body was a ruin, a hodgepodge of wounds and ice, and his eyelids fluttered rapidly. Again and again, he whispered Russian words to himself and seemed on the verge of losing consciousness. Justus, too, had closed his eyes and looked as if he were dead except for the rise and fall of his chest. His arms lay stiff and pitch-black like burnt flesh, on the armrests. Meeks barely made a sound.

"James, oh God!" he heard Mila say as she stumbled toward him. Mette tried to hold her back, but she would not be contained.

"That bad?" he mumbled, feeling a stab straight to his

heart as he vaguely realized that her face was a ruin of red and blue. He wanted to protect her, to take her in his arms and make everything okay again, but he couldn't.

"Not for me," she said, but the effort to control herself and not burst into tears was audible.

"We don't have time." He took her by the hand and hobbled with her to the nearest seat, and gently pushed her into it. "We've learned all we can about this world, and now we must leave here to unravel the final mystery."

"The Elders."

"Yes. I'm going to my seat now before Justus or Adrian die. They only have a few minutes left, I think, and it won't work without them."

"Go!" she cried in a anxious voice. It was obviously difficult for her.

"Mette..." he began, but the Dane immediately interrupted him.

"I'm okay," she assured him impatiently, pushing him in front of her until he tumbled like a wet sack, relieved to find he had fallen into a seat. Mette walked away like a ghostly shadow, and then a bright glimmer appeared in front of him. It had to be Nasaku's hologram.

"I can't prepare you for anything, James," she said. "If it works, you'll have gone farther than the Al'Anters ever could." A note of melancholy resonated through her realization. "Thank you for seeing it through."

"I think it's our only choice." Every word was infinitely difficult for him as if he had to cross a whole thicket of pain for every single syllable that left his bloodied lips.

"Have a good trip. From here on I can no longer accompany you. Justus is dying right now; I have to initiate the connection."

With that, the hologram disappeared, and James closed his eyes.

All at once, the abysmal pain that had filled every fiber of his body was gone. His world became empty because it felt as normal as after a long, restful sleep.

He opened his eyes and almost cried when he saw Mila, Mette, Justus, Meeks, and Adrian. They were standing in a circle on a green lawn under a turquoise sky with two suns at the zenith, one shimmering orange, the other slightly red. His friends were naked and completely unharmed, just opening their eyes and examining their arms and hands as if they couldn't believe it. Mila rushed up to him and fell about his neck.

"I thought—"

"It's okay," he interrupted her and returned her hug with all the love he felt.

"Where are we?"

"I don't know, but we're not on Al'Antis anymore, that much is clear."

"Then I guess we'll have to find out. This time it's best if we do it without dying," she murmured. She pulled back from his chest faced the others.

James's heart leapt with relief as they approached each other and grasped hands or hugged to express their joy at not losing anyone.

"Did we make it?" Justus asked incredulously, alternately clasping his hands over his intact arms.

"I don't know what we managed to do, but this place looks significantly friendlier than the last one."

"Let's hope appearances are not deceiving," Adrian said.

James silently agreed with him.

Could it be? Could this be the origin?

AFTERWORD

Dear Reader,

If you enjoyed this story, I would be very happy if you would leave a star rating of this e-book or a short review on Amazon. This is the best way to help authors continue to write exciting books in the future. To contact me directly, you can: joshua@joshuat-calvert.com—I answer every mail!

If you subscribe to my newsletter, I'll regularly tell you a bit about myself, writing, and the great themes of science fiction. Plus, as a thank you, you'll receive my e-book Rift: The Transition exclusively and for free: www.joshuat-calvert.com

Warm regards, *Joshua T. Calvert*

Printed in Great Britain
by Amazon

20627060R00166